THE LAST TRAIN

A DCI BOYD THRILLER

ALEX SCARROW

THE LAST TRAIN

Copyright © 2021 by Alex Scarrow
All rights reserved

This book is a work of fiction. Names, characters, places and incidents are either the product of the author's imagination or are used fictitiously, and any resemblance to actual persons, living or dead, business establishments, events or locales is entirely coincidental.

No part of this book may be reproduced in any form or by any electronic or mechanical means, including information storage and retrieval systems, without written permission from the author, except for the use of brief quotations in a book review.

Published by GrrBooks

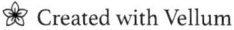 Created with Vellum

*Dedicated to the innocent victims of hate, past and present.
One day, hopefully, we'll learn.*

PROLOGUE

He stared through the slats of wood at the horror going on outside. At the body of his father lying on his back, blood pooling beneath his head as his eyes swivelled and rolled and his jaw opened and closed in a post-mortem spasm. At his mother screaming on the kitchen table, pinned down by the monster on top of her. His older sister had been raped first – she was dead now too.

The only thing stopping him from screaming along with his mother, and giving himself away in his hiding place beneath the kitchen counter, was one tiny detail. He focused hard.

There was a water bottle on the man's belt, bouncing and swinging with his exertions. It had a word scrawled across it.

He concentrated on the letters. Burning them into his mind forever. Mouthing a silent mantra...

Remember...
Remember...
Remember...

1

Friday, 11.13 p.m.

DCI Bill Boyd strode up the gentle slope of Queens Road towards Brighton station. It was gone eleven in the evening and the 'cool' side of the town centre was buzzing with bohemian life. It was September, a very warm one. Summer had arrived late this year but was making up for it now; the cafés and wine bars were still pretty busy with customers outside, sitting at the tables and chairs, laughing, drinking, eating, making Brighton look very Mediterranean.

One of the by-products of the Covid-lockdown aftermath had been an uptake in pavement seating and café culture. A rather pleasant by-product, thought Boyd. But then young and pretty people tended to make any new trend look good. Voted the happiest place to work and live in the UK God knows how many times, Brighton was heaving with university students and twenty- and thirty-somethings who'd migrated down from London to begin tech and media careers.

Boyd was a little worse for wear having shared several pints with an ex-colleague, a welcome reward for having had to sit through a whole day's worth of Powerpoint presentations on LEDS's new and (supposedly) easier-to-use user interface.

Absolutely gripping stuff.

Seeing Sunil Chandra – Sunny – presenting one of the workshops had been a pleasant surprise and after the day-long session it had been nice to sit outside with him and sip a pint or several, watching Brighton's long shingle beach being gently bathed in the evening sun to the sound of a busking skiffle band playing on the promenade.

Sunny was doing much better for himself as a consultant for the police than he had as an employee of the force, and was still insisting that his plan to remain in London and buy himself a Thames-side apartment at a bargain price was going to pay off.

Detective Superintendent Sutherland was supposed to have attended the day's training, but his phobia of all things computer-related, plus his spurious claim that his recently healed broken ankle wouldn't cope with walking from workshop to workshop had sealed the deal. Instead, Boyd would attend, learn and bring back knowledge of all the cool new computer tweaks.

And he was glad he'd gone. It had been lovely seeing Sunny again.

Boyd stepped into the station and checked the fluttering departure board. The last train to Hastings departed at 11.35 p.m. He texted Emma to say that he was grabbing that, and that she shouldn't wait up to give him a lift. She had an early shift tomorrow; he'd walk or get a cab.

He scratched his beard as he deliberated his options in the time he had left before his train departed. Time enough, he decided, to grab a coffee from the stand in the main concourse.

In the interviews to come in the next few days, he would state that this was the moment he first noticed the man, at 11.13 p.m. The man was directly ahead of him in the short queue. He had a vaguely Middle Eastern or perhaps Mediterranean appearance, with tanned skin, dark hair and a beard. He was wearing a small backpack, a baseball cap, jeans and a baggy hoodie – just like most of the male student population of Brighton. It was his manner that caught Boyd's attention, though. He was abrupt, almost to the point of being rude to the young lad serving in the stall.

He'd wanted water. Just water. Now. And nothing else.

2

11.25 p.m.

Boyd was sorely tempted to grab himself a doner kebab. He'd walked past a place just fifty yards short of the station and his tipsy – no, let's call a spade a spade – his *drunken* self rather fancied tearing into a greasy kebab. The smell of the sizzling fat-on-a-stick was driving him nuts. But, he told himself, tomorrow he'd regret the additional two thousand calories' worth of Fail. The best way to resist the urge was to recall an *eww* moment on the Hammersmith and City Line many years ago.

On a packed underground train, he'd caught the whiff of a Cornish pasty on a day when he'd not had any breakfast or any lunch and had been absolutely starving. His mouth had been quite literally watering and he'd been half seriously considering offering money to whoever was eating it for whatever was left of it. But, as the Tube train drew up at a station and a man with a very sweaty head and damp armpits pushed past him to get out, he'd discovered the actual source of the odour. The man himself smelled of pasty.

That did the trick. He decided to stick with his coffee.

At 11.31 p.m. Boyd headed onto platform seven and made his way to the four-carriage diesel train that was waiting to sputter and growl across Sussex to Lewes and then onto Hastings.

His phone rang. It was Emma.

'How was your day out?' she asked.

'Long. Brighton's nice, though.'

'Yeah, I've heard,' she replied. 'Why didn't we buy a place over there?'

'Errr... price?'

'Oh, yeah. They have jazz and stuff down on the beach, don't they?'

'Yup. Found myself toe-tapping.'

'You sound pissed.'

'I might be a little merry, maybe...'

He heard her draw in a judgemental breath. 'You'll have a sore head tomorrow, then.'

'I think that might well be. I bumped into an old colleague and had one or four.'

She tutted. 'Honestly, Dad... and you lost nearly three pounds this week.'

'Yeah, but –' he sounded like a scolded teenager – 'I managed to stay out of the kebab shop. Let's focus on the positives, Em.'

'I'm very disappointed,' she said in a mock-solemn voice. 'You let me down, you let Ozzie down, but most of all you –'

'Yeah, yeah, yeah. Up yours. Look, like the text says... Don't wait up, Ems. I'll grab a cab.'

'Right, you drunk doofus. See you tomorrow. Night!'

He looked into the rear carriage as he walked up the platform. It looked far too busy and noisy with pub-turnout passengers. The one after looked a little more promising. But, with a whistle blowing and the sound of open doors being slammed shut behind him by the guard on the platform, he decided to hop into the next carriage, second from the front, and figure it out from there.

One more casual decision, he would later realise, that would feed into the sequence of events due to unfold in the hours ahead.

3

11.32 p.m.

Boyd managed to find a table that had three spare seats and he shuffled along to sit opposite a man who had a couple of cans of Black Label on the table in front of him and was gazing listlessly out of the window. The man smiled and nodded as Boyd sat down, fidgeting to find an uncontested space for his knobbly knees.

Boyd settled for a wide knee spread, one against the carriage wall, the other angled outwards towards the aisle. His legs were like a grasshopper's, far too long and invasive to be shoved beneath one of those carriage tables. The man opposite seemed as though he was deep in thought, his dark-lidded eyes half-closed beneath a bushy monobrow of thick black hair. With his chin, jaw and mouth darkened by bristles, he looked vaguely like a raccoon... or whatever that wise-cracking little weasel-thing in *The Lion King* was.

A third person dithered beside their table as a whistle blew again and the diesel train revved impatiently, making the point it was ready to go. It was a woman about Emma's age. She looked at a cardboard slip tucked into a headrest. 'Are these reserved?' she asked.

Boyd hadn't even noticed them. He turned to see there was a card stuck in the headrest behind him too. 'Oh, bugger.'

'Not worry,' said the man opposite. 'I reserve... but someone sit in my seat.' He shrugged. 'So I sit in someone else seat. Always this happen on Friday nights.'

The woman nodded. 'When it's this busy, nobody takes these seriously, do they?'

Monobrow shrugged. 'Waste of time.'

Since he seemed to be taking up less room than Boyd, she sat down next to him.

The train left Brighton bang on time – 11.35 p.m.

Boyd gazed out of the widow and reflected on his evening. Chatting with Sunny about the old days had been good. Sunny was a part of the mosaic of memories that included Julia and Noah, and Emma when she was a precocious ten-year-old who couldn't decide whether she wanted to be a tough-as-nails copper or a fabulous princess. Sunny was a touchstone back to those times. While it had been good to laugh at the pranks and the fuckwits of the past, rejoicing in the cases that had gone well and eye-rolling at the mistakes of cases gone by, it had left Boyd feeling maudlin as he sat watching sodium-orange street lights flicker past outside the grimy window, catching snapshot glimpses of lounges and bedrooms and kitchens. *Happy families.*

They were out into pitch-black countryside within a few minutes.

'All right?' asked the man opposite. He had a thick accent. Something Eastern European perhaps, Boyd thought.

'Yeah, had a bit too much to drink, I think,' Boyd replied sheepishly.

He laughed. 'Me also. I have these –' he gestured at his two untouched cans of lager and shook his head – 'but I think I have had enough.' He huffed his *H*s like he was hawking up stuck popcorn.

'Always seems like a good idea at the time, right?' said Boyd.

Monobrow grinned and nodded. 'Beer-thinking. Not very smart, eh?'

The young woman nodded along with that. She looked up from her phone and laughed. 'Which is why I probably need to step away from Amazon right now.' She turned her screen round to show listings for designer satchels. 'The rubbish I end up ordering when I've had a couple of drinks.'

'You been to beach this evening?' asked the man.

Boyd nodded. 'Along the front. Nice. Really chilled.'

'Does Chris Eubank still cruise up and down in his big truck?' asked the woman.

'Huh?' Boyd had no idea.

She smiled. 'It's a thing... apparently. He was a boxer or something once, wasn't he?'

Boyd nodded.

'I heard that on busy summer nights he drives along the front in a pimped-up truck and honks his horn and waves at everyone.'

'Brighton's got the X factor,' said Boyd. 'That's for sure.'

He glanced at his watch. It was 11.47 p.m. The moment – he would later recall – that he spotted the man with the backpack and baseball cap again. Boyd watched him enter the carriage at the end and make his way up slowly, staring intently at the people gathered around each table before moving onto the next.

The man paused by their table, studied the passengers at the table opposite, then turned to look at Boyd and his table companions. The stranger lingered briefly and for a second

Boyd thought he was going to plonk himself down right next to him... but the man eventually moved on.

Boyd felt his copper's instinct kick in. He'd use that term in the interviews to come, although he was well aware that it was an explanation too easily used to wallpaper over prejudices and assumptions. He would look back at that moment and say it was down to the man's demeanour – he seemed edgy, uncomfortable. It was his darting eyes. The way that he studied everyone. It wasn't the backpack, or the dark beard, or the skin.

Or maybe it had been *all* those things.

Boyd's gaze followed the man as he continued in the same manner all the way through the carriage until he disappeared into the next one.

'I think he wants own table,' said Monobrow.

'Well, good luck finding that,' said the woman, 'It's packed tonight.'

Monobrow nodded. 'Very packed.' He nodded again at his unopened lagers on the table. 'Hey! You want?'

Boyd was vaguely aware the man was talking to him. 'Sorry?'

'You want beer?' He was holding out one of the cans. Boyd could see it was still fridge-cold; beads of condensation ran down the side and dripped onto the table. It was very stuffy in the train. Plus... he could feel the tail end of being slightly pissed crossing over into hangover territory.

'You sure?'

Monobrow nodded. 'Da. Take.'

Boyd took it. 'Thanks.'

The man looked at the woman. 'You want this one?'

She shook her head vigorously and puffed her cheeks. 'Got to work tomorrow. I'm bad enough as it is. But thanks.'

Boyd popped the can and chugged a mouthful, savouring how good the cold beer and the suds felt in his dry mouth.

The man sighed. 'I will not let you drink alone.' He opened

the other can and held it out for Boyd to clunk gently. Boyd obliged.

Monobrow made a toast in another language. Boyd replied with: 'Here's to getting what you want, not what you deserve.'

The young woman chuckled as she looked back down at her phone.

4

11.55 p.m.

At eleven fifty-five p.m. the train pulled into Lewes and the driver announced there'd be a ten-minute hold at the station. I looked out of the window at the platform and watched as a number of passengers stepped out to light up or vape.'

'And that's when you picked him out again?'

Boyd nodded.

'Why? What was he doing to draw your attention?'

Boyd closed his eyes to pull himself back into the hazy memory once more. It was so easy to jumble the chronology of little things. Especially when you'd had a few. Was it then that he'd thought Backpack Man needed watching closely? Why? Because he was smoking like someone about to face a firing squad? Or because he was pacing up and down, staring into each grubby window as he passed by?

'REALLY, REALLY BAD,' said Lucas – which Boyd had eventually discovered was Monobrow's actual name. He'd been talking about the Euro 2020 final, which he'd watched on a pub TV. 'Football...*Tsh!* It makes very bad behaviour when there are flags being waved around, I think.'

Boyd's attention was elsewhere.

'You okay?' asked Lucas.

Boyd turned back to him. 'Yeah, fine. Sorry.'

Lucas looked out of the window and could see Backpack Man puffing incessantly on his cigarette. 'You know this man?'

'No, I...' Boyd shook his head. 'Never met him. But his behaviour – he's acting... *off*.'

The woman glanced up from her phone and out of the window. 'That's the same guy who checked out our table, isn't it?'

Boyd nodded, eyes fixed on him.

'What are you... a *policeman*?' she said, laughing lightly.

'I am actually,' Boyd replied.

Lucas stiffened ever so slightly.

'Relax. I'm not on duty.' Boyd smiled, but Lucas seemed to have sobered right up. His jovial manner had gone.

'What is *off* with him?' he asked. 'Poor man is just smoking.'

'He doesn't look right,' said Boyd.

'Because what?' asked Lucas coolly. 'He look foreign?'

Boyd swivelled round to face Lucas. 'I'm not Border Force.' Then he turned to look out of the window again. 'He seems agitated.'

'And *that* is crime now?' said Lucas.

'I'm just keeping an eye out. That's all.'

'Well, I'm grateful,' the young woman said. 'With all those Afghans and migrants flooding in, someone's got to keep a watch-out for the dodgy ones.'

Boyd wondered who exactly she was grouping under the label 'dodgy ones'. He decided not to ask. This kind of conversation had a habit of turning ugly very quickly. As it was, he sensed the late-night commuter camaraderie around the table had been dampened and for the next hour they'd be stuck together in an awkward silence.

Five minutes later, a whistle sounded and the dozen or so smokers and vapers on the platform climbed back aboard the train.

At 12.05 a.m. the train pulled out of Lewes and headed towards Eastbourne.

5

12.30 a.m.

Boyd had been right. Not another word was exchanged between the three of them as the train rattled across the dark Sussex countryside and pulled into Eastbourne.

His woolly mind moved on to other things. He thought back over the events of the last couple of months, since the Sutton case.

Despite all assurances from Chief Superintendent Hatcher, the case had been successfully smothered and press attention was dutifully lured away with a very timely scandal involving a Premier League footballer and some inappropriate tweets.

A recent appointee to the Cabinet, Tim Portman, had been fired and the party whip had been withdrawn from him – the papers reported something to do with illegal pornography on his Westminster computer. There were no links made between Tim's sacking and Sir Jeffrey Sutton's death, and the Prime Minister's office had made some bland statement about expecting higher standards. Boyd didn't do politics, but he suspected the PM was secretly pleased the ambitious younger man had been taken out of play, making his job a little safer for a while to come.

As for Douglas Lane? There hadn't been a word about him since his arrest. The Met had the case now and he had enough compromising material on his contacts to guarantee either a sweetheart deal or an 'accident' in the remand prison showers. Boyd wondered which it would be.

The only good news to come out of the whole sorry saga was that Sir Jeffrey Sutton's will addendum looked as though it was going to be honoured and his badly injured carer and her family were going to be the recipients of his fortune rather than his well-to-do kids, neither of whom had particularly liked the old man.

That final can of lager had finished him off and he found his eyes growing heavy. The train had left Eastbourne and was now running along the coast on the final short leg of the journey to Hastings. The last thing Boyd recalled before things *began* was looking at his watch. It was 12.31 a.m.

6

12.51 a.m.

At 12.51 a.m. the emergency brakes were suddenly, jarringly engaged. The train sounded like some metallic monster being slaughtered as it ground to a lurching halt. Boyd, facing backwards, ended up with the table's contents in his lap – one empty and one half-full beer can soaking his trousers. The woman's phone skittered off the table and down into the aisle. Lucas – who was dozing at the time – was thrown forward so that his forehead almost banged the table.

The braking roused everyone in their carriage from their phones or their slumber. A final clattering lurch in the other direction concluded the unscheduled emergency stop.

'Jesus! What's going on?' Boyd heard someone exclaim a table or two up from his.

Someone else hissed. 'Oh, for fuck's sake. Seriously?'

'Leaves on the track, probably,' another muttered.

It was quiet for a few moments: nothing but the creak of bums shuffling on old seat springs and the ticking of the train at rest – then came the muffled sound of someone shouting from the carriage in front of them.

Something's kicking off.

'A policeman, yes?' said Lucas finally. The implication being that Boyd should probably get up and investigate.

A slightly pissed and very knackered off-duty policeman, yes.

Boyd shrugged. He had a warrant card in his wallet. If some drunken prat was kicking off about something, one flash of that and a few firm words would almost certainly quieten them down. He pulled himself wearily out of his seat and double-checked his phone was still with him.

He made his way up the carriage. Curious passengers on either side of the aisle looked up at him. 'Police,' he announced, trying not to slur too much. 'An off-bloody-duty one,' he added grumpily.

Pulling the sliding door aside to step into the connecting vestibule, Boyd immediately heard more than a single raised voice.

The last trace of alcoholic fuzziness cleared from his head as he passed the toilet doors and stepped over the articulated rubber mat to enter the next carriage. He could see a woman through the glass door scrabbling at the handle to slide it open. She finally got a grip on the handle and struggled to push the door to one side.

'HE'S GOT A GUN!!!' she screamed into Boyd's face as she pushed past him to escape.

Boyd tried to step out but another person pushed past him. Then another.

Two deafening gunshots echoed down the carriage like fire-crackers tossed into a tunnel. There was a brief silence, followed by everyone inside the carriage screaming in united panic.

Boyd gave up trying to enter. He backed into one of the toilets to let the stream of fleeing passengers pass him.

The Last Train

A dozen went scrambling past, one on the heels of the other, then finally he had an opportunity to take a look. He took a deep steadying breath and peered cautiously into the front carriage, the door to it left open.

It was deserted now, except for one passenger – the same man he'd first noticed at the coffee stand, impatient for his bottle of water. He had a gun in one hand and a long-bladed knife in the other. It was bloodied.

The man was standing perfectly still at the far end of the carriage. Boyd ducked back into the toilet and pulled his phone out. He dialled 999 – as an off-duty cop it was still the best and quickest way to get emergency help.

'Which service do you require?' came the voice down the line.

'Police,' he rasped.

'One second.' Then a different voice. 'What's your location?'

'Train. Brighton to Hastings. The last one. We're stopped outside Bexhill.'

'What is the nature of –'

'Live shooter. Front carriage. At least one possible casualty.'

Boyd heard the control room operator suck in a sharp breath. 'This isn't a crank call,' he whispered. 'I'm DCI Boyd, Hastings CID. We need an armed response unit and paramedics here right now!'

Boyd peeked out again and saw the man had begun to move slowly down the aisle towards him. He retreated and let the toilet door close gently on him.

He lowered his phone.

Fuck. What do I do now?

His mind flashed back to a locker-room discussion he'd had decades ago when he'd still been in uniform: *'If you were in civvies and someone came at you with a weapon... would you have a go?'*

A much younger Boyd had said something about having a

crack if he was close enough to grab the weapon. And perhaps a dozen times over the years, as he'd watched news reports about the Breivik killings in Sweden, the London Bridge stabbings, the Plymouth Shooter, he'd come to the same conclusion. If he could intervene – with a reasonable chance of success – he would.

Now, with footsteps approaching, with just a few seconds to go before the shooter would enter the vestibule, Boyd was having a rapid re-think. His whole body was trembling uncontrollably with the adrenaline and cortisol flooding into his blood.

He could almost hear Julia: *Let him go, Bill. Let him pass. Think of Emma.*

He listened, heart thumping as the slow menacing tap of approaching footsteps drew ever closer.

How many bloody times had he played out a scenario like this in his head? Visualising the encounter in slow motion, pondering what opening move he'd make: grab for the gun or knife? Go for the eyes or face? Go low and knock them off balance?

The first move would be the defining one. What happened in the struggle directly after would be down to body weight, strength, reaction time, training... a whole slew of scruffy variables that would come into play within just a few seconds in a manner that couldn't be predicted.

That first move was the only thing Boyd would have complete control over.

The sound of the footsteps changed as the man stepped onto the rubber mat of the vestibule.

Shit. Shit. Shit.

It was decision time.

7

12.52 a.m.

Boyd heard something brush against the outside of the toilet door.

It's now or never, mate.

He grabbed the handle and pulled. The door rattled noisily but refused to open.

It's a push one. Fuck. Idiot.

He pushed it open and lurched out into the narrow space just behind the man with the baseball cap. The noise of the latch and Boyd's *oof!* as he shouldered into the toilet door opposite alerted the man and he spun round.

Boyd made a split-second decision to go down low. He reached out with both hands and grabbed hold of the back of the man's legs. Then his shoulder and head impacted with the man's thighs and groin and, inevitably, they both went down in a tangle of limbs.

Get-the-gun-get-the-gun-get-the-FUCKING-gun... The words were spinning through his head as he grappled frantically with the man on the floor. If he could wrestle the gun off this bastard, it was job done, even if the fucker managed to sink the knife into one of his arms or legs.

Get the gun.

Boyd had one of his big fists wrapped around the man's gun hand. His other fist was scrabbling in the air to get a purchase on the hand that was holding the knife. The man had a slight frame; he was definitely weaker, but that wasn't the point. A free hand wielding a sharp six-inch blade could level any playing field.

Vaguely, Boyd was aware he was screaming something. *Someone help me!* maybe? But that was lost in the din of the other screaming voices just beyond. He finally managed to grasp the man's sleeve at the juncture of his elbow, clasping tightly to limit the slashing damage he could do with the blade.

Boyd switched focus back to the gun hand. The bastard was busy trying to angle the barrel towards his face.

BANG! The narrow vestibule strobed with the muzzle flash. Boyd had no idea whatsoever if he'd been hit. He tried to adjust his hold on the gun hand, but that proved to be a mistake. The man pulled free and he swung the gun hard across Boyd's face.

The blow sent Boyd backwards, knocking him senseless.

The last thing his eyes registered was the blurry outline of the man standing over him, his arm slowly straightening to take aim.

8

12.54 a.m.

'Hey, babycakes, I want to strip you naked, smother you in Heinz mayonnaise and –'

'Jay, for fuck's sake. This is my work phone.'

Okeke heard her boyfriend chuckle on the other end of the line. She could make out the beat of dance music spilling from the nightclub.

'I know,' replied Jay. 'I left a message on the other one too.'

'You bored by any chance?'

She heard him let out a long and weary sigh. 'Yeah.'

'Well, same here,' she replied. 'It's not all car chases and kicking down doors, you know.' Okeke was finally on nights this week. She'd been dodging doing her turn for months, swapping her red-eye shifts with Warren. He was happy doing the quieter stints, Okeke suspected, because it got him away from his incessantly curious and coddling mother.

'There *must* be a way I could get a job like yours, baby?'

'Of course there is, Jay – go get a degree, enrol in training for six months, and/or become a uniformed officer for five years and then try for CID. I'll see you here in, shall we say, seven years' time?'

Jay huffed. 'What about the fitness? You know I'd pass all the bleep tests –'

'But probably not in the tac vests or uniforms. Jay, baby, looking like the Hulk is not that high up on the police force's recruitment wish list.'

'I know, I know,' he said, sighing. 'I just wish I could make the business earn more.'

Jay's furniture business – essentially *The Repair Shop* but on a smaller scale and minus the TV-friendly artisans – operated out of his cluttered garage and earned him little more than pocket money each week; it was his nightclub security job that did all the heavy-lifting when it came to the bills.

'I know, love,' she replied. 'It's just one of those things you have to build gradually. It doesn't happen overn–'

Okeke saw a couple of uniformed officers sprint past the open door to CID's open-plan office. She heard more footsteps pounding down the hallway. 'Look, Jay, I've gotta go. I think something's going down.'

She ended the call and got up from her desk. The only other officer on duty tonight was DI Abbott. The handlebar-moustache-wearing eighties throwback had headphones on and was ostensibly reviewing some interview tape, but by the look of his mouse movements had been playing solitaire on the computer.

Okeke poked her head out into the corridor to see four more uniforms approaching at a sprint. All of them pulling on their tac vests and buckling up as they ran.

'What's going on?'

'Active shooter on a train outside Bexhill,' replied a sergeant without slowing down.

'Bloody hell,' she muttered.

9

1.22 a.m.

Emma's first solo shift at the Lansdowne Hotel's reception desk started at six in the morning. She'd set her alarm for five so that she'd have an hour to get up, get ready and get down the hill into town and to the hotel on time.

Patrick, the assistant manager, had shown her the ropes that Friday afternoon. Not that there was much to do until after nine thirty when breakfast had finished, then it started to get busy with checkouts and bill-settling. Patrick had drilled her on using their old computer system, which frankly looked like it belonged in another age with its DOS-like entry fields, black screen and eye-straining green text. The routine booking-in/checking-out stuff she had sorted; it was the non-routine stuff that she needed an idiot list for.

ROOM SERVICE – *kitchen staff in from 7 a.m., can make sandwiches, etc. No food after 10 p.m.*

Water/heating – maintenance engineer 24hr call out
Extra bedding/pillows, etc – storeroom beside kitchen entrance
Coffee/tea, milk, sugar, cups, etc – kitchen entrance cupboard (right)
fire alarm – assembly point car park, announcement using room phone/intercom
Anything else (urgent only) – call hotel manager
Not urgent/moral support – call Patrick

PATRICK HAD TAKEN Emma under his wing. She reckoned he was in his early thirties but he looked a good few years younger. She was amazed at how confident and relaxed he was as he handled all manner of little fires around him. He was completely unflappable as he dealt with grumpy old battleaxes complaining about lumpy mattresses, while simultaneously arbitrating a feud between two room cleaners and taking bookings over the phone... all with an easy smile and charm.

Daniel, her boyfriend, was the opposite of Patrick in every way: immature and goofy, fun and funny, but in a way that sometimes made Emma feel as though she had to be the grown-up in the relationship. She wondered why so many guys thought it was endearing to act like an impulsive child. It might have been charming with Tom Hanks playing the twelve-year-old boy magically grown to adulthood overnight, but in real life reminding your boyfriend he was twenty-four, not four, got old fast.

She was about to switch her phone off for the night to try to get some sleep when a notification pinged up on her screen.

10

1.23 a.m.

Boyd's eyes opened but refused to properly focus. He had a splitting headache, pain lancing through his head from somewhere at the back. He tried to reach up, but found his wrists were bound tightly together.

'What the f–'

'Shhhh!' someone whispered beside him.

As he blinked repeatedly, he tried to make sense of his surroundings. He was lying on the floor of one of the carriages. Beside him was Lucas. There were other passengers lying on the floor beyond him.

'What's happened?' whispered Boyd.

'Man with gun,' Lucas muttered. He nodded and Boyd followed his gaze. At the far end of the carriage he could see the door to the driver's compartment, smeared with blood. Beneath the seats he could see a pair of cheap trainers, one foot tapping the floor incessantly.

That's him. Boyd vaguely recalled the flash of white trainers on the edgy-looking man with the backpack. He wriggled on the floor, struggling against whatever his wrists had been tied with. Lucas twisted to show his bound hands.

Cable ties. Great. The movie world's handy top tip for wannabe hostage takers.

'What does he want?'

Lucas shrugged. 'He say nothing.'

Boyd saw the tapping trainer stop, then take a step forward. The man's face appeared in the aisle.

'YOU, QUIET!' he snapped.

Boyd got a glimpse of the eyes beneath the peak of the baseball cap, wide and round. There was plenty of bloodshot white to be seen.

He's manic. The young man's eyes were constantly darting from his hog-tied hostages on the floor to the large windows that showed nothing of the darkness beyond and only reflected the stark details inside the carriage. He took several steps down the aisle towards them. Boyd could see he was still holding the bloody knife in one hand and the gun in the other, a finger worryingly flexing and curling onto the trigger and then off again.

Boyd looked around at the other hostages on the floor of the carriage. They were all male, all bound. *Where's everyone else?*

He had no idea how long he'd been unconscious. Then a thought occurred to him. He'd dialled 999 in the toilet, hadn't he? The police had to be on their way; perhaps they were already assembling in the darkness outside.

He needs to be calmed down. Help was on its way. The right words exchanged with the young man could buy valuable minutes.

You're the only copper here. It's got to be you, old son.

Boyd took a deep breath to steady his nerves, then wriggled around to sit up. 'Hey?'

The Last Train

'SHUT UP!' the man snapped. The gun's aim quickly levelled on Boyd. 'You be quiet!'

Boyd fought the urge to tuck his head away and cower. He needed to project calm, not add to the hypertension. 'Look... you know the police are coming, right?'

The gunman marched towards him. He raised the barrel, wobbling, as he pressed it firmly against Boyd's forehead.

Boyd felt his heart blasting away in his chest and failed completely to keep the terror from flickering across his face.

'SHUT UP!'

'Listen...' whispered Boyd. 'Please... just listen! I'm... I'm a policeman!'

The man's twitching finger curled round the trigger.

Boyd couldn't help himself. He clenched his jaw and clamped his eyes shut, waiting for the inevitable.

'You... are... police?' The young man's voice was delicately balanced in the very small space between a manic scream and a menacing snarl.

Boyd could feel the barrel making a painful impression against his left temple. He could feel a vein throbbing back against the rough metal lip in reckless defiance.

'Yes,' whispered Boyd. A couple of seconds passed and he felt the pressure against the side of his forehead lessen ever so slightly. 'They're going to be outside this train any minute.'

Boyd dared to crack open his eyes and saw that the gunman's finger had eased off the trigger.

'There'll be a negotiator outside,' he continued, 'and he'll need to know what you want.'

Lesson Number One in the negotiator's handbook: *if they're busy talking, they're not busy shooting.*

Boyd repeated himself. 'They'll need to know what –'

'Shhhut the fuck up!!!' the man snapped.

Boyd nodded quickly. He'd said all that he wanted to say right now. He'd given the man something to think about.

There was a protracted silence in the carriage, the kind of silence that was deafening. Boyd could hear the faint sound of waves outside, gently crunching against the breakers in the dark.

'What... do I want?' repeated the man softly.

From the front of the carriage came a soft moan. A pair of legs in dark trousers and dark shoes scraped across the dirty floor every now and then. The smear of blood across the driver compartment's door was the only clue to the injured man's identity.

The driver had been shot or stabbed. Either way, it was clear he was bleeding out and needed help, if he wasn't already past the point of no return.

Just then someone's mobile phone started playing the ticking theme tune to *Countdown*. Boyd saw their captor's damp face flicker and tic. *Fucking stop, for Christ's sake!*

It did, thank God, before the *dudda-dudda diddly doop* sign-off – and before the phone owner's brains were smeared across the chequered pattern of the train's seats. Boyd could pretty much smell the sweat coming off the guy who'd rejected the call coming from his back trouser pocket.

'You,' said the gunman to Boyd. 'Get all phones.'

'I need my hands,' said Boyd.

The gunman squatted down and, with a flick of his knife, sliced through the cable tie. Boyd's wrists fell apart from each other. He couldn't help but let out a wheeze of relief. Having hands again made him feel less vulnerable.

'Get phones,' said the young man, backing a few steps away, gun raised at Boyd once again.

Boyd nodded. 'Okay... right, okay.' Slowly, very slowly, with his hands raised to show he was simply complying, he struggled to his feet and turned to face the other men in the carriage.

'I need your phones,' he announced. 'If you've got one on you, could you nod your head?'

11

1.27 a.m

Okeke listened to the radio chatter that was feeding into the control room from the first police officers to arrive at the scene. She was also getting live video streamed to her computer screen from one of the uniformed officers who'd arrived at the trackside.

He was some distance away from the scene. She could see a stationary four-carriage train on the track right beside the sea. On the inland side was a static caravan park. Officers with high-vis jackets and torches were knocking on the caravans closest to the track, hustling half-dressed occupants out and away. The whole scene flickered with the headache-inducing blue lights flashing from the top of the patrol cars that had pulled up inside the campsite.

'Fuck me,' wheezed DI Abbott. 'It's going full-on *Die Hard*.' That was one of Jay's favourite films. Lots of blam-blam, lots of crash-crash, lots of dead-dead. Okeke sincerely hoped it wasn't going full-on *Die Hard*.

She recognised the Chief Super's voice over one of the radio channels. Her Madge had been roused from her bed and had arrived at the station only a few minutes ago. She was now somewhere on the floor above, monitoring events, but no more. Active control was down in Bexhill. Chief Inspector Bailey was the force's incident manager, consulting with the tactical firearms officer on the next step forward. They operated a Gold–Silver–Bronze command structure. Hatcher was Gold; the sergeant in charge of the armed officers was Bronze. The 'go' command had to come from Gold, but once things were in motion it was Bronze who took over.

The streaming chest-video-cam spun away from the campsite and settled back on the stationary train. Okeke could hear the officer's whispered commentary.

'... the last train out from Brighton. Departed Eastbourne without incident at zero thirty hours and was stopped at about zero fifty hours. We have most of the passengers in the rear carriage and about a dozen or so hostages in the front carriage...'

Okeke's phone vibrated in her jacket. She pulled it out to see Emma Boyd's name flash up on the screen.

'Emma? What's –'

'Dad's on that train!' Emma blurted out.

It took Okeke a few seconds to wrap her head around the fact that Emma knew this was going on already. 'The train incident?'

'It's on TikTok!' said Emma. 'Someone's filming it! *That's Dad's train!*'

'Did he call you?'

'No. I got a bulletin alert. Then I saw someone's streaming it on social media.'

Okeke swore under her breath. *That's right. Shit... Boyd was in Brighton today – the LEDS workshops.*

Emma's voice was shaking. 'It's on TV now as well. I don't know if Dad's all right.'

The Last Train

'It's okay, Emma, it's okay. The train is surrounded by police. They've got it locked down. There've been no reports of gunshots. It's all quiet at the moment.'

DI Abbott nudged her arm. 'Shouldn't be telling her sit-rep stuff,' he muttered.

Okeke gave him dagger-eyes. 'Nothing's happening right now.'

'Are you there?' asked Emma.

'No. I'm at the station. I'm watching streamed video from the responders.'

'I'm so scared. I can't believe Dad's on it!'

'It's okay, Emma. He's going to be all right. He's had training for this kind of thing; he'll know exactly what to do.'

'Oh, God...'

'Don't worry, Emma. You know your dad. He'll be keeping his head down.'

12

2.01 a.m.

Boyd could see the flashing blue lights outside. The multiple strobing effect really wasn't helping to keep things calm. Any muppet could see that the increasing number of flashing lights and high-vis jackets were pushing the hijacker towards the edge. Boyd was sitting closest to him on the aisle floor, halfway down the carriage; the rest of the hostages were sat on the floor at the rear, their hands still bound behind their backs.

At least with everyone's mobile phones tossed outside onto the track, there were going to be no more surprise ringtones to wind him up even more. Once the police had organised themselves outside, they'd try to engage him via a loudhailer. And that, Boyd imagined, was only going to make things worse. It was almost as if the hijacker had not planned beyond the part where he stopped a late-night train and took some hostages. He seemed unsure as to what to do next.

You need to talk to him, Julia whispered. His late wife could sometimes be Queen of the Bleedin' Obvious, but her advice had always been sound.

'Hey, mate...' Boyd rasped softly. The gunman turned away from the activity going on outside to look at him. 'You got a name?'

'Fuck. Silent!' the young man hissed. The tip of the bloodied knife swung towards Boyd.

He couldn't take his eyes off the blade. For some reason, knives had always scared him more than guns. Perhaps it was because something so non-descript as a kitchen utensil could become an instrument of death in a heartbeat. A gun was always a gun. But a knife could be a Jekyll and Hyde.

Boyd took a quick deep breath to clear the fear out of his voice. 'A word of advice... keep your head low and don't wave that or the gun around. The police may already have a green-light on shoot-to-kill.'

The man took a second to digest that, then hunched a little further down.

'Better,' Boyd added.

The gunman turned to peer up at the window. It was practically opaque with the build-up of condensation. It was getting cold outside, but inside the fuggy warmth persisted. If the police had marksmen positioned outside, getting a clear ID on who was a hostage and who wasn't was going to be difficult with the windows all fogged up.

Keep talking to him.

'So what's your name?' asked Boyd.

The man's eyes flashed angrily at him from beneath the peak of his cap. 'Silent.'

'Look –' Boyd decided to press his luck – 'you need to give them a name. So they know who they're dealing with. They'll want to know what your demands are.'

Please bloody have some. If he didn't, that didn't bode well.

The man glared at him again and Boyd nodded to indicate

he got the message. His question had been timely, because just then he heard the pip of a loudhailer being switched on.

'THIS IS THE SUSSEX POLICE FORCE. HOSTAGE NEGOTIATOR SPEAKING. PLEASE INDICATE THAT YOU CAN HEAR ME!'

The gunman hunched further down in his seat, then turned to Boyd.

He's looking at me for advice?!

'You should wave a hand at the window,' said Boyd. 'Let them know you hear.'

The man didn't respond, his eyes narrowing.

'If they're talking, they won't try entering,' Boyd added.

The gunman raised a hand above his head and waved it around beside the window.

'GOOD! THANK YOU!' came the voice outside.

Boyd managed a tight smile. 'There you go, mate. You've got some breathing space.'

'Riz,' he replied.

'Sorry?'

'Riz,' he repeated. 'Name is Riz.'

'Okay...' Boyd nodded. 'Boyd.'

'Boy?' the man said, one brow raised.

'Boyd,' he repeated, emphasizing the 'd'.

'DO YOU HAVE A MOBILE PHONE WE CAN COMMUNICATE ON?!' called the negotiator.

Again, Riz turned to Boyd, who mimed using a phone.

Riz shook his head. 'No phone.'

'Tell *them*,' said Boyd, nodding at the window. 'You'll need to open it.'

Riz slid the top window panel open, letting in a blast of welcome cool air, and yelled, 'NO PHONE!'

'OKAY. UNDERSTOOD.'

Boyd glanced over at the legs of the train driver; they were

The Last Train

still moving. He was alive. Just. 'You need to let that man get some help,' said Boyd.

Riz turned to look up the aisle at the driver, then back at Boyd and nodded. 'How?'

Boyd pointed at himself, then up at the fogged window. 'Let me talk to them?'

He looked suspicious.

'I'll shout,' said Boyd. 'That, okay?'

Riz hesitated a moment, then nodded.

Boyd cupped his mouth towards the window. *'CAN YOU HEAR ME?'* he bellowed slowly.

A moment later the negotiator replied: 'YES. WHO IS THIS?'

'My name's Boyd. I'm an off-duty copper. I'm speaking on behalf of the hijacker!'

A few seconds passed. Then:

'OKAY, BOYD. WHAT DOES HE WANT?'

Riz nodded at the driver.

'The train driver is injured and needs urgent medical assistance. He will allow someone on to the train to take him off!' Boyd double-checked that with a glance at Riz. He nodded.

'OKAY. GOOD. STAND BY!'

'What is happen now?' asked Riz.

Boyd wasn't entirely sure. The negotiator now knew there was only *one* armed man to deal with, but, because they had no idea what *he* looked like, they probably weren't going to risk using the wounded train driver as a cover to storm the train. Nothing so bold just yet.

Boyd pointed at the window again, then at himself, then said to Riz, 'I should show myself. Let them see me.'

Riz frowned suspiciously again.

Boyd persisted. 'I'll need to let the paramedics onto the –'

'Stay!'

Boyd tapped the seat beside him with one hand. 'If I sit up... Show myself? I can help you communicate with them.'

Riz paused, then nodded. 'You. Can. Sit.'

Boyd smiled briefly, raised his hands where Riz could see them, and struggled up off the floor and onto the seat.

'*Hello! Can you see me?*'

'WE SEE YOU.'

Boyd waved a hand, hoping the fogged glass wasn't making his hand look like it was waving a gun. '*This bloke's going to allow paramedics on, to get the driver.*'

'UNDERSTOOD. STAND BY...'

13

2.27 a.m.

Emma had the TV on the BBC News channel, her laptop open on the Hastings Old Town Facebook page, and the TikTok app open on her phone. Out of all three sources, it was her phone that was delivering the most information.

The train had come to a stop just outside Bexhill, alongside a caravan and static trailer camp. She was watching a livestream video coming from some kid's phone inside the camp. The pictures were grainy, shaky, frequently drifting in and out of focus and accompanied by the voice of some teenager repeatedly whispering 'No way! No way!'

Emma could see two figures in paramedic-green manoeuvring a stretcher out of the front carriage's door and down onto the track.

'Oh, God,' whimpered Emma. 'Oh, God... no, no, no...' She was absolutely certain that if anyone was coming out of that train on a gurney, it was going to be her dad, simply because she knew he was dumb enough to announce himself as a copper-off-duty.

She'd tried his phone several times already and each time it had gone to voicemail. She hoped to God that tomorrow morning he'd be moaning at her for all the messages he was having to delete. She swiped the screen to try calling again, and, as she did, the phone buzzed in her hand.

She saw Okeke's name and answered.

'You watching this on TV, Emma?'

'On TikTok. Is that my dad on the stretcher?'

'No, love. No. It's the train driver. He was shot or stabbed. The hijacker's letting medics take him off the train.'

'Has anyone else been hurt?'

'I don't know, Emma. I don't think so. Your dad's okay, though.'

'How do you know?'

'He's speaking for the hijacker.'

'What?!!'

'It's okay, Emma. He's doing a good job. There's a dialogue open; this'll be over soon. I promise.'

~

BOYD WATCHED the paramedic jump onto the track, then, with his colleague, ease the stretcher down to the ground.

He pulled the door to the carriage closed and returned from the vestibule, walked towards Riz and took his seat again.

'That was the right move,' he said to the young man. 'You bought yourself some time and goodwill.'

Riz nodded.

Boyd opened one of his hands and showed him a small radio handset. 'They gave me this, so you can talk directly to the negotiator now.'

Riz shook his head. 'No more talk.'

The Last Train

'You need to talk to them,' said Boyd. 'You need to tell them what you want.'

Riz looked at Boyd and said nothing.

'What's this about? Riz?'

He shook his head. 'You not my friend.'

'Well, no... okay. But this situation doesn't need to end with you dead. Do you understand?' Boyd nodded out of the window and pointed. He knew the police outside could see his gesture and hoped that the FTOs that undoubtedly had scopes on the window knew that he wasn't the man they were after.

'If the train driver dies... they'll definitely have a shoot-to-kill order if they can get a clear shot on –'

'I am ready to die,' Riz said.

'Well good for you. The rest of us have still got some shit to sort out, though.'

Riz smiled. Boyd hoped for a moment that was because he found him funny.

'Tell police... if they shoot me, *all* die.' He lifted his sweatshirt to reveal wires and a row of what looked like cigarette packets wrapped in foil and taped to his skin.

'Fuck!'

Riz nodded and repeated that. 'Yes. Big fuck.'

It felt as though the seat beneath Boyd had dropped away – he was weightless for a vomit-inducing moment. His scalp and neck prickled and for a second he really did think he was going to throw up the beer and crisps he'd filled his belly with earlier in the evening.

Riz lowered his shirt and Boyd realised the other men down the far end of the carriage probably hadn't seen it. Only he knew how utterly fucked they all were right now.

Clear your head, mate. Clear your head. Then talk.

He blew out several fluttering breaths. 'You want me to tell the negotiator that there's a bomb in here?'

Riz shrugged.

'It's probably a good idea, mate,' said Boyd. 'They'll give you a bit more thinking time.'

'No more thinking time.'

'Riz... c'mon, mate, why? What's this about?'

The man shook his head as if that was the world's dumbest question. 'You not understand.'

'Try me.'

Riz curled his lip; his face had the look of someone tired of explaining himself to fools. 'I die. No problem.'

'Riz... shit, what do you want? Why are you –'

He smiled. 'Revenge.'

'For what?'

He shrugged. 'Enough of talking.'

'But, Riz –'

'No more "Riz",' he snapped irritably.

'I'm trying to help.'

'Shut fuck up now!' The tip of the knife swung towards Boyd's face again. 'You not help me. Only help *you*.'

'I'm trying to save lives.'

He sneered at that. 'Only care some lives.' He held the blade closer to Boyd's face. 'You stay here. Or I kill you.'

'What're you going to do?'

The blade came right up to Boyd's chin and tickled the bristles of his beard.

'Finish job,' the young man whispered. He took the radio out of Boyd's hand and stuffed it into a pocket. 'You silence now.'

Riz crawled down the aisle towards the others, keeping his head low. He stopped a few yards short of them and slowly studied them.

'You!' he said after a minute. He pointed his gun at one of them. 'Come.'

The man was in his mid fifties, balding, plump with a face that was ashen and waxy. 'Me?'

The Last Train

Riz nodded. 'Come!'

The man shook his head. 'Please!'

'Come or I shoot!' said Riz, raising the gun.

The man struggled up to his knees. 'Okay! Please! Don't shoot! Please!' He managed to get up onto his feet, despite his arms being tied behind his back.

'Stay low,' called out Boyd, nodding at the fogged windows. The man's eyes widened and he quickly lowered himself back down onto his knees and advanced reluctantly up the aisle towards Riz. He stopped. 'God. Please... I... d-don't...'

'SHUT UP!' Riz aimed the gun at him. 'Closer!'

'Riz,'said Boyd. 'Whatever you're thinking of doing, this is –'

'ENOUGH!' He swung his aim round to Boyd. 'I said no more talk!!'

Boyd raised his hands again in a gesture of compliance. *He's beginning to lose it.*

He could see a finger curled on the trigger again. If he put any more weight on it, whether his shot hit anyone or not, the sound would trigger a storming of the carriage. And, if that vest bomb was the real thing, lead to a lot of dead people.

'Riz... be careful. Don't fire that gun.'

'I shoot you!' he snapped back, then turned to face the man he'd picked out from his group of cowering hostages. He was on his knees in the aisle just a yard from the hijacker.

'Please...' The man shook his head, becoming tearful. 'Please... don't... sh-shoot me.'

Boyd heard Riz muttering something in his own language. It could have been some sort of prayer. Or it could just as easily be him talking himself into proceeding with what he had planned.

'Turn,' he said, holding his knife out.

'Please! I haven't done anything!'

'TURN AROUND!'

'No! Please!'

45

'DO THIS OR I SHOOT!'

Is he going to... cut his throat?! The thought came to Boyd's mind along with the horrific recollection of images from fifteen years ago of various terrified men in orange boiler suits kneeling in a desert.

The man shuffled slowly round, sobbing.

Riz stepped forward, tucked the gun into his waistband and grabbed the back of the man's shirt. 'This is for justice...' muttered Riz. 'This is for revenge.'

With his knife, he sliced through the material up to the back of the collar, the blade nicking the man's skin near the top, between his shoulder blades. The man screamed with the sting of the unintended laceration. A trickle of dark blood ran down his pale back.

'PLEASE!!!!'

Riz sliced at the man's leather belt, then the waistband of his trousers, pulling the material down to expose the man's underpants, now wet with urine.

That was where Boyd's recollection became a little hazy. One minute he was fixating on the knife in Riz's hand; the next, all hell broke loose.

14

2.37 a.m.

Someone suddenly lurched to their feet. Boyd saw over the screaming man's bare shoulder that it was Lucas. He screamed something in whatever Eastern European language he spoke and lunged forward. In the split second that followed, Boyd honestly couldn't see what Lucas was hoping to achieve. The exposed man was hunched over on his knees in between Lucas and Riz and, now that Lucas was on his feet, Boyd could see that he was quite a short and stocky man. He was going to crash into the other hostage and send both of them sprawling to the floor.

Boyd had underestimated Lucas's agility. Lucas put a foot on the man's arse, stepped up and catapulted himself towards their hijacker.

Riz had reached down to his waistband and had just got a handle on the gun when Lucas landed on him head-first like a human cannonball. They both crashed to the floor of the aisle. Boyd was on his feet and charging forward to help Lucas before he had time to think that the smart thing to have done would have been to dive for cover.

'HE'S WEARING A BOMB!' Boyd bellowed as he dropped down to join the flailing bodies.

Once again he found himself frantically scrabbling to get his hands on one of Riz's wrists. The gun or the knife hand were an equal priority. Riz could ditch either weapon, reach into his pocket and flick a toggle switch at any second.

Lucas was using his head as a weapon, swinging it down again and again trying to headbutt the gunman while his bound arms flexed and contorted, trying to pull free of the cable tie.

Boyd had his hands on the knife hand, one holding the wrist, the other trying to peel Riz's fingers off the knife – all the while certain the gun was going to go off again, this time finding his head.

He finally got the knife free and let it clatter to the floor, still holding Riz's wrist. 'WHERE'S THE OTHER HAND!!!' he yelled.

Boyd heard him let out a piercing scream and turned to see Lucas had sunk his teeth into the side of his neck like some ferocious zombie. Riz was bashing at the side of Lucas's head with the handle of the gun, trying to get him off.

The gun fell out of Riz's hand and spun off into the darkness beneath one of the seats. Boyd reached to secure Riz's other hand. He got a purchase on his wrist and Lucas wriggled across the man's chest, using his bulk to weigh him down.

Boyd pushed Riz's left arm down and, kneeling on his wrist, he reached across to grab the knife. With a quick flick, he sliced at Lucas' cable tie, and now, finally, between them they had four hands to deal with the squirming bastard.

Lucas, his mouth wet with blood, was now screaming in his own language while repeatedly punching Riz in the face. Boyd pulled Riz's sweatshirt up to get a look at the vest bomb. The

The Last Train

packs of foil, a dozen of them, had a red wire running from one to the next and then up towards his shoulder.

Boyd jerked the shirt higher to see where it led. It could be a switch, a timer, a small phone – there were any number of ways to trigger it.

He was dimly aware of other voices shouting now. Glass smashing. Chaos unfolding from all directions. There were bodies swarming into the carriage as he fumbled inside the man's shirt, all the way up to his shoulder, trying to trace where that red wire was going. He felt his fingers prick on something sharp and realised he'd found a frayed end taped to Riz's collar bone. It was a dead end.

It's fake. He felt a flood of relief.

He turned to see two armed police staring at him down the barrels of their assault rifles.

'STEP BACK! STEP BACK! STEP BACK!' they were both shouting over each other.

'The vest's fake!' yelled Boyd. 'It's FAKE!'

'STEP BACK!' both officers screamed at Boyd. He scooted backwards on his bum, his shoes slipping in the growing slick of blood on the floor. He felt the gun beneath his buttock and scooted further back to allow the officers to see it was out of Riz's reach.

A third officer pulled Lucas back in a neck-hold, away from the discarded knife.

'It's okay! IT'S OKAY! He's a hostage!' Boyd shouted before they mistakenly put a bullet in him.

Lucas was dragged roughly all the way back to where the other hostages were seated.

And then it went bizarrely silent.

Riz was gurgling on his back. Legs splayed out, arms clutching the ragged bite wound on his neck. He was no immediate threat.

'PARAMEDIC!' someone shouted behind the two officers,

whose guns were still aimed at Boyd. The word rippled down the carriage, out into the vestibule and then out into the night.

That should have been the end of it. But Riz flopped over onto his side and looked at Boyd, his mouth opening and closing, trying to say something. It sounded like he was repeating the same word, over and over.

'For fuck's sake, stay still!' Boyd hissed.

But Riz didn't. His hand slid across the grimy floor towards the gun.

He tried again to say something – but it was drowned out by the gunfire.

15

Boyd woke up late to the sound of seagulls flying low over Ashburnham Road and the clatter of glass bottles tumbling down the gullet of a rubbish truck. He remembered it was bin day today. The gulls were there to remind everyone.

He looked at his watch. It was quarter past ten. They were late this morning.

But then so was he, albeit with one hell of an excuse.

He'd managed to hit the sack at 5 a.m., having been taken to Conquest Hospital first to be looked over, then quickly, informally, interviewed by Sutherland and Hatcher, who'd come to the hospital to check on him.

Then Emma had brought him home. She made him a mug of over-sugared builder's tea, which he probably hadn't touched, and now he was lying in bed, listening to the rubbish truck slowly make its way uphill past his house.

He got up, pulled on a T-shirt and a pair of tracksuit bottoms from the 'clean pile' sitting on top his chest of drawers, and headed downstairs.

He entered the dining room. Emma was at the table on her laptop. 'Hey, Dad, what're you doing up so early?'

'It's gone ten.'

'Hello?' she replied. 'Earth to Dad... You were hostage to a crazy guy last night...'

A small part of him had been hoping it had been one of those vivid dreams that have a tendency to linger for a while. A dream so real that you found yourself wondering if it had actually taken place.

'It's top of the BBC's Most Read list,' she said. She turned her laptop round and showed him some grainy stills of a train silhouetted by floodlights, and the heading 'Train siege on South coast'.

'And it's all over Facebook,' she added. 'And the TV. And, like, everywhere.'

Boyd sighed. 'Wonderful.' Emma had made a cafetiere of coffee so he poured himself a cup and sat down opposite her. 'Please don't tell me my name is splashed everywhere?'

She shook her head. 'No names yet. Just that it happened outside Bexhill, early hours, armed police involved, single gunman subjugated and pronounced dead at the scene.'

Boyd tried to wind his jumbled memory backwards: him and Emma talking last night, the hospital, the ambulance from... the campsite... beside the stationary train... The further back he delved, the more chaotic and jumbled it all became.

I must have been in shock.

He pushed his memory harder and recalled the gunman – his name suddenly came back to him. Riz, lying on his back, gasping for air. Then, yes... the gunshots. *Shots*. Plural.

'I was right beside him,' said Boyd.

Emma reached out to squeeze his arm. 'I think you're expected to have to go and see someone about this, you know.'

'Huh?'

'Some sort of immediate counselling?'

Dr Munroe had been assigned to him by the HSE following the Sutton case. Then, last night, Chief Superintendent Hatcher had thrown some additional sick leave at him, along the lines of 'Don't you dare turn up at work for at least a fortnight, Boyd'.

So, he was already seeing a psych. One session a week on a Wednesday morning.

At least they weren't going to run out of things to talk about now.

The front door's knocker clacked loudly and Ozzie fired off a couple of ear-splitting barks in case they hadn't noticed. Boyd went to answer it.

He pulled the door open to find Charlotte reaching for the knocker, about to try again. Her eyes rounded as she looked up at him. 'Thank God!' She placed a hand on her chest. 'I thought... there were no replies. I thought you might be on that train.'

'Ah, I'm so sorry. Shit, sorry.' Boyd shook his head as he remembered. His phones along with those of the other men in the front carriage had been tossed out of the window. Even if they were still working, they would have been bagged and tagged and in an evidence room by now.

'My phones were chucked out of a window,' he said.

'Were you on it? The train?' she asked.

He nodded. 'But it's okay.'

Neither of them seemed to have figured out yet quite what their friendship was – a casual dog-walking acquaintance, or something else – nor what the boundaries and rules of their association were. She reached out with both hands and he grasped them in his fists and then waved them up and down in the odd way a boxing referee will grab a boxer's mitt to announce the winner.

'Oh, God,' she gasped.

'I'm okay. I'm okay,' he said. He stepped backwards into the house, pulling her clumsily so that she staggered over the threshold. In his head, the manoeuvre was meant to culminate in some kind of manly embrace, but instead they must have looked like a pair of kangaroos squaring up to fight.

He let her go before he pulled her right off her feet and onto the floor.

As he released her hands, Charlotte said breathlessly, 'I rang and texted as soon as I saw the news this morning!'

Of course. He'd told her earlier in the week about his looming trip to Brighton on Friday.

'I'm okay,' he said again, softly this time. 'A little shaken up but still in one piece.'

If he'd been a little better at judging moments and moods, he might have leaned in for a hug, but the moment passed and Emma appeared in the hallway.

'Oh, hello. Charlotte? I've just made coffee. Fancy a cup?'

∼

LATER THAT MORNING, after Charlotte had left to go back to her job at White Rock Theatre and he'd persuaded Emma to head into work too, Boyd surfed through the news channels on his Sky box. He settled on BBC News 24, which was showing a live image of the train he'd been held captive in last night, surrounded by police in high-vis jackets keeping the public and the press well back from the taped area around the track.

'... *as far as we know, there have been two fatalities: the driver of the train is one, the other is said to be the hijacker. At the moment, the police are not saying whether or not the attack was terror-related. It's thought that the incident could have been far worse; an eyewitness from the Shingle Beach Caravan Park heard a number of gunshots inside the train and there are rumours that the gunman may have been wearing a vest bomb...'*

The landline phone trilled on the bay windowsill. He muted the TV, reached over and picked it up. 'Boyd?'

'Guv, when are you getting a replacement phone? I had to hassle Emma at work to get your house line.' It was Okeke.

'Umm... I'm hoping to get at least one back from evidence at some point.'

'Ha! Good luck with that,' she replied. 'Anyway, how are you doing?'

He vaguely remembered speaking to her in the early hours after Emma had brought him home from the hospital. 'Fine. Knackered. A bit shell-shocked.'

'I bet you are. Her Madge and Sutherland asked me to find out when you were planning to come in. Not that they're nagging,' she added quickly. 'They made a big thing about saying that you're taking as long as you need... but they also want to get a full debrief as soon as possible.'

He bet they did. This was another headline-grabbing incident on Sussex Police's turf. The Sutton case might have been all but forgotten – the UK press had moved on from the unfortunate 'accidental' death of a former government minister – but a story as emotive and visceral as a 'terrorist hijacking' was going to have legs.

'Monday morning,' replied Boyd. 'They've both interviewed me already and I'm having my weekend.'

Now that the adrenaline had deserted his blood, he felt as though he was nursing a hangover. But at least he was thinking a little more clearly now. The jumbled narrative of events was beginning to settle down and he was having momentary flashbacks of intense detail.

And the delayed emotional responses were finally kicking in too.

Fucking hell. I could have died.

'Yeah, I need the weekend.'

'That's what I thought,' said Okeke. 'And Monday morning's pushing their luck, to be honest.'

'No. I'll be good to come in then,' he replied. 'I just need a couple of days to clear my head.'

16

Lucas Pesic's right shoulder had been dislocated in the struggle with the gunman. After being dosed up on gas and air, the doctor had popped it back into its socket and put his arm into a sling to protect the damaged soft tissue from further harm. The nurse informed him that he should give his right arm complete rest for a few days to give the muscles and tendons time to settle down.

'Do you have a partner who can help you at home with things like unscrewing bottle caps and jars?'

'No. I live alone.'

'Well, perhaps you can ask a neighbour or a friend to help you with things like that,' said the nurse.

Lucas was on nodding terms with the Albanian man who rented a bedsit on the top floor of the house he lived in. Perhaps if he got into any difficulties he could knock on his door and ask for help.

'What is the bill for this?' he asked grimly.

The nurse smiled. 'We're not America yet, thank God. No charge.'

He nodded gratefully. 'Thank you for your kindness.'

'It's what we do, pet.' She patted his back. 'Now, if you go and see the A and E registrar, you'll get the doctor's discharge letter to take home with you, which you can show your employer to get sick leave.'

'I have no boss. I work for myself.'

'Ah.'

'I am delivery driver for pizza shop.'

'Ah, I'm afraid you won't be able to drive for a bit.'

Lucas sighed. 'But I need the money.'

'Perhaps you can take the letter to the benefits office? Maybe there's some sort of financial assistance you can get?'

He suspected the young woman had no idea really. It wasn't her fault. There was no point pleading his case to her. He nodded and began to gather his things.

'Hold on,' she said. 'A word of warning. There's a whole load of journalists making a nuisance of themselves at the main outpatients' exit.'

The last thing Lucas needed right now was people jostling and haranguing him about last night. 'Oh, shit,' he muttered.

'You might want to use the geriatric patients' exit.'

She helped him pick up his bits and pieces and led him out of the triage ward and down a hallway. She pointed to the sign. 'Follow that – it's quiet and leads straight to the taxi ranks and bus stop.'

Lucas thanked her again and, clutching his canvas bag, he shuffled down the hallway towards the smaller exit.

His ribs ached painfully and one ankle had been twisted badly during the scuffle. His whole side was purple, but the scan had shown no broken bones.

It could have been far worse, one of the police officers who'd brought him in had told him. The vest bomb could have been very real. He could have suffered life-changing injuries – or, more likely, been decorating the inside of the carriage.

Lucas realised how lucky he'd been and thanked the Virgin Mary for watching over him last night.

The sun was shining again today and dazzled him as it streamed in through the glass doors. He decided to take the bus instead of walking home. And... once he got back to his room, he was going to have a long lie-down and try to work out how he was going to make ends meet over the next month.

No work meant no money. No money... meant no room. It was a simple straight line of consequences that he was going to have to figure out a way around. Lucas had slept on the streets before and was determined he'd never have to face that ordeal again.

He emerged from the dimly lit lobby into the sunlight and, blinking back the glare, noticed a cluster of about a dozen men with cameras waiting at the bottom of the wheelchair ramp.

'Hey!' one of them called out. 'You're one of the passengers from the train hijacking last night, aren't you?'

The question caught Lucas off guard. 'Yes... I...'

Which was enough to trigger the avalanche. They surged forward, obstructing his way down the ramp. Their cameras snapped like machine guns, lenses all but jammed into his face.

'Please! I... Can you let me pass?'

The questions came at him all at once.

'Was it an ISIS terrorist?'

'What nationality was he? Afghan? Syrian?'

'Was it a jihadi? What did he want? What did he say?'

'Are you one of the passengers that tackled him?'

'Do you know where the terrorist came from? Was he black, mate? Middle Eastern?'

Lucas was making little progress. 'Please! Let me pass!'

'What's your name, mate? Do you want to give me your story?'

'Leave him the fuck alone!' shouted someone at the back. 'Give him some space!' A woman pushed through the men, roughly shoving them aside.

'Hey, fuck off!' shouted one of the journalists.

The woman – with boyishly cut short, dark hair, and dressed in black trousers, a leather jacket and a white blouse – had the swagger of someone who was used to crowd control. 'No, *you* fuck off, you parasite!' she replied, placing herself between Lucas and the scrum. 'Don't talk to these scumbags. Here... I've got a cab waiting for you!'

'I don't have money for –'

'Don't worry, it's pre-paid. Just get in and get yourself home.' She put an arm around his shoulders, then, with her other arm reaching out to prevent anyone coming too close, she cleared a path for him and walked him over to the waiting car.

'Thank you! Thank you, Miss...'

'Ruth.' She pulled a business card out of her jacket and dropped it into his canvas bag. 'I'm here to help. Call me when you've had a chance to get some rest.'

She pulled the door open, bustled him in and slammed it shut. He caught one last glimpse of her through the window as she turned round and began shouting at the journalists.

'Where to, mate?'

'West Hill Road, St Leonards, please.'

17

'Thank you for coming in this morning. How're you doing, Boyd?'

'All right, ma'am.'

He had expected to see only Chief Superintendent Hatcher and Detective Superintendent Sutherland in the meeting in Her Madge's office, but there was a third person, a woman, sitting beside Sutherland. She turned in her seat and nodded a greeting to Boyd.

'This is DCI Yolanda Williams,' said Hatcher.

Boyd walked over and offered his hand. 'Good to meet you,' he said.

'Williams is from CTPSE,' said Hatcher.

Boyd wasn't surprised that someone from counter terrorism had been sent down from Thames Valley Police. There'd been noises about each force setting up their own CT unit, in an attempt to look as muscular on the issue as the recently beefed-up Border Force, but for the moment resources were still split across eleven regions, and Sussex came under the wing of Counter Terrorism Policing South East.

'DCI Boyd,' Williams said in greeting. Her hair was clipped

short and business-like all over. He noticed a little silvering around her temples. She looked tough and confident, Boyd thought. He guessed she'd had to be.

'I've learned how brave you were last Friday,' she said.

'Not out of choice,' he replied.

'It *was* a choice,' she countered. 'You weren't in uniform or on duty. You didn't have to volunteer that you're a policeman. And you rushed that terrorist not knowing that the gun and vest were fake.' She nodded respectfully. 'I think that qualifies as brave.'

'Take a seat, Boyd,' said Hatcher. She waited until he'd settled into the spare chair before she began. 'So, as I'm sure you're aware, the train hijack has been all over the news this weekend. Normally a leading story in its own right, but even more so because of the "passenger intervention" aboard the train, which, I believe, involved you and one other man, Lucas Pesic.'

She pronounced his name *Pes-ick*, rather than *Pes-ich*, Boyd noted. That was going to bug him.

'Pes-*ich*,' he clarified.

Hatcher bristled slightly.

'Pesic was the one who acted first,' he continued. 'I happened to be close enough to offer some assistance.'

'Right.' Hatcher cupped her chin. 'So this Pesic –' she said it correctly this time – 'was our main have-a-go hero, was he?'

Boyd nodded. 'He was. If he hadn't made the initial move, I... I, well, it was looking very much like the hijacker was getting ready to...' Boyd nearly said, *butcher the passenger*. The removing of that poor man's shirt had had a ritualistic quality about it, the muttered words almost like a prayer.

'Kill him?' prompted Hatcher.

'Yes, ma'am.'

'Very bloody brave,' muttered Sutherland, nodding his head. 'That must have been terrifying.'

'It was.' Boyd suppressed a flash memory of it: the man begging, crying, on all fours.

Hatcher looked down at her notes. 'This incident is a bit of puzzle, though. We still haven't been able to ID him. The hijacker.'

Williams cut in. 'That's correct. We've got an extensive watch list of young men on the path to becoming home-grown and radicalised; and another watch list of returned ISIS fighters. We're working our way through them as best we can with the information we have.' Williams leant on her arm rest. 'You said in your statement that he said his name was Riz?'

Boyd nodded. 'I've got no idea if that's a first name, second name or a nickname.'

'Riz is a common shortening of Rizwan, which is a Pakistani name,' said Williams. 'We have a few of those on our radar, but unfortunately we don't have a match so far.'

'We don't really know anything about him,' said Hatcher. 'Apart from his first name and what he looks like. We don't know what his intentions were, who he was affiliated with... or sympathetic to. Or even whether it can be officially classified as an act of terror.'

'Good God, I'd call it terrorism,' Sutherland scoffed.

'It was *terrifying*, if that's any help,' said Boyd. 'I'm not sure what the exact definition is.'

Williams nodded. 'That's what lies at the heart of this. The legal definition is *an attempt to influence or overthrow a government or induce public fear by using violence*. It's a broad definition that covers jihadis, alt-right fanatics, racists, homophobes, incels... Terrorism isn't always about God's will.'

'Right,' Boyd agreed.

'Some of the other hostages,' continued Williams, 'said you spoke with this Riz for a little while?'

'A little. I was trying to calm him down.'

'Did he say anything that sounded agenda-driven?'

Boyd shrugged. 'Such as?'

'Anything that might identify a cause? A crusade?'

'Not really no. He said something about revenge.'

'What exactly?' asked Williams.

Boyd struggled to recall. 'Something like, *This is for revenge.*'

Williams nodded thoughtfully. 'That's woolly.'

'Hmmm,' agreed Hatcher. 'It doesn't help us much. The problem is that we have the majority of the media leaning into the idea that he was a radical Muslim because of... well, the obvious *visuals*. He had a backpack and a vest bomb and he wasn't white.'

'He had a beard,' Sutherland offered. Hatcher gave him a withering glare.

'The method was very much Lone Wolf,' added Williams. 'The gun was a disguised athletics starting pistol, the orange plastic sprayed to look like gun metal. The vest-bomb explosives were clumps of modelling clay. The knife was a standard kitchen knife. There was nothing in his "arsenal" that couldn't be bought in any high street.' She settled back in her seat. 'With Lone Wolf radicals, they usually operate, as the name suggests: alone. No support network, no contacts; it's all DIY... it's all improvised. Which is why they're so difficult to spot before they decide to act.'

'There are no red flags?' asked Hatcher.

Williams shrugged. 'If we're lucky, a social media platform might alert us to content posted in the days that lead up to ideation becoming action. But it's usually too late. We find the final message, the justification rant, whatever... in the aftermath.' She sighed. 'Which is why I really hate social media. It's a breeding ground for troubled malcontents and we're increasingly playing whack-a-mole with angry young men who just suddenly pop.'

'Anyway,' Hatcher said, clapping her hands together. 'Let's focus. The point is... DCI Williams is here to find out whether this incident falls into the terrorism definition and thus becomes a case for CTPSE to run.' She turned to Boyd. 'I'm afraid you won't be on that team... because you were involved directly.'

He'd expected as much.

'And what's more, we –' she glanced at Sutherland to indicate it wasn't just her decision – 'we think you should take a couple of extra weeks' sick leave.'

Sutherland, taking the hint, piped up. 'Yes, Boyd. You've been through three traumatic incidents in the last six months. Then there's that awful stuff that happened to you a few years ago. And of course this last Friday on top. It's too much for anyone.'

Hatcher leant forward onto her desk. 'You're an excellent officer, Bill. I don't want to lose you to emotional burnout or a nervous breakdown. Is that clear?'

Boyd wondered if they were genuinely expecting him to argue with them. Some additional paid leave sounded just fine to him.

'Okay.' He clasped his hands together with a soft, concluding clap. 'Free paid leave,' he said with a smile. 'I'll take that.'

Hatcher looked relieved.

'Seriously,' Boyd added, nodding, 'I think I need this.'

18

Lucas tugged aside the net curtain and peered out of the window of his bedsit. Once again there was a flurry of activity down on the street. There were twenty or so journalists with cameras, smartphones, microphones, all of them peering up at his window and calling at him to come down and give them a few words.

Frederik, the Albanian man from the top-floor bedsit, was making them both a coffee. He came over to join Lucas at the window. His mop of black curls that tumbled out from underneath his Metallica baseball cap, his straggly beard and his tall, beanpole-skinny frame contrasted in every way possible with Lucas's short-clipped hair and squat physique.

'You very famous man now, eh?' Frederik said, nodding at the press mob below.

Lucas shrugged unhappily. 'I just help policeman on train. This is all.' He raised his arm in its sling. 'And now I can't work. What do I do?'

'I bet they give you much money,' suggested Frederik. 'Serious. Much money.'

Lucas shook his head. He wasn't after fame. His mother, if

The Last Train

she'd still been alive, would have said he was painfully shy. Always a quiet boy. He never wanted to be the centre of attention.

    Frederik grinned. 'Or maybe you be on TV?'

    Lucas shook his head again. 'I don't want to be on TV.'

    'Illegal?'

    Lucas nodded. 'I do not have the settled status.'

    He'd been living in the UK for just over ten years now, most of them in Hastings. And at no point in all that time had his path crossed with the authorities. Not once. He'd managed just fine living entirely within the twilight world of the cash-in-hand economy. Unlike back home, there was always work to be had: picking fruit during the summer months; takeaway meals to be delivered to folks every night. The owner of this house was happy taking a cash payment, so really, so far, Lucas had managed to avoid the need to enter his details on any government department form.

    And, now with this Brexit thing all done, it would be foolish to put his name down on any piece of official-looking paper. Why in the Sacred Mother's name would he? He'd been coping all this time without state money, without the benefits that everyone seemed to think his kind were hungry to get their 'grubby hands' on.

    As for healthcare, Lucas thought he was in good enough shape. He'd only needed medical help twice in the last ten years. Once for an infected cut, and the other time was last night. He'd avoided the Covid jab partly because he feared appearing on some official's paperwork and, if he was honest, partly because of the rumours about it having some tiny surveillance chip. Anyway, he had bought a forged vaccination card, which he could show employers when they asked, which was rare.

    But this… this situation was going to expose him as an illegal. There was no doubt about it.

'I try to do good thing,' Lucas muttered. 'Now I am fucked.'

Frederik stroked his beard. 'Maybe they help you?' he said, gesturing at the noisy pack of journalists.

Lucas wasn't so sure about that. The things that ended up in the papers about people like him were decidedly unhelpful. Hostile even.

The kettle snapped off and Frederik went to make the coffee. Lucas looked down again through the gauze of the net curtain at those people gathered outside. They really didn't look too friendly to him.

19

Boyd wasn't sure if dogs were allowed in the White Rock Theatre. At least, not the general public's dogs. He pushed the lobby door inwards, with Ozzie confidently leading the way inside before stopping suddenly to sniff at some faint stain on the burgundy carpet.

'Ozzie,' Boyd growled under his breath. 'If you're even thinking about leaving a gift...' He gave the lead a gentle tug and, as Ozzie put the brakes on, half dragged him over to Charlotte's office and tapped his knuckles lightly on the door.

'Come in!' she called out.

He pushed the door open and stuck his head in. 'Surprise.'

She looked up from her monitor and her face lit up with delight. 'Bill! What are you doing here?'

'It's nearly lunchtime.' He checked his watch. It was quarter to twelve. Not nearly. Not really. 'Fancy some fresh air and chips?'

Charlotte's dog, Mia, emerged from beneath her desk, shook herself down and came over to greet Ozzie in the appropriate manner – nose to his butt.

'It's early for you, isn't it?'

'I'm off duty,' he replied with a carefree grin. 'For the next two weeks, in fact.'

'Goodness, because of the train thing?'

'Yup. I'm officially on sick leave.'

'Good,' Charlotte smiled. 'I think you've been roughed up enough for now.'

∼

'So they just said go home?' she asked.

'Yup.' He picked up a flattish stone and prepared to skim it across the top of another lazy incoming wave. Ozzie danced in a circle with anticipation ready to chase it down, but it disappeared into the wave's belly without a single bounce. Ozzie looked from the sea to Boyd and back again with such an unimpressed look on his face that Boyd couldn't help but laugh.

'They told me to take two weeks off on full pay – but I've got to continue seeing my therapist.'

Charlotte glanced at him.

'Because of the train incident and all the other recent malarkey,' he clarified.

'Malarkey?' She raised her eyebrows. 'I don't think your Emma would just casually dismiss it as malarkey.'

Emma had single-handedly organised moving him out of London to Hastings; she'd even helped him fill in his re-deployment application because he'd been, well, next to useless last year. She'd moved him here, because apparently Hastings had been voted one of the nicest towns to live in along the Sussex coast. The idea had been to get him back into his job somewhere quiet. Somewhere not too challenging.

Well, that hasn't exactly gone to plan.

Charlotte sipped her cappuccino. 'I think time off is a really good idea.'

'Well, I'm not exactly complaining,' he said as he bent down for another stone. 'If September's weather holds out – that's two weeks in the garden on my lounger with an ice-filled beer bucket.'

'Lucky for some,' she replied with a friendly nudge. Then she added, more circumspect this time: 'How are you doing?'

'Okay.'

'No. Really.' She stopped in front of him, blocking the waves, stalling his next throw. 'I suspect you're one of those men who doesn't tend to talk about things.'

He wondered whether Charlotte, Her Madge, Dr Munroe and Emma were all in some WhatsApp group entitled 'We Need To Talk About Boyd'. Munroe had been saying the exact same thing to him for the last six weeks, trying to coax him to vomit up the last three years of grief and trauma.

'I'm not the whinging type,' he conceded. 'It's not a good look.'

Charlotte's brows locked together into a severe, scolding ridge. '*Whinging?*' she echoed.

He'd known it was completely the wrong thing to say as soon as the words had left his mouth.

He paused for a moment before saying. 'I just find talking about things too much stirs everything up. Brings memories up that I don't... that I'm not ready to conduct a post-mortem on.' He was thinking about Julia and Noah. He hadn't told Charlotte in great detail what he'd witnessed, just that it had been a fatal RTA.

'I'm not talking about *grief*, Bill,' she said, correctly guessing what he was referring to. 'Take it from me... it takes a lifetime to get over losing someone, and sometimes even a lifetime's not enough. I'm talking about *trauma*. Shock. Fear. Anger. Those aren't scars; they're tumours. You need to dig them out, or they'll eat you up.'

'Christ, when did you swallow a psychologist?' he said, unable to suppress a smile.

'I've been around awhile.' She smiled back at him. 'One or two more years than you. But who's counting, eh?'

Ozzie had given up waiting for Boyd to throw the next stone and was now doing zoomies and play-bows with Mia. Between them, they were kicking up rooster tails of wet sand and sea spray as they ran in circles through the retreating waves.

Charlotte nudged his arm. 'I'm just saying I'm here if you need to offload. I'm quite good at tea and sympathy, you know.'

～

BOYD RETURNED HOME AT THREE, after walking Charlotte back to work and lingering on the seafront with Ozzie for a while longer. There was no rush to get back to work, no cases to mull over nor calls to return. It was surprisingly cathartic, sitting on the pebbles with the beach largely to himself and watching the waves slowly retreat and reveal a wet petticoat of dark virgin sand.

The road outside his house was cluttered with vans parked one wheel on the curb and a small scrum of press waiting in the afternoon sun for something interesting to take a photo of. He managed to get almost all the way up Ashburnham Road to his house before someone spotted his approach.

'Mr Boyd?'

He made the mistake of looking at whoever had called out. A moment later he was wading through a mosh pit of pencil microphones and waggling smartphones, trying to keep Ozzie from being trod on, or, more to the point, from taking a bite out of someone for stepping on one of his paws.

'Are you the other passenger who helped take down the terrorist?'
'Do you see yourself as a have-a-go hero, mate?'
'What happened? How did you take him down?'
'Did you use anything as a weapon? A bottle? A brolly?'

Her Madge had firmly instructed him to stick to 'No

comment' if he got ambushed outside the station or his house. Boyd opted for 'Piss off!' as he shouldered his way through the ruckus to reach his front door.

He dug out his keys as Ozzie fired off a volley of warning barks. Then he let himself in.

'Fucking hell,' he muttered. He looked down at Ozzie. 'You all right, mate?'

Ozzie looked as though he was ready to trot back outside to give them another piece of his mind.

'Jesus,' he said to himself. *'Brolly?* Seriously?!'

20

'Hello?' Lucas checked the name on the business card. 'Is this Ruth Cadwell?'

'Is that Lucas Pesic?' she replied.

'Yes.' Wearing Frederick's Metallica baseball cap as a makeshift disguise, he was using one of the few public telephone boxes in Hastings that still functioned. 'Please. Can you help me?'

'Of course I can, Lucas. Where are you?'

'I am in phone box in Saint Leonards. There are reporters all around my home.'

'I'm not surprised. You're a hero. They want your story, Lucas. Look, give me a street name – I'll come and pick you up immediately.'

'I am at the front. Warrior Square.'

'Warrior Square. Give me ten minutes. And, Lucas?'

'Yes?'

'If anyone approaches you, asks you any questions, say nothing, okay? Absolutely *nothing*. Is that clear?'

'Yes.'

She hung up.

The Last Train

Lucas looked around. He felt like that poor man Brian in that famous British Monty Python film. He half expected to see a swarm of ancient Judeans holding sandals aloft while barrelling down the road towards him.

'I do not need this,' he muttered unhappily. 'I really do not need this.'

He had six pounds in change on him, clothes he'd worn earlier this week but was yet to take to the laundry, and his house keys. He felt like a fugitive on the run. Not a hero.

As Ruth had promised, ten minutes later a car pulled up on the far side of the road. A horn beeped once. He recognised the person driving it as the woman who'd got him the cab outside the hospital.

She waved him over, and he peered around. There were a few families strolling along the seafront, all bucket, spades and dripping lollies. But luckily no baying packs of reporters. He crossed the road quickly and got into the car.

'Thank you for your help,' he gasped.

'It's okay, Lucas,' said Ruth. 'Look, you're going to be chased down by everyone over the next few days. Newspaper reporters, TV stations, photographers, and they're going to want to know everything about you.'

'I do not want.'

'I know.' She smiled. 'I get that. So, if you can trust me... I'm going to take you to stay somewhere quiet and out of the way. And then we can talk about your options...'

'What are options?'

'Choices,' she said. 'How much money you can make from this. How much you want people to know about you. You're an illegal, aren't you?'

Lucas closed his mouth tightly.

'It's okay,' said Ruth. 'I don't work for Border Force. I'm not from the government.'

'But what if all the other people find out I am –'

'They inevitably will, Lucas. I'm sorry. You've stumbled into a big story and I know you were only trying to do the right thing on the train, but now...'

He turned to look at her. 'They will send me to ship camp?'

The holding ships that the Home Secretary had touted as a vote-winning policy before the last election had finally turned into a reality: three repurposed cruise ships had been stripped out and refitted to hold several thousand detainees at a time – and they had started filling up.

Ruth shook her head. 'Not if I can help it.'

'Are you the... legal advice?'

She smiled. 'Not quite, but I can *get* you some legal advice. I can help you organise an appeal. And, if we're cautious about how your story is told, we can get the Great British Public on your side, Lucas.'

'So I can stay?'

She nodded. 'So you can stay. And not in a floating detainment camp.'

21

DCI Williams had been given the Incident Room in which to hold her post-mortem briefing.

'Good afternoon, everyone.'

She had invited everyone from Hastings CID, including DCI Flack and his seven county-lines team regulars. She also had in the firearms officers who'd boarded the train and witnessed the climax to the siege. There were enough people in the room that the table had had to be pushed to the side and a dozen rows of seats set out.

'I'm DCI Yolanda Williams, CTP South East. This, I'm hoping, is going to be a very quick operation. We have a murder victim: the train driver. And we have our dead murderer. What we don't have, however, is his identity, or a clear motive. And regarding the motive... specifically we need to identify whether this was an 'act of terror' or otherwise, which will in turn define whether this continues as a Sussex Police case or comes over to the CTP.'

She picked up one of the many tabloids folded on the table beside her. 'This headline pretty much sums things up.' She turned it round to show her audience a photograph of the train lit up by floodlights and the headline **WHY?** stamped in capitals across the top.

'Why?' she said. 'That's the question. Why? What the hell was this all about? Was this an act of terrorism? Did he act alone? Was he a returned ISIS fighter? A home-grown radical? Or was he simply a... a wack job?'

There were a few wry smiles at that.

Williams set the paper down. 'We're going to be under pressure to answer those questions immediately. Not tomorrow, next week, but *now*. Every time we answer a press query with "We don't know yet", we look like a bunch of idiots. And we don't want that.'

Most of her audience nodded in agreement.

'So "Why?" is the most important question to answer as a matter of urgency. If this wasn't terror-related ... then –' she smiled – 'you'll be relieved, I'm sure, to have me out of your hair. I head back to Thames Valley Police and it becomes a Sussex Force murder. Until then, I'm afraid, I'm your SIO. Now then –'

'If it does turn out to be an act of terror,' interrupted Okeke, 'will the investigation relocate?'

Williams frowned at the interruption. She picked Okeke out of the audience – which wasn't difficult seeing as how she was the only other woman in the room. 'Like I *just said*,' she answered, 'it heads back to Thames Valley.' She returned her attention to the audience as a whole. 'Now then, we need to pursue two lines of enquiry. The first is to find out the hijacker's identity. We need a name and we need an address. If we get those, we may get a laptop, a phone, social media... and we'll know what we're dealing with. The second line of enquiry will be looking at the incident itself. The methodology used by our hijacker, behaviour markers and so on. We'll be interviewing the passengers, the hostages, including your colleague – what's his name?'

'DCI Boyd,' said Sutherland.

Williams nodded. 'We'll be looking for any indication of the hijacker's background, his behaviour, his state of mind... why he selected only white males to take hostage.' She paused. 'Yes. You heard that correctly. Only white males were taken as hostages...' She let that hang in the air for a moment. 'This could be a racially motivated crime. We need to handle this very carefully. We can't be seen to jump to the assumption he was some home-brew jihadi. I want an action log that clearly demonstrates that we've made no assumptions whatsoever. That we're not guilty of confirmation bias. Racial profiling. Islamaphobia. Is that clear?'

The room filled with a chorus of 'yes, ma'ams'.

'*Division*... is what shitty rags like this thrive on,' she added, tapping the stack of tabloids. 'It's what sells their papers. The longer we take... the more room they have to stir things up.' She picked up a notepad from the table. 'So, your D-Sup has given me a list of names he has available for my core team. Since I don't know any of your faces, can you stand up when I call out your name?' She looked at the scribbled names. 'DI Abbott.'

Abbott slowly stood up, grinning self-consciously at the rest of the officers in the room.

'You're going to be my second and operations manager.'

He nodded. 'Ma'am.'

'No more easy nightshifts, mate,' someone called out. The room filled with laughter and DI Abbot gave the room at large a withering glare before sitting back down.

'DS Minter?'

Minter stood up.

'You'll lead the first line of enquiry, the hijacker's identity.'

'Yes, ma'am.'

'DC O'Neal?'

O'Neal stood up, his cheeks beetroot red.

'You're in charge of collecting and collating information

from passenger and hostage interviews. I want to know every little detail of what happened on the train during the incident and in the time leading up to it.'

'Ma'am.'

'DC Okeke?'

Okeke stood up.

Williams looked at her sternly. 'Legwork. Right. That's all for now, everyone. You four,' she said to Abbott, Minter, O'Neal and Okeke, 'you've got until the end of your shift to find homes for any outstanding casework. I want your undivided attention from tomorrow morning onwards.'

22

'Great, thanks so much for picking me,' Okeke muttered to herself. 'Bitch.' She finished logging off and grabbed her jacket.

'Do I detect a note of resentment there?' Minter enquired, eyebrows raised.

'I just don't like the cow.' Okeke got up and shrugged her jacket on. 'Bloody *legwork*.'

She had been quietly stewing for the last couple of hours, barely giving any thought to the idiot-proof handover notes she was writing for Warren.

'I know exactly why she did that,' she huffed.

'No. But I expect you're going to enlighten me?' Minter replied.

'It's because I'm black and female.'

Minter's mouth dangled open.

She turned to look at him. 'You look shocked, Minter. Hadn't you noticed?'

'What? No. It's... I don't think Williams has got anything against you,' he said.

'Oh, you don't?' Okeke spat. 'Well, why did O'Neal get a specific role, and I'm the bloody gopher?'

He didn't have an answer. 'It's just, Okeke, I'm not sure how to say this...'

'*She's* also black and female?' Okeke said it for him. 'And why the fuck would she publicly humiliate a "fellow sister"?' Okeke added bitterly.

Minter sighed. 'I wasn't going to say it like that.' The usually unflappable DS looked like a deer caught in headlights. 'Well, I wasn't going to say it was anything to do with colour. I mean...'

Okeke pulled her bag off the back of the chair. 'Then what?'

'I mean... she's another woman in an all-male environment. Why would she deliberately do you down?'

'Who knows? Because she thinks the only woman in the room should be *her*? Because she sees another black woman and doesn't want to be seen showing the slightest hint of favouritism?' Okeke pushed her way through the double doors into the foyer and jogged down the stairs.

Minter hurried after her. 'Surely she would see another...' he faltered.

Okeke turned and half smiled over her shoulder. 'Go on, I'll let you say "black".'

'Okay then... another black woman as a good thing. Someone to be encouraged.'

Okeke pressed her ID against the reader and stepped past the barrier into the rear-exit foyer and out into the vehicle compound. 'See, that's just it, Minter... We're told, *We want you – We really want more BAME officers in the force, woman especially!*' She stopped and fumbled in her bag for her pack of cigarettes. 'But once we're inside, we're blame magnets. We're only in the force because we're black, because we're Muslim, because we're female. Some nice person held the door open for us to sneak in.' She pulled out a fag and lit up. 'And if something goes tits up and there's one of us on the team, it's like, *Ah... well, there you go... Standards dropping... What did you expect?'*

'Ah now, come on, Okeke... That's not true. You fuck everything up on a daily basis and you're still the boss's favourite.'

Okeke laughed. 'I'm serious, Minter. If something does go wrong or we don't come up with anything useful, the blame-finger will always point downwards – and guess who it'll end up pointing at! Williams won't want anyone accusing her of going easy on me. That's why she's going to ride my ass like Shergar.'

'Much as I'd like to see that...'

'MINTER!' Okeke said, shoving him hard. 'You are everything that is wrong with the force – can't you be serious for one minute?'

'OW!' Minter yelped. 'I was just going to say that I don't think that's what's going on.' He frowned. 'Seriously, Okeke. You don't need to worry. I'm only going to say this once: you're a good copper and I'd want you on my team every time.'

She patted his shoulder affectionately. 'Aww thanks, Minty – you're not as dumb as you look.' She smiled. 'Anyway. Enough of this, eh? Shall we go see the guv?' SHE shot him a sideways glance. 'I could put a good word in for you...'

~

BOYD OPENED THE FRONT DOOR, still half asleep. 'Minter? Okeke?'

'All right, boss,' said Minter.

'That's a good look,' said Okeke.

Boyd glanced down at his khaki shorts and flip-flops. The afternoon sun had pinked his shins and knees, adding the first bit of colour to his skinny legs for quite some time.

'I was grabbing some rays, before, you know, it buggers off

until the middle of next year.' He stuck his head out of the door. 'Ah good, looks like they've pissed off for the day.'

'The paps?'

Boyd nodded. 'They started to give up earlier this afternoon.' He pulled the door wide open. 'Come on in.'

His flip-flops slapped against the wooden floor as he headed down the hallway to the dining room. 'You two want a cold beer?'

'Thanks,' said Okeke.

'You got a diet-something?' asked Minter.

Boyd turned to look at him.

'Got the gym later, boss.'

Boyd rolled his eyes. 'Of course you have.' He reached into the kitchen fridge and pulled out a small bottle of beer for Okeke and a diet Coke for Minter. 'Come on outside.'

He led them into the garden where his lounger was half shaded by an umbrella. Ozzie lay flat out beneath it, too hot and bothered to get up and greet anyone.

'Any sign of my phones yet?' Boyd asked.

Okeke nodded. 'Ah, yeah. I've got this one.' She reached into her bag and pulled out his personal phone. The screen was shattered. 'It was pronounced dead on arrival, guv.'

'Great,' he said, inspecting the dented back before tossed it onto the lounger.

'Here.' Boyd pulled out two collapsible garden chairs before sitting down. 'To what do I owe the pleasure?'

'It's semi-official, semi-social, boss,' said Minter. 'There's a DCI Williams down from the counter terrorism unit at Thames Valley.'

'A real charmer,' added Okeke.

'I've already met her,' Boyd replied. 'You probably wouldn't want to spill her pint,' he added.

'Quite,' said Minter. 'She's running the enquiry. First port of call is finding out whether this was an act of terrorism or not.'

'She's tasked us with ID'ing the gunman, old-school style. Shoe leather and door-knocking in Brighton,' added Okeke.

'So far the counter terrorism lot have got nothing on this guy Rish,' added Minter.

'Riz,' corrected Boyd.

'I know you've already given a statement, guv,' Okeke added, 'but would you mind walking us through what happened on Friday again? Just the bits when you first became aware of him?'

'Sure,' Boyd said, and recounted his story from the moment he first noticed him at the coffee stand to seeing him again on the train. 'At first I thought he was just looking for a seat. You know how it is... Crowded train – you don't want to be stuck next to someone eating chips, or too loud, too sweaty. But, yeah, looking back on it now, he was definitely scoping everyone out.'

'And then the next time you spotted him, boss?' asked Minter.

'Eleven fifty-five p.m. – the train had pulled into Lewes and the driver announced there'd be a ten-minute hold while they uncoupled the rear two carriages. Riz was walking up and down the platform, looking into each of the windows.'

'What do you think he was looking for?' pressed Minter.

Boyd shook his head. 'Hostage candidates, maybe?'

Okeke took a slug of her beer. 'He was being selective?'

Boyd nodded. 'I think so. Very deliberately. And apparently I fitted the bill.'

'Which was?'

'Male. White. Middle-aged. There were eleven of us. We all fitted that same profile.'

'Was there any other overlapping descriptor?' asked Okeke.

He cast his mind back. The men had all varied in size and shape. 'Not really. It might have been some other selective thing... A behaviour? An activity? I don't know...'

'What were you doing, boss?'

'Not much. Dozing. Chatting.'

'What about clothes?' asked Okeke.

'I was wearing some, yes.'

She smiled. 'I mean...'

'Nothing eye-catching. Work clothes. Jacket, shirt, tie.'

'He stripped down one of the hostages, didn't he? Pretty much slashed his clothes off.'

Boyd nodded.

'Why?' she pressed.

Boyd still had no idea. 'Humiliation, possibly?'

'Humiliation... then what, boss?' asked Minter. 'We read an eyewitness report that said the hijacker looked like he was getting twitchy with his knife. The next step would have been execution, would it?'

Boyd reluctantly cast his mind back. As he reached back into the early hours of Friday morning, he felt goosebumps on his skin, and his stomach churned and flipped over. 'He had a knife in one hand. Yeah... maybe he was about to, you know...'

Minter blew out his cheeks. 'Scary stuff.'

'Fucking terrifying,' agreed Boyd.

'How are you coping?' asked Okeke.

Boyd took a long swig of his beer.

'Guv?' she prompted.

'I'm okay,' he replied. 'I mean... it's strange. While it was going on, I was okay. Kept my head. Stayed calm.' He shrugged. 'Now... I'm relaxing here in the sun with a nice cold beer, I'm getting the bloody shakes.'

'PTSD,' said Minter.

Okeke looked at him with heavy-lidded eyes. 'You think, sarge?'

'I prefer the term *after-shock*,' said Boyd, 'if that's even a medical term. It's just... when you think back, you realise it could easily have been much worse.' He took a deep breath to clear his head and settle his gut. 'Look, I've got a question for you two. Any idea which twat in our force leaked my name to the press?'

They both shrugged.

'You know how it is, guv. Just takes one flapping mouth.'

'Yeah, well, I've had a huddle of paps outside my house since it happened. Her Madge is lucky I haven't lost my shit with them, to be honest.'

'I think they're all after that little hairy fella who made the first move,' said Minter. 'Have-A-Go Hugo.'

Boyd rolled his eyes. 'Lucas. His name's Lucas. But I suppose they won't let something as boring as getting a name right ruin a catchy strapline.' Boyd picked up the *Mirror* from the ground beside his lounger and showed them the front page. 'This one's my favourite.'

There, taking up a quarter of the page was a picture of a bewildered-looking Lucas, emerging from Conquest Hospital with his arm in its sling. The headline was: HOLD MY PINT, SERGEI!

Okeke tutted. 'What's with the whole meerkat thing?'

'Look at him,' said Boyd. 'It's those thick dark eyebrows, probably. The dark stubble.'

They laughed. Minter pulled the conversation back to police work. 'So this guy, Riz... What was your impression of him, guv?'

'He was young. Nervous. Confused... at first. I'm not sure how committed he was to going through with whatever it was he was trying to do.'

Minter nodded. 'Did he fit the SLATE profile?'

SLATE was a clumsy acronym that Border Force and CTP had sent round at the start of the year: S for stressed appearance, L for loose clothing, A for alone, T for tense, E for eyes – shifty ones. Boyd had seen a few of those things in Riz. That was probably why he'd noticed him at the coffee stall in the first place.

'Yeah, he did.'

'Williams is especially keen to know if he's a radical or not,' said Okeke. 'Did he say or do anything that pushes the answer one way or the other?'

'Nothing overtly.' Boyd tried to remember what Riz had said and done. There'd been no declarations about his faith, none of the usual go-to phrases called out. No muttered prayers. 'I really don't think this was a religious thing,' he said.

'Then racial? Political?' she asked. 'Any kind of agenda?'

Again. Nothing. Boyd shook his head. There'd been no declaration by him that his action was in the name of anyone or anything. 'I don't think so. He... except...'

'What?' asked Minter.

'He said something about revenge.'

'What exactly?'

'That it was about revenge,' Boyd replied. 'I think.' His mind jumped to the last few seconds, to Riz lying on the ground gurgling blood and gasping at him.

'I remember he was trying to say something to me when they shot him.'

'What?'

'He was saying the same word over and over. It sounded like *zishad*.'

'Zishad?' Minter repeated.

Okeke's eyes narrowed. 'Well, hold on... if you want, I'll be the one to say it.'

The other two both looked at her. 'Say what?'

'Um... that it sounds a helluva a lot like... *jihad*.'

Boyd shook his head. 'No, definitely not that. He was looking at me as he said it. I think he was trying to tell me something important.'

'What?'

Boyd shrugged. 'I really don't know.'

23

Ruth Cadwell booked Lucas Pesic into a Premier Inn under her name, then settled him into his room. She put the kettle on.

'You want a coffee? Tea?'

Lucas nodded. 'Coffee, please.'

While she tore the sachets, he looked around the room. 'How long I am stay here?'

'For the next couple of days, Lucas. You saw what it was like outside the hospital, outside your bedsit. No one knows you're here and that'll give us time to work out the way forward for you.'

'Am I in trouble?'

'No.' Ruth turned round to look at him. 'Well, for what you did on the train, no. That was incredibly brave. You're a hero now.'

He shook his head. 'No... Not hero. I just did what need to be done.'

She studied him as he wandered around the room. *He's gold. Absolutely twenty-four-carat gold.* The public were going to lap him up. The *Mirror* was right: he *did* look a little like Sergei

Meerkat. He had a vaguely similar-sounding Eastern European accent. Most of all, he seemed charmingly humble. None of that after-the-event pumped-up machismo; none of that 'yeah, I totally decided to take him down' BS.

Ruth Cadwell had, in her tender care, a very, *very* marketable person.

The kettle finished boiling and she made him his coffee. 'Here you are, Lucas.'

'Thank you, Ruth.'

'Now, sit down. You and I need to talk.'

Lucas perched on the end of the bed as Ruth pulled out the chair from beneath the small dressing table.

'What you did, Lucas... Everyone – I mean, *everyone* – wants to hear about it. They want to know exactly why you did it, how you were feeling at the time. Then they're going to want to know about you, Lucas. What kind of man are you? What makes you tick? What makes you happy?'

Lucas nodded along to all that.

'Basically they'll want to know your whole life story,' Ruth went on.

He looked decidedly less happy about that idea. 'I do not want this.'

'Why?'

She could see his empty hand clenching into a fist and unclenching. 'Lucas, if I'm going to help you, you need to tell me if there's anything I should know. Are you in trouble? Have you broken the law?'

His eyes met hers and he gave her the slightest nod.

'Are the police after you?' she asked.

He took a moment with that question, then finally shook his head.

'Who then?'

'The Border Force.'

'Because you're here illegally? You told me this already. Is that it? Have they been in contact with you?'

He shook his head agin. 'Not in contact. No. I come here ten years ago. It is a long time.'

'Smuggled?'

He nodded. 'Back of truck.'

Ruth had covered numerous migrant stories for the *Daily Mail* in years past. She was glad to be well and truly out of that business and working for herself these days. She'd called her business Cadwell PR – it was a little boutique public relations agency that comprised herself and her office minion. The niche in which she operated was often referred to by hacks and paps as the 'Kyle Pile'. As in Jeremy Kyle. Everyday folks unintentionally caught up in news stories, completely unaware that for the duration of the news-worthiness they'd be ensnared; their every uttered word carried a monetary value. Ruth was in the business of putting a tap over their mouths and metering the output. Sometimes spinning it a little too.

'Lucas, listen very carefully to me...' She leant forward on her seat. 'In the public's eyes, you are a superhero. When they hear your story, they'll back you; they'll campaign for you, and Border Force and the Home Office will have little choice but to offer you settled status, perhaps even some kind of honorary citizenship. Do you understand what I'm saying?'

Lucas nodded. 'I will be legal? In UK?'

She nodded, then smiled. 'Better than that... Legal and with some decent money for once. How does that sound?'

For the first time in what felt like ages he managed to produce the flicker of a hopeful smile. 'Yes. That sound good.'

'Good. So, okay... the first thing is we need is some paperwork. A contract between me and you to say I'm acting as an agent on your behalf. Then... I need you to tell me everything about yourself. From your childhood, right up until now. I need your life story, all of it. That way I can figure out the best way to sell your story to the people of Britain.'

24

'*Z*ishad? Are you sure?' DCI Williams looked at Minter.

'Boyd was pretty sure,' added Okeke.

'Not *jihad*, sergeant?' she asked, addressing Minter again. 'The word gets pronounced in a variety of different ways and it's a similar word across a lot of Asian, Arabic and Middle Eastern languages.'

Minter glanced at Okeke. 'He was pretty clear about it, ma'am,' he said. 'He thought the gunman was trying to tell him something.'

'Like what?'

Minter shrugged.

'Well, that's just DCI Boyd's guesswork, isn't it?' Williams stood up and straightened her jacket. 'But it might make sense to explore it anyway. *Zishad*.' She cocked her head. 'All right then. Good work, detective sergeant, you better see what intel that stirs up in LEDS.'

'Yes, ma'am,' he replied, and he and Okeke both watched Williams head back to Boyd's desk, beside the window with the fossilised spider plant. The Incident Room was largely empty. The only other two in this morning were DI Abbott and DC

The Last Train

O'Neal. Abbott was busy clacking away, one-fingered, at his keyboard and frowning at the screen. It looked as though O'Neal was still arranging his desk.

Okeke turned to Minter. 'See? She didn't even fucking acknowledge me. You saw that right? She wouldn't even make eye contact,' she whispered.

Minter shrugged. 'Look, just... keep your head down and don't make a big thing out of it. She's not going to be your boss forever.'

Okeke ground her teeth.

'Good God, I can hear that,' said Minter.

'Better this than what I'd like to say,' she muttered.

Minter picked out a workstation, hung his jacket over a chair and placed his water bottle on the desk. 'All right then...I suppose we'd better crack on. I'll push the word through LEDS and let's see if we get a hit.'

Okeke picked the next desk along. 'I'll research it as a name,' said Okeke. 'We might get to narrow down a country of origin.'

'Good idea.'

She hung her jacket on the back of the chair and grabbed her purse. 'Gonna get a coffee. D'ya want one?'

'I'm good thanks,' Minter replied, indicating his bottle.

'Wait a sec, Okeke!' It was Williams. She had a phone to her ear and was mid-conversation. 'Uh-huh, right. Well, it's looking more and more like it. I'm going to need some more CTP bums on seats down here if you can spare them.' She held up a fiver and pressed the phone to her chest. 'Okeke, if you're going up to the top-floor canteen, I'll take a cappuccino.'

Okeke managed to hold back a *fuck you* behind a tight and economical smile. 'Yes, ma'am.'

∼

Around mid-morning, Okeke went outside for a smoke and found O'Neal nearing the end of his fag.

'All right?' he said.

She nodded as she sparked up.

O'Neal blew out a cloud of smoke. 'Williams is a bit of an old bag, isn't she?'

'Tell me about it,' replied Okeke, rolling her eyes.

'She bollocked me for being too scruffy.'

Okeke looked at him. O'Neal was wearing dark jeans instead of suit trousers, and trainers instead of proper shoes. 'No offence but you are. You may be a plain clothes copper, but that's not an excuse to come in casual.'

'I thought she was going to send me back home,' he huffed. 'It's like being back at school again.' He pointed to his collar and tie. 'She made me do up the top button and tighten my tie. I bloody hate that; it feels like it's choking me.'

Okeke shook her head. 'Thank God we don't all have your problems, O'Neal.'

'You don't have to wear a fucking dog leash. It's not fair,' he moaned.

She blew out a breath. 'I know. Lucky me.'

'And you get a choice... Shirts or blouses, flats or heels, skirts or trousers.'

She huffed and smiled. 'You want to wear a skirt, O'Neal? Because, you know, it's okay to express your –'

'No! I'm just saying you ladies get more wriggle room than us guys.'

'Right. Of course we do.' The irony in her voice was wasted on him.

'Female bosses are a fucking nightmare,' he muttered. 'They get a total power trip.'

Okeke was about to open her mouth to tear into him, but then stopped herself. There was too much ignorance, misogyny and plain old dumb-fuckery for her to be arsed to even begin to unpick.

~

AFTER A COUPLE of hours of staring at her screen, Okeke had accumulated a little more wisdom on the name Zishad. There were a variety of approximate spellings that might account for the misinterpretation or mishearing of the word that the hijacker was uttering as he died. For example, Zihad could be a Bangladeshi name; the word itself meant 'war for Islam' – but it could also be Muslim name, meaning 'pious and abstinent'. Zeeshan was a Turkish name, a first name mostly for boys but some girls in Turkey were called Zeeshan too, meaning 'moon' or 'magnificent'.

The 'Riz' part was even more problematic. It could have been a shortening of a common first name like Rizwan, or a nickname taken from some other part of a given name like Ariz, Tavorris, Damaris, Idris...

Okeke touched base with Minter after lunch and all he had to show for several hours of trawling through LEDS was a long list of near-miss names too. Luckily most of the hits had a booking-in photograph for them to compare against the shot taken of Riz's dead face. It wasn't an easy side-by-side comparison to make, since one of the gunshots had been to the side of his head and had caused a purple-hued subdermal swelling around one of his eyes.

Most of the rap sheets featured young Asian men who'd been charged with drug- and gang-related crimes. Most of them could be ruled out as too young to be their Riz, being mere teenagers. A few of the older hits were down for non-violent crimes like fraud, embezzlement, theft. Likenesses aside, or lack thereof, there was no one in the list of names Minter had that felt like a lead worth chasing down.

They presented their findings to Williams.

'The research on the names is useful,' she said. 'But I'm not surprised the database hasn't given us any likely go-to leads. His MO has Lone Wolf written all over it, which tends to fit. They're usually educated. Studious. And not in gangs.'

'You're certain he was acting alone?' asked Okeke.

Williams acknowledged her for once. 'Yes, Okeke, at this point I very much do. The vest bomb was fake, the gun was an easily available starter pistol, and he acted alone. That suggests a bedroom jihadi who looked up a whole load of "How To" websites for aspiring martyrs. He was probably still living at home with his parents and watching too many ISIS videos up in his bedroom.' She scooped up the printouts and handed them back to Minter. 'All the same, get DI Abbott to collate what you've got into the action log.'

'You still think this is terror-related?' pressed Okeke. 'You don't think we should explore other avenues, say... something mental-health-related? Perhaps look at a motive via his victim selection?'

Williams sighed. 'Policing is about working your way down a list of plausibles. Not jumping from assumption to assumption. I know that sounds dull, but that's how it is. If a perp barks like a dog, we go through every breed of dog first, then... and *only then* do we start looking at cats.'

'That can bark?' queried Minter.

Williams smiled. 'Quite. Not the greatest metaphor, but you get my point?'

Minter nodded; Okeke didn't.

'Boyd seemed to think the guy was a bit uncertain,' Okeke pointed out.

'And what does that actually mean?' asked Williams. 'Uncertain as in not sure how to proceed? Uncertain as in... having second thoughts? Uncertain as in... this was his first time?'

Okeke shrugged. It wasn't the most compelling counterargument against someone like Williams.

'For every wannabe martyr, it's their first time,' Williams said sarcastically. 'Victim selection, all male and white, is a pretty clear marker in my book that this had, at the very least, a racial factor to it. The stripping of one hostage was about humiliation, control. And, from what I'm getting in the hostage statements we've gathered, he was about to slit that man's throat.' Williams narrowed her eyes. 'Now that sounds very much like barking to me... so shall we start by looking at the dogs first?'

25

'Don't take the piss, Giles – you know he's worth way more than that,' said Ruth.

Ruth Cadwell lit up a cigarette in her car. She was parked facing the Premier Inn reception so that she could see if Lucas decided to step out for a wander. She'd left strict instructions that he wasn't to leave his room.

'Thirty thousand, then,' he countered.

She was talking to Giles Fullerton, features editor of a particular tabloid. She knew that he'd have to refer anything over fifty thousand to his boss, which meant he'd be out of the loop and unable to take any credit for the exclusive.

'Sixty,' said Ruth.

'Oh, come on.'

'Everyone's after him, Giles. Everyone's door-knocking to find him. It's not just the UK press either; there are some US news stations that want to peg an interview with him too. And they've got very deep wallets.'

She took a long draw on her cigarette. 'This conversation ends on sixty grand, or I'm just going to dial the next number on my very long list.'

'For God's sake, Ruth...'

'Go on, off you fuck and talk to Scotty about it.'

'I'll put you on hold,' he grumbled.

'That's okay. I can wait.'

Giles's voice was replaced with Kylie Minogue's 'Better The Devil You Know'. Ruth turned on the speaker and let the phone rest in her lap.

Sixty thousand for an exclusive with Lucas Pesic was an ask. Yesterday she would have gone for forty, but, just looking at the headlines and the increasing noise on social media, she could see his stock was rising fast. However, like any story, there was such a thing as peak value. Interests waned. Attention spans were short. If another member of government was caught shagging his Westminster office assistant, or another mouthy celebrity dropped another ill-judged Twitter bomb, the feeding frenzy could evaporate overnight.

With Lucas, though, Ruth figured she had about a fortnight's window to play with; after that, the offers would taper off sharply.

She glanced at the window of Lucas's room. It was ajar and the net curtain was flapping inside. She'd bought him a KFC bucket for lunch and some cans of Coke to keep him happy while she made her calls.

The music snipped off and a male voice barked down the phone: 'Richard Scott.'

She picked it up and turned off the speaker. 'Hi, Richard. It's Ruth Cadwell. I presume Giles has just briefed you?'

'Forty-five thousand for Have-A-Go Hugo and that's only if you keep him under wraps and frogmarch him straight into our office for the exclusive.'

'Sixty,' she replied. 'You know this is still fresh for another week.'

She heard him sigh.

'You're a jammy bloody bitch. Getting your claws into him like that.'

'Right place, right time.'

'Yeah, right. Well, look, fifty's my final. I've got a cracking front page for tomorrow as it is.'

'Bollocks you have. It's Slow September; the best you've got is something old and recycled or copied-and-pasted from Facebook.'

The *UK Daily* was almost certainly running something about the late summer heatwave driving the sales of beer and ice cream sky-high.

'He's trending on pretty much all the platforms, Richard,' Ruth continued. 'I was listening to Nick on LBC this morning and, despite being Eastern European, Lucas apparently represents 'the best of British'. You know as well as I do, he's a perfect catch. You want a piece of him or not?'

She heard Scott suck in some air, then finally let it out. 'Fifty-five, then. Final offer.'

'Done.'

'When can we have him?'

'Tomorrow. I'll drive him up myself.'

'If anyone gets a snap of him before we have him, that price drops, Ruth. You understand? Even if Sergei's in the back of your car and it's a blurry picture. He's pristine for us or we're out.'

'Relax. He's hidden well away.'

'Fine. Get him here tomorrow morning. Ten a.m.' He hung up on her.

'Charming,' she muttered, and settled back into her seat to finish her fag.

Lucas really was a perfect catch. Not only the hero of the hour in a dramatic hostage situation but one with a powerfully sad backstory. An illegal immigrant trafficked into the UK in the back of a container truck ten or so years ago, who'd lived on the streets, eaten out of supermarket bins, drifted from one ghastly cash-in-hand job to another and, after a decade of living as a ghost in the shadows, finally had enough work that he could afford a crummy bedsit in St Leonards.

She'd been almost touched at the way he'd explored his Premier Inn room – like it was the presidential suite of some Dubai hotel. And that, by the way, was his star quality: the humbleness, the joy he'd expressed at all the little luxuries in the room... the wall-mounted TV, his own bathroom, the crisp sheets.

Just like with *The X Factor*, or any other of those factory-farm talent shows, the best contestants were the ones who could sing AND had a sad story to tell. And the best of those looked the part too. World-weary and worn down to a nub by the slings and arrows of life. Lucas's round face featured heavy brows that arced to look permanently, melancholically bemused by everything.

To be fair to Scotty, it really *was* a pity his name wasn't Sergei.

∼

'Tomorrow?'

'Tomorrow,' she repeated. 'I'll take you to their offices in London and they'll interview you there.'

'You be with me?' asked Lucas.

Ruth nodded. 'Oh, you betcha, I will.' She helped herself to one of the hot wings he'd been unable to finish.

'They will ask me about what happen on train?'

'They will, Lucas. Now... here's the thing. They're going to want every damned detail. They're going to want to get the whole story. Not just what happened on the train but all about your story... your time over here in the UK.'

He shook his head. 'I will be sent to camp!'

She reached out and grabbed his arm. 'No. Lucas, we talked about this right. Listen to me. That's not going to happen. Not if we play this the right way.'

'But I am illegal.'

'Yes... but that kind of thing can be flexible. It's all down to public opinion – well... it can be if it's done right.' She leant forward. 'You're a hero. What you did saved the lives of all the other guys in the carriage. You didn't know the bomb wasn't real, or the gun. That's an incredibly brave thing you did... and the people of Britain aren't going to let some Border Force officials bundle you up into a van and take you to a detention camp. You have to trust me, Lucas. I know what I'm doing.'

Lucas nodded. 'All right.'

'Good. But here's the thing about tomorrow's interview... They're going to want to know *every* detail – but we won't give them *every* detail. We won't give them too much about what happened on the train.'

'Why not?'

'Because I'm negotiating with some people to find the best place for you to tell your story. Your *whole* story. We're going to save it for TV. And there'll be some serious money for you for doing that.'

'I get even more money than this?'

'Yes, Lucas. Much more.'

Lucas' eyes all but popped out.

She couldn't help smiling. *He really is perfect.*

26

'It does seem quite impossible to keep you from getting into trouble, Boyd.'

Dr Munroe seemed, to Boyd, to have learned everything he knew about psychology practice from watching episodes of *Frasier*. He had a warm gravelly voice with just the slightest hint of a transatlantic accent, a mustard-coloured cardigan over a checked shirt, and a bit of a Salman Rushdie look going on with his clipped beard and his slicked-back thinning hair.

'It's not exactly through choice,' Boyd said. 'Anyway, I'm on enforced sick leave for a fortnight, so no chance of trouble in the near future.'

'Was that your Chief Superintendent's idea?'

'Yup. She said she was worried about burnout.'

'Burnout?' Munroe laughed. 'That's what Instagram celebs get. Wimbledon tennis players. Rock stars. You have *psychological trauma* to work out of your system.' He shook his head. '*Burnout*, God help me...'

'That's just it: I don't feel traumatised.' Boyd examined for a moment how he *did* feel. 'I feel numb – to all the recent stuff, that is.'

Munroe nodded. 'All the things that have happened since you moved from the Met?'

'Yup.' Boyd chuckled. 'Emma forced me to pick a quieter, easier posting. That went well.'

'And how about the things that happened before that? The loss of your wife and son?'

'Well, that still hurts like fuck,' Boyd answered honestly. 'And I don't think there's any danger of that changing any time soon. I live with it.'

Outside the small window of Munroe's top-floor practice, a gull was tapping at the glass with its beak. Munroe got up out of his armchair and approached the window to shoo it away. 'Go on! Get out of here!'

'Back in London, it was bloody pigeons,' said Boyd. 'Birds don't like me. They're always hassling me.'

Munroe banged a hand against the glass and the gull reluctantly fluttered away.

'Maybe in a previous life you were Saint Francis?' said Munroe, returning to his seat. 'And they're just trying to remind you?'

Boyd looked at him. 'Shit... and I'm letting *you* rummage around inside *my* head?'

Munroe smiled. 'Let's talk about what happened last Friday.'

Boyd settled back into the leather chesterfield – the obligatory treatment couch.

'What I want us to review,' continued Munroe, 'is your perception of it all in the moment. How you felt during the ordeal. What thoughts were going through your head?'

'Well, for starters... I genuinely thought he was a suicide bomber and in an enclosed space like a train carriage you get directed blast damage. I didn't think that much of me was going to be left if he detonated it.'

'And that realization made you feel...?'

Boyd cast his mind back. 'Terrified, obviously. At first.'

'At first?'

He frowned as he picked his way through the debris pile of his memories. 'Well, then I just... got used to the idea that I was probably going to die; that when it happened it was going to be quick. There one second, gone the next.'

Munroe nodded. 'When a person experiences that kind of a scenario, they can have a moment of clarity... Everything that is unimportant is stripped away and what you're left with is what you truly value.' He stroked his carefully sculpted Frasier Crane beard as he spoke. 'Often, after incidents like this, people make substantial course corrections in their life. Because they've got a glimpse of what it is they want to get out of life. Why don't we try that? Settle back, close your eyes... Go back to Friday night...'

Boyd closed his eyes and tried to put himself back in that train compartment, back into those moments just before Lucas made his run at their captor and it all kicked off.

He pictured the carriage, empty except for a dozen terrified men... and Riz.

Fleeting, fractured thoughts came flooding back to him. That night, on the train, he'd thought about all the moments he'd *nearly* surprised Julia with an impulse gift, or an unplanned evening out... but then just hadn't, because there was a bill to pay, or something needed repairing or replacing... or because he'd been simply too tired to make the effort and he'd kicked it down the road as something to do on another evening.

His mind had been full of things he could have done better. Moments that could have become memory treasures. What he wasn't recalling, though, was some fleeting epiphany, some nascent ambition or desire suppressed by the baggage of responsibility. No deeply buried desire to motorbike across the Saharan desert or live off-grid in a rainforest, or track arctic wolves in Norway.

None of that bucket-list stuff.

Boyd's moment of clarity had been a litany of *Why the fuck didn't I do THAT when I had the chance?*...

He realised that what this was telling him was that a few years ago he'd had it all. Had everything he wanted: his wife, his family, his career... He'd been utterly content. His biggest regret was that he'd taken it all for granted at the time. And that hurt. A lot.

Boyd took a breath and shifted his focus back to the scene on the train.

Lucas was sprawled across Riz, trying to wrestle control of his hands, while Boyd frantically traced the course of that red wire up his bared torso. This was followed by the sound of glass breaking and boots clambering aboard, the other men screaming in terror.

And Riz was sprawled on the floor of the carriage, blood spilling from his gurgling mouth, from Lucas's blows, as he locked his eyes on Boyd and whispered that cryptic word over and over before the fateful gunfire.

–had-zhishad-zhishad-zhishad-zish–

And, yes, it did sound a little like *jihad*. But... it wasn't quite that word... The softly slurred 'zsh' wasn't the more affirmative sound of a 'J', not like *judge* or *jagged*... More like...

'What's that you're saying?' said Munroe softly. 'Boyd?'

Boyd's eyes snapped open. 'Bollocks,' he muttered. 'He wasn't saying *zishad*; he was saying something like *hadzish*.'

'The suicide bomber?'

Boyd looked across at Munroe. 'Yeah. *Hadzish*. Does that word mean anything to you?'

Munroe shook his head. '*Hasish* maybe, but...'
'*Hadzish*,' Boyd repeated. 'Is it even a word?'
Munroe shrugged. 'Could it be a name?'

27

'This is DI Hermione Smith. She's an expert in criminal psychology, and this is DI Matthew Connor, an expert in organised crime gangs and terror networks.' DCI Williams gestured at her two colleagues who had just travelled down from Thames Valley Police HQ.

'What they don't know about radicalization and lone-wolf psychology probably isn't worth knowing,' she added.

Okeke nodded at both new arrivals to the Incident Room. They looked almost as young as O'Neal and Warren. Having recently broken into her thirties, Okeke suddenly felt very old as she watched them return to the task of settling themselves in at neighbouring desks. DI Smith was petite and pale with a long perky ponytail of ginger hair that Okeke felt oddly compelled to tug. Connor was short and slim with a Tintin flick of hair held perfectly in place by product. They both looked like smug six-formers who'd just landed the A-level results they'd been hoping for.

Williams, having made the introductions, addressed her wunderkinder directly. 'Hermione, Matthew... when you're both plugged in, I'll get you up to speed,' the DCI said. 'Would you like a coffee? Tea?'

Minter looked at Okeke and muttered, 'Milkshake?'

She smirked. 'Or perhaps a Sunny D?'

Williams turned and said, 'Okeke, would you mind? Two teas. White, no sugar.'

Okeke raised her brows and glanced meaningfully over at Abbott and O'Neal, both of whom were much closer to the kitchenette.

Williams raised her own brows, thicker, heavier and, most importantly, higher. 'Now please.'

~

'IDENTIFYING this man Riz remains our top priority,' began DCI Williams.

Okeke realised that they'd subconsciously arranged themselves around the conference table in two camps: Sussex Force on one side, Williams and her two young experts on the other.

'We're planning to go public with CCTV footage of him, most likely the day after tomorrow to see whether we can pull in any leads. Somebody, hopefully, will recognise him. But the image we have isn't particularly good.'

She looked at Minter. 'I want you and DC Okeke to go over to Brighton to do some door-knocking. Your starting point is the train station and the coffee stall on the concourse, where DCI Boyd said he saw our man. I also want you to look for overlapping CCTV cameras outside the station, so that we can build a camera-path leading up to it. If we can get a better image before Friday that would be useful.'

'Ma'am,' Minter said, nodding.

'Meanwhile, Hermione... I want a scratch psychopathology profile for him. Does he fit the Lone Wolf profile? Was this a racial thing? You know the drill.'

'Yes, ma'am.'

'Matthew, you're on digital markers.'

'What are digital markers?' asked DI Abbot.

Williams nodded at Matthew to explain.

'We may be able to track down his online identity by analysing keywords and phrases used on social media in various forums that we monitor.'

'We're looking for signs of "leakage and fixation",' DI Smith cut in. '*Leakage* is the term we use for the behaviour that terrorists exhibit when they're on the cusp of acting. They want to let people they trust know what they're about to do. They start posting manifestos, explanations, as documents, videos and so on. They want to leave behind a documentary record of what they've done and why they did it.' She absently stroked the frame of the tablet in front of her. 'When a suicide bomber blows himself up, he's no longer around to justify his sacrifice. But he wants to leave behind some record of his action. A memorial of sorts.'

'It's an act of vanity,' added Williams. 'But also an attempt to inspire others to do the same thing.'

'What about the other thing you mentioned?' asked Minter.

'*Fixation* occurs during the planning stage,' Smith continued. 'In this case, Riz may have been doing a lot of online searches to do with train timetables, the train line, the stations along the way. He may also have been researching the passengers – when's the busiest time? How many people he'd have in the carriage with him. That kind of thing.'

Williams nodded. 'Hopefully we'll be able to identify a particular user, an IP number and an address. Then we'll know exactly who he was and why he did it.'

28

Lucas Pesic stared goggle-eyed at the refreshments laid out on the long glass table: crust-less sandwiches, vol-au-vents, filled bagels, doughnuts and a platter of fresh fruit.

He turned to Ruth. 'All this is for me?' He looked shocked.

She nodded and smiled. 'Yes – well, mostly.'

'Is too much!'

'Don't worry. I'm sure you'll get some help.' She led him over to the table and pulled out a chair for him. 'Why don't you take a seat?'

He sat down and eyed the selection in front of him before reaching out for a doughnut. 'May I?'

'Knock yourself out,' she replied.

Through the smoked-glass wall she could see Richard Scott emerging from his office with Giles and a couple of junior flunkies in tow. Like the Pied Piper he weaved across the open-plan office floor towards the meeting room.

'Now remember, Lucas... today you're talking about who you are, your story, and just a little about what happened on the train, okay?'

'Da.' He nodded, mouth already bulging like a hamster's.

A moment later Richard Scott entered the room. 'Aha, there he is!' he exclaimed, hands spread wide. 'The man, the legend... the hero!'

Lucas got up as Scott strode over and grabbed one of his hands, pumping it up and down. 'It's an honour to meet you, Lucas. An absolute honour!'

Lucas nodded and smiled as best he could, his mouth still too full to talk.

Scott laughed. 'You carry on! Enjoy! Good to see you've brought an appetite!'

He sat down in the chair next to Lucas, and his minions rounded the end of the table and sat on the far side.

'Ruth,' Scott said, nodding at her. 'Thanks for coming to us first.'

She smiled. 'I know you've got deep pockets, Richard.'

'For the right stories,' he replied. His assistants began setting up a microphone. 'Lucas, do you mind if we record this interview?'

'Sure.' Lucas nodded. 'Is fine.'

'For editorial purposes only,' cut in Ruth. 'Our arrangement doesn't cover audio broadcast and streaming rights – you understand that, right?'

Scott raised a brow. 'And who's got those? LBC? BBC Radio 4?'

'Currently in negotiation,' she replied.

He rolled his eyes. 'Why doesn't that surprise me.' He turned to Lucas. 'We're going to go front cover with this interview for tomorrow. With something like "Spunky Train Superhero" or "Balls of Steel" as the strapline.'

Lucas finished his doughnut and popped open a can of Coke. 'I am not superhero.'

'Oh yes, you bloody well are, sunshine,' said Scott. He

reached for a smoked-salmon-and-cream-cheese sandwich. 'Now look, Ruth tells me you have an issue with your legal status in this country?'

'Lucas nodded. 'I am illegal. I do not have the settled status.'

'Well, good. Because we're going to champion that for you. All right? We're going to launch an appeal to raise some money for you and set up a petition online to have your status reviewed and sorted as soon as possible.'

Lucas looked at Ruth uncertainly and she gave him an encouraging smile. 'That's right, Lucas,' she confirmed. 'The *UK Daily* is going to get behind you and they have *millions* of readers.'

Scott took a bite out of his sandwich. 'You're precisely the kind of person we want in this country. Courageous. Hardworking. Modest...' He nodded his head, having run out of descriptors.

'You epitomise the kind of immigrant we want to welcome in,' added one of the men on the other side of the table. 'And the mad bastard you took down epitomises the kind we don't.'

'Really, Giles?' Ruth cut in, looking at the man who'd just spoke. Then she turned to Scott. 'That's going to be our angle?'

'In a more nuanced way,' Scott replied, eyeing his features editor sternly. 'Yeah.'

She nodded. 'I like it.'

'Well,' Scott said, 'I assume we're not going to get a blow-by-blow account of what happened on the train, are we?'

Ruth offered him a tight smile. He'd guessed how she wanted to steer this.

'Who's getting that? Sky? GB NEWS? FOX?'

'It's currently in negotiation,' she said again.

'As I thought,' said Scott, nodding. 'So we're going to focus on his backstory. We'll go with the "what makes a hero" angle. That okay with you, Lucas?'

The question was met with a shrug. 'My story is –' Lucas shrugged again – 'I am not so special.'

Scott wagged a finger at him. 'Why don't you let us be the judge of that? Now then... let's start at the beginning. Where were you born? Tell me all about your childhood, Lucas.'

29

'Are you sure you're remembering it correctly?' asked Charlotte.

Boyd watched Ozzie and Mia circling around an empty McDonald's burger carton discarded on the shingle. Both seemed convinced there was something left inside to snaffle.

'No,' he replied, 'not really. It's getting hard to discern between what I remember and what I *think* I remember. If you get what I mean.'

She nodded. 'Oh, I do. The mind plays tricks on you. Makes you doubt your sanity sometimes.'

'It does. I mean he could have been saying *zishad* over and over or *hadzish*.'

'*Hadzish*? With a soft 'g' at the end or the 'ish' ending. Like *hadge-zish* or *had-jish*. Which one?'

Boyd shook his head. 'Hard to say... I guess he was slurring his words.' He didn't want to elaborate further and explain that the man's mouth was filling with blood.

'*Had-zish*, I think.'

'So it could have been *hadzish-hadzish* or *zishad-zishad*?'

He nodded. 'Over and over.' He sighed. 'But then... shit... I don't know... It *could* have been *jihad*.'

Charlotte changed the subject. 'So how did your therapy session go?'

'Good. Good. We discussed how nearly getting killed can help focus your mind on what's important to you.'

'And what's that?' she asked.

He looked at her. '*Not* getting killed... for one.'

She laughed. 'Well, that's a positive sign.'

He knew what she meant. He was finding reasons to look forward. It wasn't just about being there for Emma and any potential grandkids any more.

He sneaked a sideways glance at Charlotte as she called Mia away from yet more weekend rubbish that had been dumped on the beach. In so many ways Charlotte was the exact opposite to Julia. Julia had been headstrong and outgoing. The extrovert in their marriage. And he'd been the more-than-willing sidekick. They'd been opposites. And, consistent with that old truism, they had been good together.

Charlotte, however, was gentle, reflective, an introvert.

Until you accidentally get her stoned. He smiled at the memory of the barbeque back in June. At the wild woman unleashed by the secondary fumes of marijuana coming from his garden-clearance bonfire.

∼

AFTER THE LUNCHTIME walk on the beach, Boyd returned home and fired up his old PC. Although this wasn't his case and he had no business sticking his nose into some other SIO's investigation, the word he thought he might have heard the gunman gasping with his final breath felt as though it was important.

He tapped 'hadzish' into the search bar and immediately got a 'Did you mean' message from Google.

'No,' he grumbled at the screen, 'I'm not after *hashish* or *hadzici*.'

Below Google's helpful message, the nearest to a hit was a Gordon Hazich's profile on Facebook and a recipe for some sort of yoghurt salad dressing.

He tried 'zishad'. Again, no bullseye, just a few near misses. 'Zihad' was a common Bangladeshi name derived from the word Jihad. And of course, Suchard, was a very nice brand of Swiss chocolate.

He spent another half an hour buggering around with various spellings and sound-a-likes but got nothing at all useful back. He finally decided he'd had enough and picked up the landline phone in the lounge. He flicked through his work notepad and found the number he was after, scrawled at the bottom of a page of notes on LEDS.

Sunny answered after a couple of rings. 'Yeah?'

'It's Boyd.'

'Boyd!' Sunny answered. 'Shit! I heard you were involved in that train thing!'

'Yeah, I was.'

'I called you, man. No answer.'

'I know. My phone took one for the team,' Boyd said ruefully.

'You okay, mate?'

'Yup, no injuries. A little shaken maybe.'

'Were you there to witness the Russian dude do a Crazy Ivan at the jihadi dude? Apparently he beat the guy up just with his head!' Sunny sounded impressed.

Boyd couldn't help a wry smile. This story was going to run and run and slowly evolve into a caricature of itself. 'Yeah. I was there,' Boyd replied. 'Pretty sure he's not Russian, though.'

'Whatever, they're all nuts over there. Shit, though, what a thing! Scary, huh?'

'Very,' Boyd confirmed.

'If I hadn't kept you down the pub so late –'
'I know. But it could've been any train, so... look, Sunny?'
'Yeah?'
'Can I ask you a favour?'
'Sure.'
'I'm trying to work out a word I heard someone say. I'm not even sure I heard it correctly, but you know what I'm like with foreign languages and spelling.'
'What's the word?'
'Something like hadzish. Or it could be *had-zshish*. The *sh* bit might have been pronounced with that guttural sound like when you're clearing your throat.'
'What, like *hch*-alepeno peppers?'
'Yup, like that.' Boyd made a mental note to stop calling them 'j-alepenos'.
'What's this to do with? A case?'
Boyd sighed. 'My sanity maybe. I just want to make sense of something I... think I heard.'
Sunny paused. 'Wait. Is this do with what happened on the train?'
Boyd was reluctant to give him any more context. It wasn't that he didn't trust Sunny to keep it to himself, but... it was becoming a bigger news story by the day, and he was in danger of encroaching on DCI Williams' turf. 'Sorry. Can't comment on where and why, Sunny. Just something I heard and I'm not sure how to spell it or what language it is.'
Sunny laughed. 'You poor dumb monolinguistic ape.' He spoke three languages and probably programmed in a dozen more. 'So let me get your monkey-fingers spelling, Boyd...' he said, still laughing.
'I would spell it *hotel–alpha–delta–zulu–india–sierra–hotel*,' Boyd said.
'Got it.'
'You in Brighton still?' asked Boyd.

'Nah, came back to the Big Smoke over the weekend. I'm taking some leave later on this week. Three days of explaining LEDS to you lot has totally done my head in.'

Boyd laughed.

'Leave it to me, mate,' said Sunny. 'I'll give you a call if I find anything.'

'Thanks, Sunny.'

Boyd hung up and grabbed a beer from the fridge. His garden was calling him. He wandered out into the backyard to find that his lounger, still catching rays from the late-afternoon sun, was occupied by a very hairy, loudly snoring spaniel.

30

'The terrorist attack last Friday night aboard a train near Bexhill, East Sussex, was brought to an end by passenger intervention, the police officially confirmed yesterday. In a stand-off between the terrorist and armed police officers that lasted several hours, it was the action of a couple of courageous hostages that brought the incident to a close.'

Ruth looked up from the paper at Lucas. He was already grinning at the word 'courageous'.

She continued reading: 'A number of witnesses aboard the train, have confirmed that the attack against the as yet unnamed terrorist was led by Lucas Pesic (fifty-four) an Albanian worker, currently residing in Hastings. Robert Punt, a fellow hostage, claimed the Albanian launched the attack despite having "both hands tied behind his back" when it became clear the terrorist was getting ready to kill one of the other captives. "It was absolutely insane – he charged at the gunman using his head like a battering ram," said Punt, "knocking him down to the ground where he began headbutting him on the floor. I've never seen anything like it!"

'Simon Collingham, another hostage, said that Pesic's attack "saved the life" of fellow passenger Martin Bartrum, who had been stripped naked by the gunman in what appeared to be a ritualistic effort to humiliate him before attempting to kill him with a long-bladed knife.

'Pesic, a resident in the UK for ten years now, was reluctant to comment on the incident saying that "he is not particularly special" and that he was only doing what he thought was the correct thing to do at the time. See page three for more on the have-a-go hero.'

Ruth looked up from the paper. 'There's a bit more speculation in this article on the terrorist ... but let's go take a look at page three, eh?'

He nodded, and she flicked to the third page.

'So there's an article here on domestic terrorism, and *ahh* – here it is!' She turned the paper round to show him the photograph they'd taken of him in the meeting room: all smiles, a bulge in one cheek and a half-eaten doughnut in his fist.

'I look like greedy pig,' he said, laughing.

Ruth laughed too. 'Relax. You look great.' She began reading once again: 'Lucas Pesic is a cheerful and charming example of the kind of person we welcome into our country. Originally from a small village in Albania, he has offered his skills as a handyman across Europe and ten years ago he arrived in Britain. He says he came to the UK to build a life in an "exciting country" full of "hope and opportunity". Talking with this humble man yesterday at our offices in Fulham, it quickly became apparent that he is exactly the kind of foreign citizen we need to be attracting to our country. In so many ways he represents the core values of our country: diligence, modesty, fairness and, most importantly, courage.

'"I am not [a] special person," was one of the first things he wanted to tell us. "I am just an ordinary man."

'But his life in the UK hasn't always been easy. He explains that he was trafficked into the country in the back of a container truck and consequently represents one of the many undocumented foreigners still present in the UK. As he explained, his situation has been challenging from the very beginning. "When I first come, I live[d] on the streets for many months, because I did not know if police would come for me." Indeed, Lucas, a man used to having a proper home and family life back in Albania found himself living in the twilight world of London's backstreets, shop doorways and underpasses, alongside many people with alcohol, drug and mental-health issues.

'The main problem for Lucas, and people like him, is that, despite having work and earning money, he remains an undocumented citizen of this country, which means on the one hand he pays no taxes, but on the other he has had no access to the services and support we all take for granted in the UK. For example, he tells me that he was concerned that the injury he sustained in attacking the gunman (a dislocated shoulder) would put him into thousands of pounds of debt that he would have no chance of paying off. He has always assumed – correctly – that attempting to access these services would attract the attention of the authorities and land him in an immigration camp. The irony is, that if he had made himself known to the authorities and applied for settled status before July 2021, he would undoubtedly have qualified to live and work here.

'Which is why we here at *UK Daily* want to put things right for Lucas. The deadline may have long expired but that shouldn't mean that someone like him, one of *the right people*, should be forced to live the life of a fugitive, always surviving in the margins, always worried about attracting unwanted attention. In many ways, Lucas represents the VERY BEST OF BRITISH values. Therefore, *UK Daily* has launched a Fund This Now campaign to pay for legal counsel to have his case retrospectively evaluated by the Home Office and to appeal against the expired-registration penalties.'

Ruth set the paper down on the table and slapped the kettle on. 'Well, Lucas, what do you think about that?'

Lucas was getting preferential treatment now the hotel manager knew who he had staying there. The refreshments tray was brimming with freshly stocked sachets and complimentary biscuits. The bed had double-thick cushions laid on it. He also had the premium Wi-Fi package – complimentary, of course.

He shrugged. 'They like me?'

She leant forward and nudged his arm. 'They love you.'

31

'The *right people*?' Okeke repeated. 'That's what it actually says?'

Minter re-read the last paragraph of the article. 'The *right people*.'

'Jesus.'

Minter looked up from the paper. 'What's up?'

She indicated left for the slip road off the A42. 'So there are *wrong* people to allow in?'

Minter nodded. 'Doesn't seem that unreasonable. Crooks. Murderers. Rapists. Mafia. I wouldn't want people like that allowed in.'

Okeke sighed. 'When editors in papers like that say the "right people", you know exactly what they mean.'

'What?'

She glanced at him. 'It's dog-whistle racism.'

Minter pulled a face. 'I've never quite got the point of that expression.'

'Like a dog whistle, Minter.'

'Like –' he whistled as if summoning a sheep dog – '*Here, boy?*'

'No, you muppet. The kind of whistle you blow through. Too high-pitched for humans to hear; just the dog hears it.' She pulled off the A42 and slowed to a stop for the roundabout. 'It's about using language that isn't going to get you into trouble... but your audience know exactly what you mean.'

He lowered the newspaper and folded it in his lap. 'Oh, come on. I'm not going down that rabbit hole. Every time someone says "those people", they're not always talking about an ethnic minority.'

She glanced at him again. 'Aren't they?'

Okeke found a narrow space in Brighton train station's car park, right next to the entrance, and slid the Vauxhall pool car in effortlessly. She placed the car's police logbook on the dashboard, so that they didn't get ticketed, then they climbed out and entered the station's concourse, quickly finding their first port of call: the coffee stand.

Minter dug into his jacket for his notepad and pen. 'I'll go and interview this guy; you go and find out what cameras cover the station's entrance.'

Okeke flashed him a look.

'Please,' he added.

She headed towards the ticket office, scanning the iron girders above for the station's CCTV cameras as she crossed the concourse.

Minter, meanwhile, came to a halt in front of the coffee stand.

'What do you want?' asked the man beyond the counter. Minter pulled up his lanyard and let the barista look at his ID card. 'DS Minter, Sussex CID. Last Friday...'

'This about the train attack?' the man cut in.

Minter nodded. 'Last Friday night, coming up to midnight. Were you serving here?'

'Yeah. I do Fridays. Most of them, anyway.'

'Excellent.' Minter smiled. 'Can I ask you a few questions about that night?'

'Sure – go ahead, chief.'

Minter consulted his notes. 'Just before the last train to Hastings set off, you had a few customers?'

'Friday night at closing time? We always do. Everyone's trying to sober up.'

'Well, we have a witness who was on that train, who bought himself a coffee before he got on, saying that he spotted the hijacker buying some bottled water from you.'

'Really?' The barista looked surprised, and just a little thrilled. 'Yeah, I s'pose it's possible. Can't say I remember any individual customers, though.'

Minter pulled out a couple of pictures to show him. One was the grainy image they had of their man from a distance, wandering around the station with his backpack. The other was an image of his face taken on the pathologist's slab.

The barista leant across the counter and studied them both. He winced at the second image. 'You guys got a name for this dude yet?'

'That's precisely what we're working on,' replied Minter.

The barista studied both pictures a moment longer. 'Can't say I actually remember him meself, but we've got a cam in the stall.' He turned round and pointed at a discreetly placed lens, glinting between two jars of coffee beans. 'Safety cam, for our benefit. We get abusive customers sometimes, especially at closing time.'

'Will that have last Friday's footage on it?'

'Sure. I guess so. I've never fiddled with it, really, so I don't know how it works. Want to look?'

Minter nodded.

'Step into my isolation cell,' said the barista, and opened a side door to the stand. Minter went around the side and climbed a couple of steps. The stand wobbled slightly under his weight.

The barista grinned at Minter. 'You've got to be small to work in one of these, mate.'

'I can see that.' He turned round in the narrow space behind the small counter. It was no bigger than a small aircraft cockpit and the tight space was cluttered with spouts from the coffee machine, handles from stock cupboards and a panini press.

'It's pretty bloody sm— Ouch!' Minter quickly retracted his singed elbow from the water heater.

'Yeah, you might want to watch that. It's hot.'

'Jesus,' he said, rubbing his arm, 'how the hell do you cope being stuck in this trap all day?'

'It's a job,' the barista replied. 'Could be worse, right?'

Minter wondered how. Even murderers in prison had more elbow room than this. 'What do you do if you need a piss break?'

'We aren't allowed to leave the stall unattended.' He shrugged. 'We just have to, you know, hold it in.'

Minter frowned. He wondered whether that contravened some sort of employment law. Probably not these days.

The barista nodded at the station toilets. 'Sometimes I just quickly nip over there when no one's around. Anyway... the camera.' He pushed aside the coffee jars and eased the camera out for Minter to take a look.

'Thanks.' Minter turned it round in his hands and carefully ejected the memory stick from the back. '*Et voilà* – it's all stored on this.' He pulled an evidence bag out of his jacket pocket.

'Uh... dude, what're you doing?'

'I'll need to upload what's on here back at the station. Don't worry – it'll be returned.' He dropped it in the bag and scribbled his initials and date on the label with a Sharpie.

'Look, I'm not sure you can take it. We're not going to be

able to use the cam now. I reckon I'll need to call my boss.'

Minter pulled out one of his cards and handed it to him. 'I'm sorry, but it could have vital evidence for the case. I'm sure your boss can get you a replacement memory stick for tonight's shift. My number's on there if he gives you any grief. We'll drop it back in a day or two, okay?'

The barista took the card and reluctantly replied, 'All right.'

Rather than attempting to turn round inside the cramped space and risk burning himself again, Minter backed out of the stall. 'Thanks for your help...' He peered at the young man's plastic name label. 'Luigi?'

'We share the name tag. Steve,' he replied. 'Steve Hopper.'

Minter jotted the name down in his pad. 'All right, Steve, thanks for this. You got a mobile number?'

Steve gave it to him.

'We may need to contact you if there's anything useful on this.'

'Sure. I'm always shackled in here... pretty much.'

With that, Minter wandered over to the entrance and emerged from the concourse to the square outside. To his left was a taxi rank, ahead Queens Road sloped gently downhill towards the seafront. To his right were a few bus stops and a number of kiosks selling sandwiches, burgers, kebabs and cheap phones. The square was overlooked on all four sides by tall town-centre buildings that bristled with anti-pigeon spikes on every likely perch and was crowded with lunch-breakers soaking up the remains of the late-arriving summer.

He spotted Okeke walking back across the square, scribbling away in her notepad and muttering to herself as she did so.

'Okeke!' he called.

She looked up and adjusted her trajectory. She came to a halt just in front of him. 'Fourteen public-space cameras; two of them, fixed, are aimed on us right now.' They were standing in a square of bollards right outside the main entrance. 'So we should start with those for the breadcrumb trail. Any luck with the coffee stall?'

Minter raised his evidence bag.

She saw the memory stick inside. 'Nice one. From the stall itself?'

'Yup, right over the vendor's shoulder. Hopefully we'll get a usable face shot.'

'With our guv's ugly mug leering over his shoulder, no doubt.' She smiled. 'Hopefully not caught on camera picking his nose if this is going to end up on the news.'

∽

MINTER HAD the contents of the memory stick uploaded to their secure server as soon as they got back to Hastings. Annoyingly, the camera was one that recorded twenty-four hour files. So there were fourteen large files, one for each day.

He picked the one dated last Friday and opened it. Thankfully the cam recorded high-resolution images with a timecode in the corner. However, captured at the rate of about four or five images a second, the playback created a migraine-inducing stuttering effect. Minter fast-forwarded through the video until the time code showed 23:25 and decided that, no matter how much he wanted to punch the stuttering screen, there'd be no more time-skipping until the end of the media file.

He recognised the back of Steve 'Luigi' Hopper's head as he shuffled around in the claustrophobic space behind the counter. When he wasn't serving, he was doing make-busy tasks – cleaning the frother's spout, sorting through inventory. There were no moments when he seemed to switch completely off and pull his phone out for a quick scroll. Minter was beginning to wonder whether the installation of a camera had more to do with snooping on the baristas than protecting their safety.

In the background he could see the station's concourse, an ebb and flow of passengers arriving home from London, or departing Brighton for Hove, Eastbourne, Lewes, Bexhill and Hastings. All in glorious high-res full-colour jerk-o-vision. Minter checked his notes. Boyd had said that he'd gone to grab a coffee at about 11.35 p.m..

The seconds ticked past 23:35 on the timecode and Minter, cursing internally, was about to go back to five minutes earlier, when he saw a figure approaching the coffee stall.

It looked like their man.

Ahead of him, two girls had ordered coffees that looked more like desserts, and Hopper appeared to be chatting them up as he squirted aerosol cream and drizzled toppings over their drinks. Minter spotted Boyd, shambling impatiently into view. He grinned. He couldn't recall actually seeing his boss *this* hammered before. The Friday-night pint at the Bier Garden was usually just that for him, one pint, or perhaps two halves to make it last a little longer, then back to the station to pick up his car.

Hopper finally passed the girls their top-heavy frothy drinks and then their man stepped forward. Minter paused the video and stepped through a dozen frames, one at a time, before he had the clearest-looking shot of their man's face.

'Bingo,' he muttered as he screen-grabbed the image before letting the video resume. The man pointed at the fridge – asking for water, just as Boyd had said. It was hard to determine his demeanour without sound, but he certainly didn't offer anything like a smile as he prepared to pay.

Steve leant forward and said something to him. The man cupped his ear. Steve pointed at something off-screen.

Okay, Steve my man, what's all this all about?

The man seemed to understand, then dug something out of his backpack. He held it up to show Steve, but the edge of the coffee jar obscured his hand. Steve nodded at whatever it was,

The Last Train

then the man took his water and turned away, stepping past Boyd and quickly disappearing from view.

Minter paused the video, opened his notepad and leafed through the pages until he found Hopper's number scribbled down. He dialled and waited.

After half a dozen rings, Steve answered. 'Yeah?'

Minter could hear running water; Steve's voice was echoing as though he was standing in a tunnel.

'It's DS Minter. We spoke earlier.'

'Oh, right, yeah.'

Minter heard a toilet flush. 'I'm having an emergency piss break. Can't talk long.'

'That's okay. It's just a quick question. I've just been watching the CCTV video and the man we're after did come to your stall.'

'Whoa. Okay. That's fucking creepy.'

'Yeah, but there's something going on that I don't quite understand. He bought a water, but it looked like you were drawing his attention to something?'

He heard a door creak on its hinges, then the echoing sound was gone, replaced with the hubbub of the station's concourse. 'Oh, probably the thing we're doing right now.'

'What thing?'

'Just for younger drinkers – water's free if they're a student. The manager thinks it looks good that we're, like, doing our bit to sober folks up before they board a train.'

'So it looks like he pulled something out of his bag to show you.'

'Yeah, sometimes I ask for proof, so we're not handing water out to, like, everyone.'

'Proof? That they're a student?'

'Uh-huh. It's Brighton, dude. Nine times out of ten it's a student union card.'

32

'A student, eh?' DCI Yolanda Williams gave Minter a stiff nod. 'Good work, sergeant.'

'Thanks, ma'am.'

She looked down at the printed screen grab. 'This looks like it's going to be clear enough to work with.' She turned round and clicked her fingers. 'Matthew?'

DI Connor got up and came over. 'Ma'am?'

Williams handed him the printout. 'A picture of our perp.'

Connor nodded approval. 'That's really good. Really clear.'

She looked at Minter. 'Sergeant here says he may be a student. He thinks he flashed a student union card.'

'You want me to run Cyclops through the student union database?'

Williams nodded. 'If the card isn't a faked one, is that image hi-res enough for Cyclops to make a face match?'

'Easily.' Connor looked at Minter. 'Can you send me the digital file?'

Minter nodded and Connor headed back to his desk.

'How are we doing on the CCTV trail in Brighton?' asked Williams.

'Okeke's on it. There are two fixed public-space cameras outside the station that catch the entrance. She's going through those first to catch which direction our man came from. Then she'll expand the search.'

'Good. I'll get your CID colleagues Abbott and...?'

'O'Neal.'

'They can get off their tasks to give you a hand with that. Chances are we'll have an ID and an address within a few hours, but if the student union card's a fake, we'll need all hands on camera-tracking.' She offered him a clipped smile – a rare currency. 'Excellent work.'

Minter returned to his desk and Okeke looked up from her screen. 'So? Is the Wicked Witch of the East happy?'

'She seemed pleased.'

Okeke glanced at their SIO as she pulled up a chair between DIs Connor and Smith and began discussing strategy with them. 'I notice *they* get the first-name treatment and the friendly face.'

Minter followed her gaze. 'They're her protégés.'

Okeke nodded. *Her babies, more like.* She watched the exchange furtively. Williams was all smiles and eye contact as she discussed the next steps with them. A stark contrast to the hard face and barest acknowledgement that Williams afforded her.

'How's it going, Okeke?' asked Minter.

She turned back to look at her screen and hit play. The footage was taken from the camera mounted outside and above the entrance to the Budgens store. In view was the station entrance, the bollards outside and part of the taxi rank. If their man had taken a taxi to the station, then he'd still need to walk into shot to go in. This would mean trawling back to catch the reg numbers of every taxi that had arrived over the previous couple of minutes to be sure she got the right one.

'Slowly,' she replied.

'She's going to assign Abbott and O'Neal to help with eyeballing,' Minter informed her.

Great, Okeke thought. Abbott was likely to moan all the while as he did it, and probably wouldn't do it properly anyway. He was the kind of copper who claimed he'd rather be out on the street fighting crime, but was, in reality, far too lazy to step out of the station. He was CID driftwood that lingered at his desk, trying to look busy moving paperwork from one tray to another. God knows why Sutherland had put his name forward. Since he was a DI, he was also likely to pull rank over Minter and try to direct their efforts.

Her grumbling thoughts were suddenly blown to one side by the appearance of their man on the screen; he was approaching the station entrance from the opposite side to the taxi rank.

'Got him,' she said, pausing the video.

Minter slid his chair over to join her. 'Oh yes! That's our man.'

Okeke consulted her notes. She'd drawn a rough map of the area in front of the station, marking the two fixed public-space cameras and their approximate cones of view. 'He's entered coming in from the left.' She checked out Google Maps on her phone. 'That's Guildford Road.'

Minter wheeled himself back to his desk. 'I'll call Brighton Council and see what cameras they've got up. Can you canvas the shops along there for outward-facing cams?'

'On it,' she replied, keen to get a cam-trail established before DI Abbott waddled over and messed things up.

33

'It's going to be Thursday next week. They'll record the interview in front of a small audience, then the show will be broadcast on Friday evening,' Ruth informed Lucas.

She was going to have to move Lucas somewhere else pretty soon. It was surely only a matter of time before one of the cleaning staff or the Premier Inn manager let slip who they had staying and there'd be no way she could organise his press appearances from here. She wouldn't be able to hear herself think, let alone have a conversation with anyone, with reporters hammering on the window 24/7. Lucas, the poor sod, could probably do with a change of scenery too. He'd been holed up here for nearly a week.

He was thumbing through the channels on his TV. 'It will be on the Sky?'

'On Channel Four, *The Greg Norman Show*. You know it?'

Lucas shook his head.

'Greg's a really nice guy,' she said reassuringly. 'He used to have his own news and current affairs channel on YouTube. You know YouTube, right?'

He nodded. 'Yes. The PewtiePie man.'

'Nearly,' she accepted.

'And the funny ice-bucket videos.'

'Right, so the twenty-first century hasn't completely passed you by, then?'

Lucas looked her way. 'Huh?'

'Never mind. Anyway, Greg's famous for being on YouTube. Now he does his show on Channel Four on Friday nights. It's a big audience, Lucas. If there's anyone in the UK who doesn't know you by now, they will by the weekend. And then it will go on to YouTube and everyone in the world is going to know how brave you were.'

Lucas turned from the screen to look at her. 'In world?'

'Uh-huh.' She smiled. 'But I'll tell you where the money's going to come from, Lucas. It'll come from endorsements, sponsorship, advertising. I had a call from an advertising company who've been commissioned to do a campaign for a supermarket – they want you as the main character.'

'Supermarket? Like Co-op?'

She pursed her lips. 'Bigger. International. Very exciting, eh?'

He nodded, but she wasn't feeling that buzz coming back from him any more. 'What's up?'

'It was not just me.'

'Well, it was, Lucas. That's the point. That's why you're the hero. You got up and charged when no one else did.'

'Boyd,' he said. 'Boyd save my life.'

'The off-duty policeman?'

He nodded. 'Yes.'

'He helped, Lucas, yeah. But only after you'd knocked that bastard off his feet. It was you who made the first move.'

Lucas muted the TV. 'I would be dead man without Boyd. He did the have-a-go too.'

Ruth sighed. 'Lucas, look... the whole point about this story, what makes *you* so special, is that you led the charge.'

'We both took terrorist man down. Boyd should be with me.'

Ruth felt that she could quite happily throttle him right now. All those lovely zeroes, and, most importantly, her inflated commission, were beginning to vanish in front of her eyes. 'Lucas, if we make a big deal about what happened being a *team effort*, we're going to lose some of that "star appeal". Do you understand?'

'Less money?'

'Oh, yes. Much less.'

He shrugged like that wasn't such a big deal.

'Shit, what is it?' asked Ruth. 'Are you nervous? Is that it? I'll be there, you know. Right there in the studio audience cheering you on. And Greg's a pro; he'll ease the interview along. There won't be dead air or –'

Lucas shook his head. 'I want Boyd on show with me.'

'No... it's you. Just you.'

'Uh-uh. Boyd – or I not do it.'

Oh, for fuck's sake...

34

Okeke watched from the far side of Stonecross Road as the armed officers assembled in the dark outside the terraced house. Number 34 looked just like any other student flat along the same road – green recycling wheelie bins overflowing with pizza boxes, cans and bottles.

They'd picked a crap night to go crashing in. It was a *very* mild night this Friday; windows were open all the way down the street, and several front yards were populated by students in noisy clumps sitting out and putting the world to rights over coffee and late-night munchies.

Already the two police vans that had pulled up and spilled two dozen black-clad and Kevlar-plated FTOs out of their rear doors had begun to attract attention.

Okeke didn't think the sight looked particularly great – a group of officers looking very militarised and ready to storm some terrorist stronghold... and an increasing audience of onlookers, many of them holding up their smartphones and filming the operation.

DCI Williams had selected Okeke to come with her to the raid alongside her two Bright Young Starlets. That had both confused Okeke and caused her to re-evaluate Williams somewhat. Maybe her SIO wasn't such a bitch, after all.

The CCTV image Minter had obtained from the coffee stall had, after being run through the NUS's membership database using CYCLOPS facial recognition software, produced an address and a name – Rizmet Hadzic.

Okeke, Williams and the others watched as the armed officers filed up the path to the front doorstep, then, with just a few moments of silent hand-signalling between them, they began the raid.

The door ram went in hard, only twice before the old wooden front door splintered and gave way. The officers stormed inside one at a time, all bellowing '*Armed police!*' at the tops of their voices. Okeke couldn't help but think that they looked like some weirdly awkward, slowed-down conga as so many of them trooped into such an impossibly small space.

Lights winked on inside the house and she caught glimpses of shadow figures behind net curtains being roused from their beds. Williams hadn't been anticipating finding an active terrorist cell in the student-heavy Moulsecoomb area of Brighton. She was a hundred-per-cent convinced that their man was a loner, but it made sense to be cautious, hence the two van loads of boots. Stonecross Road, or at least the vast majority of its denizens, were now emerging from their homes to see what the hell was going on.

Williams turned to the uniformed officers nearby and told them to spread out on either side of the road and shoo everyone back into their houses.

Good luck with that, thought Okeke. Some of the students had already made their way onto the pavement and were hurling abuse in the direction of the police.

The first of Number 34 Stonecross Road's tenants began to emerge from the front door, cuffed and led towards the patrol cars waiting to whisk them away. The spectacle wasn't helped by the fact that the arresting officers were white and the tenants being roughly dragged out weren't. Okeke glanced at Williams, and the DCI shrugged. The expression on her face seemed to say, *It is what it is.*

The next tenant to be pulled out of the house was a petite Asian girl, crying for help and squirming and wriggling against the firm grip the officers had on her arms as she was escorted to and pushed into the back seat of another patrol car.

'Racist wankers!' someone shouted out from the gathering crowd of onlookers.

Williams tutted and shook her head. 'They had a terrorist living right next door to them... and *we're the bad guys*?'

The hasty pre-raid briefing had mentioned that their man, Rizmet Hadzic, a Brighton University student, was renting a room right in the middle of studentsville. Williams had been mindful that the raid could look like another of Border Force's heavy-handed swoops for 'illegals', and had briefed the men going in and the crowd-control officers to not let it look like eighties-era policing. 'We want smiles and manners please, gents.'

Now, Williams' radio crackled in her hand. 'The house is clear.'

'All right – out you lot come,' she replied. 'Quick as you can, please.'

Okeke looked at the growing crowd of students that had emerged into the road. 'Ma'am, we're going to be all over social media.'

'Then let's be mindful of how we act.' Williams turned to DIs Smith and Connor. 'Hadzic's room is all yours. Matthew: digital forensics, laptops, phones, tablets, memory sticks. Hermione: photos of the room first, then it's all eyeballs. Off you go.'

'Yes, ma'am,' they chorused. Okeke watched them pull on their blue forensic gloves and cross the road.

'Okeke?'

'Ma'am?'

'Those kids... I want to know who's had any contact with Number 34: borrowed some sugar, shared a bus, swapped mix tapes, shared a joint, whatever they do these days... clear?'

Okeke nodded, although she doubted she was going to get much cooperation out of anyone tonight. 'Maybe I'm best coming back tomorrow to do that?'

'No, now. Tomorrow this'll be in the news. Rizmet Hadzic will be identified as the train terrorist and everyone's responses will be heavily skewed by confirmation bias. So get on with it... please.'

Okeke looked at the students all around them, phones raised and barking out insults, trying to provoke reactions from the uniformed officers holding them back. Every last one of these kids was an instant 'citizen journalist' by virtue of their waving smartphones.

'What are you waiting for?' Williams said.

'I'm going to be filmed by all of them,' Okeke said cautiously. 'Every word I say is going to be recorded.'

'So ask very nicely.' Williams turned to look at her pointedly. 'You'll be just as much a part of the optics this evening. Go and make this work for us.'

Okeke nodded, pulled out her notepad and was nearly at the police cordon when she realised why Williams had sent her over.

I'm female and black.

She changed course and headed instead into the front yard of Number 32, the terraced house next door. 'Fuck you,' she muttered under her breath. She rang the doorbell and a young bleary-eyed man answered it almost immediately. He looked as though he'd just woken from a deep sleep. He glanced at Okeke, then over her shoulder at the goings-on in the road.

'Shit. What's happening out there?'

Okeke planted a rigid smile on her face. 'It's okay – you're not in trouble.' She pulled out her warrant card and showed him. 'DC Okeke, Sussex Police. Do you mind if I come in for a minute and have a little chat with you and your housemates?'

'What about?'

'Your neighbours.'

35

Okeke found herself in a small front room dominated by a wall-mounted 52-inch OLED TV screen with a PlayStation beneath it. The only furniture was an old armchair, three brightly coloured beanbags and a low coffee table covered with crisp packets and empty Redbull cans.

'Have a seat,' said the lad who'd let her in. 'I'll call the others.'

Okeke chose the armchair.

'Joy! Sal!' He bellowed up the stairs. 'Police are here!' he added, then returned to the front room.

'Can I get you a brew? I think the milk's okay.'

'I'm good, thanks,' replied Okeke. 'I'm just going to be a few minutes with you.'

'All right.' He slumped down in the beanbag nearest the TV. 'This is about the freshers' party last week, right? Because we already spoke to a policeman about it and he said it was just –'

Okeke waved him silent. 'No – like I said, you're not in trouble.'

She heard the tumble of footsteps coming down the stairs

and the two other tenants of the terraced house appeared. 'Who's this?' asked the tallest of the two.

'I said already. Police.' He gestured at the tall girl. 'This is Joy Parker. This is Saleena Vikram. I'm Lawrence.'

'Hi,' replied Okeke. 'I just want to ask you –' she nearly said *kids* – 'about the people living next door at number thirty-four.'

'They're all first-year students,' said Joy. 'They only moved in at the beginning of the month.' She perched up to peer out of the window. 'Is this to do with all the racket outside?'

Okeke nodded. 'In a way. Have any of you spoken to any of them? Interacted at all?'

'Well, yeah,' said Lawrence. 'We invited them to our party a couple of weeks ago since they're all new. Break the ice and that.'

'Right.' Okeke smiled, *genuinely*. There might be some useful titbits, after all. 'Did they come round?'

'Yeah, all four,' said Joy.

'Can you recall their names?'

'Sure... Rani, Alessandro, Kyle and the quiet one... What's his name?'

'Riz,' said Saleena.

Joy grinned as she flopped down onto one of the beanbags. 'Oh, yeah – you got on pretty well with him if I remember rightly.'

Okeke jotted the names down. 'And they're all first-year students?'

'Yeah, they moved in as a group fairly recently,' said Joy.

Okeke addressed the next question to Saleena. 'Do you know if they knew each other before moving in together?'

Saleena settled down gently on the last available beanbag. 'I think two of them are brothers,' she replied. 'Rani and Alessandro.'

'What about the other two?'

'I don't think they already knew each other. They'd told us that they'd arranged the houseshare through FratMate.'

'FratMate?'

'It's an app that new students can use to organise house-shares,' said Joy. 'It's got a checklist of habits, likes, dislikes – matches you up with people you'd want to share with.'

Okeke laughed. 'Wow, there's an app for everything these days, eh?' She realised too late how old that made her sound. 'So, Saleena, you got to have a chat with the lad called Riz, eh?'

She nodded.

'What's he like? Nice?'

She shrugged. 'Yeah, I s'pose so. Quiet, I guess.'

'He's old,' Joy smirked. 'At least thirty.'

'He's a mature student,' Saleena corrected her. 'And what's wrong with that?'

'Absolutely nothing,' Okeke said. 'What kind of stuff did you guys talk about?'

'Music. Films. Tattoos. Missing home. Families. Faith.'

Okeke tried to not react to the last word. 'General getting-to-know-you things, huh?'

Saleena nodded again.

'Why are you so interested in him in particular?' asked Joy.

Okeke decided to answer with a little woolly obfuscation. 'He's been missing for a few days now. We're concerned.' She turned back to Saleena. 'Did he seem upset about anything?'

'No. Actually he was really excited about getting a tattoo done. I bumped into him outside our house, maybe four, five days ago, and he was buzzed about it.'

'A tattoo? What kind of tattoo?'

'He drew it for me,' she said. 'Kind of like a lobster in a circle or something.'

Okeke held out her pen and pad. 'Could you draw it for me?'

She shook her head. 'Not really. I don't really remember it. It was just a really bad drawing.'

'All right.' Okeke noted Saleena's description on her pad. 'You said you two talked about faith. Are you religious?'

'I'm Muslim,' she replied.

'Riz too?'

Saleena nodded. Okeke's mind blanked. She wanted to ask how strong his faith was without sounding provocative. 'Was he very…'

'Very Muslim?' Saleena eye-rolled and shook her head. 'You either are or you're not,' she replied. 'It's not a fashion choice.'

Okeke nodded. 'You're right. I'm sorry.'

'But you're asking whether I though he was a *radical*, aren't you?' pressed Saleena.

'Yes,' Okeke said carefully. 'Yes, I suppose I am.'

'I don't think he was,' Saleena replied. 'He wouldn't have let himself be alone with me. He wouldn't even have spoken to me if he was.'

Lawrence interrupted. 'Hold up… Has this got anything to do with that train thing?'

Okeke weighed up how much she could reveal. As DCI Williams had said, it was going to be all over the papers tomorrow. 'We think he might be involved somehow, yes.'

'You're totally shitting me!' gasped Lawrence. 'We had a fucking *jihadi* at our party?'

Joy looked at him with disgust. 'Lawrence, for God's sake, grow up.'

'No,' said Saleena softly.

Okeke leant forward. 'No… what?'

'No… I *don't* think he was a jihadi,' she replied icily.

'Fuck it,' Lawrence cut in again. 'I *knew* he was dodgy. I told you, guys. I said –'

'I've had enough of this.' Saleena got up and headed towards the stairs, then paused on the bottom step. 'If he did do it... I really don't think he did it in *God's name*.' With that, she hurried up the stairs to her room.

'Okay, I've got enough for now,' said Okeke. She took down their full names and phone numbers, then handed Joy one of her business cards. 'Can you give this to Saleena? If there's anything that she thinks of that might be helpful...'

'She should call your number?'

Okeke nodded, then stood up. 'You will probably have a lot of press bothering you outside over the next few days.'

Joy turned to Lawrence. 'Oh, you'll love that.'

He spread his hands. 'It's gonna boost my TikTok.'

Okeke closed her notepad and put it away. 'I'll let myself out.'

36

'I know it's a Saturday morning and some of you Hastings lot are in doing an unscheduled shift, but I'm afraid terrorists don't take weekends off.'

DCI Williams studied her team around the table. A couple more fresh-faced detectives from CTPSE had joined them. Minter had whispered a comment that they were breeding like rabbits.

Okeke had no idea what one of those was. As far as she was concerned, they were more like Pixar's yellow minions – except with criminology degrees and all looking young enough that they'd be ID'ed in any pub keen to keep its licence.

'Last night's raid on Hadzic's house has satisfied me that this should remain a counter-terrorism operation. Let's start with what you guys turned up...' She glanced at DIs Smith and Connor.

Smith opened her laptop and turned it round to present the screen to everyone. She brought up a scanned image of Hadzic's passport.

'Rizmet Hadzic was thirty-five years old and Albanian. We're having the passport inspected by their embassy to see if it is valid. Until we hear otherwise, we'll assume it's real and that his name *is* Rizmet Hadzic. We've checked with Brighton University and he was enlisted on a computer sciences course but had only turned up for the registration day and the first lecture. So it seems as though he was just going through the motions of being a student.'

She tapped the keyboard and another image came up: a photograph of his small bedroom.

'We found no Koran, nor any Koranic verses or notes. But his passport, phone and door keys were all there… all indicators that he had no intention of returning to this room.'

She nodded at her colleague to continue.

DI Connor cleared his throat. 'Okay, on the digital forensics side, we have a laptop and a smartphone. The laptop has been sent up to our regional office for analysis. His iPhone, however, we've managed to unlock and –'

'How?' interrupted Okeke. 'Doesn't that require some kind of permission from Apple?'

Connor glanced sideways at Williams.

'We have a licence to use Pegasus-Plus in cases such as this.'

There had been a stink in the *Guardian* a year or so ago about that software. Developed in Israel, it was a suite of tools that allowed a licence holder to hack into any smartphone and use it as a comprehensive surveillance device. The *Guardian*'s point had been that a lot of the 'licence holders' had turned out to be totalitarian regimes with less than admirable human rights records, and their victims tended to be critical journalists, human rights activists and, in a few cases, other foreign leaders.

'We sent a text to his phone,' Connor explained. 'The text carries the embedded access programme and with that we can get administration rights to unlock the phone.'

'Jesus,' muttered O'Neal. 'That's pretty cool.'

'Not if you've got something to hide,' said Williams. She nodded at Connor to continue.

'We're going through the data right now,' he said.

'Have you turned anything up yet?' asked Williams.

Connor paused. 'Nothing that's jumping out at us so far. Hadzic's phone is a recent purchase. A couple of months old, and he's only used it to make a few calls and texts.'

'Such as?'

'Ordering takeaway food. Contacting FratMate members and the other occupants of the house. Presumably communications about viewing the room and setting up the houseshare.'

'What about social media?' prompted Williams.

'None,' replied Connor. 'He's not active on any of the social media platforms.'

'Which is extremely odd for a student attending university in another country, isn't it?' said Minter. 'What about friends? Family back home?'

Williams nodded. 'Obviously he wasn't a typical foreign student. He was on a mission. Keeping a low profile and going through the motions to appear like a legitimate student.'

'Which makes him sound trained,' said one of the eager new faces. 'ISIS-K have been doing a big push to extend their influence out of Afghanistan via the internet. Grooming and training online. Picking an Albanian ID for an operative makes sense.'

Williams nodded at that suggestion.

'I'm hoping we'll get a lot more from the laptop,' said Connor.

'And we have Hadzic's housemates,' said Williams. She looked at her watch. 'We've got about eighteen hours left with them; they've had their rest-recovery period and breakfast, so we're good to start interviewing again.'

'What's the interview strategy, ma'am?' asked Smith.

'At the moment, we're on a general fishing expedition,'

replied Williams. 'Let's get a more inked-in picture of Rizmet from them. Was he a devout Muslim? Was he secretive? Did he interact with his housemates or was he a loner? Was he spending his time up at the train station? Was he interacting with people who *weren't* fellow students?'

'Ma'am?' Okeke lifted her hand.

'Okeke?'

'You saw my interview notes from the neighbouring house, number thirty-two?'

'The students next door that had a party, yes?'

'One of them, Saleena Vikram, seems to have had a chance to interact with him at a more meaningful level. Perhaps that's worth following up on?'

'I noticed you made a big thing of a tattoo he was talking to her about?'

'Yes, Saleena said it was a design he was planning to have done on his arm. She said he seemed quite excited about it. She gave a pretty good description – maybe there's something in that? Some symbolism? I'd like to interview her again.'

'He had the tattoo done, Okeke. It's in the post-mortem report. In fact, there's a photograph of it.'

'Oh, I didn't know...'

'It's in the investigation log,' said Williams tonelessly. 'It's a scorpion. Apparently it's some sort of gaming thing. Matthew?'

'Yeah, it's just one of the logos from a PlayStation game. *Bug Pit*. It's this year's *Fortnite*,' Connor supplied.

'Yeah. My nephew plays it,' said another of the team's new arrivals. 'It's what all the kids are playing. They join clans and have team battles online.'

'Hold on,' interrupted Okeke. 'Well, doesn't that jar? He's a thirty-five-year-old, not fifteen. Also, if he's some ISIS-groomed jihadi... why was he so hyped about getting a gaming tattoo?'

'It's just role-playing,' replied Smith. 'He was undercover. He was playing a part.'

'Going to a house party next door? Being alone with a girl?' pressed Okeke. 'Really? Someone groomed to the point that he's ready to die for his faith would do that?'

'The 9/11 attackers spent the week before they hijacked those planes visiting Las Vegas,' countered Smith. 'It's not unheard of for a martyr-in-waiting to indulge himself a little.'

Williams cut back in. 'Let's not lose our focus here, Okeke. We have a recognisable operational MO. A recruit posing as a mature student, doing a computer course, into his gaming, making all the right noises so that he doesn't draw attention.'

'But Saleena's impression of him was –'

'It fits that MO,' said Smith, a little too forcefully. 'How many times have you heard people say, *'He seemed very nice... very polite... very helpful'*?' She shook her head. 'It's a standard tactic. It's ISIS training one-oh-one. Don't attract attention. Keep your head down. Act more western than a westerner.'

'But hold up,' said Okeke. 'I mean... are you suggesting that, because he didn't look or act like a radical terrorist, that makes him even more suspicious?'

Williams answered: 'It suggests training and given that he's not British, and he's not a home-grown bedroom radical, we have to consider that he's actually had some experience of being covert.'

'Isn't that witch-trial logic?' said Okeke. 'Only a true witch would deny so strongly that she's a witch?'

'Don't be ridiculous, Okeke,' Williams said, glaring at her.

'I'm just –'

'Terrorist groups are much more savvy these days. The beards get shaved off. They're picking more western-looking candidates. They can hide their faith. Go to parties. Play computer games –'

'Behave *exactly* like us?' said Okeke acidly.

'Yes,' replied Williams. 'When in Rome...'

Okeke shook her head in disbelief.

William's patience finally hit zero. 'Are you an expert in radicalised psychopathology, Okeke?'

'No.'

'Then shut up and stop making a fool of yourself.'

Williams turned her attention to the rest of the team. 'Right. We have eighteen hours with Hadzic's housemates. These will be the interview teams...'

37

Boyd was attempting to throw together a paella for his lunch. He'd been watching a chef throw some bits and pieces into a frying pan on TV this morning and that, alongside the unseasonably warm weather, had inspired him to improvise something Mediterranean.

He found himself rummaging through the freezer for a bag of frozen prawns that he was certain was hiding somewhere at the back behind countless half-empty bags of garden peas. Ozzie was hovering by his feet, studying the floor at the base of the freezer for any fallen contraband that might tumble from the over-stuffed drawers. He'd cottoned on to that trick pretty damned quickly.

'No, mate... there's nothing for dogs today,' Boyd said as he carefully pulled out an upside-down bag of sweetcorn. 'Bollocks.'

Several corn kernels, frozen together into boulders, clattered onto the floor and were hoovered up by Ozzie before Boyd could recover them.

'Okay. Maybe there is.'

Ozzie's attention remained resolutely on the bag dangling from Boyd's hand.

Just then, the landline rang from the lounge and Boyd stuffed what was left of the bag of sweetcorn back into the freezer and hurried down the hallway, flip-flops slapping at his heels.

'I'm coming! I'm coming!' he muttered. He really needed to get a new smartphone sorted out. He picked up the house phone. 'Boyd.'

'Hey, mate. Good time? Bad time?' It was Sunny.

'Just doing some lunch. I can talk.'

'I ran that name you gave me, along with various most-likelies as well. It looks as if the word is most probably a surname.'

Boyd had thought that it might be.

'Hadzic is a relatively common Bozniak name,' Sunny continued.

'Bosniak. As in Bosnian?'

'Bosnian *Muslim*,' Sunny emphasised. 'That's an important distinction, Boyd. Bosnia–Herzegovina is really made up of three distinct peoples bundled into one nation: Bozniaks, Serbs and Croats. And, because of the ethnic cleansing that happened, they're very much regionally grouped.'

'Right.'

'So,' continued Sunny, 'Hadzic is a surname that is associated with the Višegrad region of Bosnia. That name ring a bell?'

'Vizzy...what-what?'

'Višegrad.'

'Not really, no. The "grad" bit sounds Russian.' Boyd gazed out of the bay window at Ashburnham Road and the hazy blue sea beyond the roofline of the houses opposite. 'So what's Vize-grad and why am I supposed to recognise it?'

'It's the location of one of the worst atrocities during the Bosnian War. Bosnian Serbs on Bosnian Muslims. It was fucking medieval, Boyd. I've been reading up on it this morning. The slaughter of something like three thousand people in just one town.'

'Shit.'

'Yeah, I won't give you the grisly details now. Not if you're cooking.'

'That bad?'

'Yeah, it was pretty fucking bad.'

'Can you text me how to spell Hadzic? And this Viz-place...?'

'Višegrad. Sure.'

'Thanks, Sunny.'

'No probs. Hey... look, it's pretty dark stuff. You sure you want to take yourself down that rabbit hole?'

'I'm okay, but thanks for the heads-up,' said Boyd.

'Well, look, it was good catching up with you again properly. You coming up to London any time soon?' Sunny asked.

'If I do, I'm buying. I owe you.'

Sunny chuckled. 'Yes, you do! Sounds good, mate. Old times, big man.'

Boyd smiled. 'Yeah. Old times.'

He ended the call and put the phone back on charge.

The Bosnian War? That was early nineties, wasn't it? About thirty years ago now. History almost. If Hadzic was the hijacker's surname... then was that war relevant to him in some way? More to the point... why had he been so damned desperate to pass his name on?

∼

BOYD'S LUNCH ended up looking passably Mediterranean and he ate some of his almost-paella out in the back garden with Ozzie overseeing each mouthful. His plan was to have an old-man nap afterwards and then fill the latter end of the afternoon with some research on the Bosnian War. His landline rang again.

'For Christ's sake,' he grumbled as he hurried back indoors. He picked the phone up. 'Yup?'

'Is that William Boyd?'

'Who's asking?'

'My name's Ruth Cadwell. *Are* you William Boyd?'

'Just Boyd,' he said. 'What can I do for you?'

'You're the guy who helped Lucas Pesic take down the hijacker?' Ruth said.

Oh, for fuck's sake. Some pap must have dug out his phone number. 'Look, I'm not doing interviews or –'

'I'm calling on behalf of Lucas Pesic. He asked me to ring you. He wants to meet up with you.'

Boyd paused. He hadn't been expecting that. They'd exchanged a manly handshake and a 'take care' as both of them parted company and were escorted to different ambulances by their paramedics and they hadn't had any contact since.

'Who are you in relation to him?' Boyd asked.

'I'm his PR manager,' Ruth said. 'As I'm sure you're aware, he's becoming a bit of a celebrity.'

Boyd laughed. And why not? It took a pair of stones to do what he'd done. 'I'm glad for him,' he replied. 'He's a ballsy guy.'

'Yes. Yes, he is. But... I'm a bit worried about him, to be honest,' said Ruth.

Ozzie started barking outside and Boyd wandered over to the doorway to peer down the hall. 'What's wrong with Lucas?' he asked.

Through the dining-room window he could see Ozzie, pacing up and down the dividing fence between his garden and the Parrot Lady's next door. Between the barks, Boyd could hear the bird calling Ozzie all sorts of rude names.

'I think he may be suffering some kind of post-trauma backlash. This last week has been quite an intense experience for him, and I think he needs to decompress with someone.'

'Family and friends are usually a good place to start, Ms Cadwell. Not some random bloke he met on a train.'

'He has no family. He has literally no one. He's an illegal and he's had a pretty tough few years over here.'

Boyd recalled reading something along those lines in the papers. There'd been a picture of Lucas's chubby round face making short work of a doughnut.

'He asked me to ask you whether he could meet you somewhere for a pint and a chat. Just the two of you. No press, no PR. No one else.'

Boyd gave that a moment of consideration. The man had been pleasant and friendly before things had kicked off. A likeable chap. And Boyd had to admit there'd been several times over the last week when he'd felt it would have been helpful to process the experience with someone else who'd actually been there.

'All right,' he said. 'I don't see why not.'

'Thank you. I'm managing his exposure to the press, but also I'm rapidly becoming his mother, I think. He's in quite a fragile mental state right now and I think this will really help him.'

'So how do you want to do this?' asked Boyd.

'Could you meet him tomorrow evening?'

'Yeah, I suppose I could. But where? His face is as well known as the bloody Go Compare guy.'

Ruth laughed. 'He's staying in a Premier Inn at the moment. You're in Hastings, aren't you?'

'Yup. In the old town. Well, uphill from it anyway.'

'Are there any pubs that you know of? Ones that are tucked away? Discreet?'

The Old Pump House came to mind. He gave her the pub's name and the address.

'All right,' she said. 'Seven in the evening okay for you?'

'Just me and Lucas, right? This had better not be a pap ambush.'

'I promise,' replied Ruth. 'I'll be his taxi there and back. But I'll give you two all the room you want.'

'Fine.'

'Thank you, Mr Boyd. Lucas will be made up to hear this.'

'Give him my best. Tell him the first round's on him.'

She laughed again. 'I will.'

38

Boyd tapped 'Visegrad massacre' into Google and began to read about the most horrific episode in the three-year-long war. The war had effectively only just started in the spring of 1992 when the Serbian-dominated Yugoslav army moved into the town of Višegrad in Bosnia. They occupied the town after a couple of days fighting Bosniak separatists and declared it a Serbian stronghold. A month later in May the army left Višegrad in the hands of the local police and some hastily recruited paramilitary groups.

And that's when it turned ugly.

All non-Serbs – two thirds of the population – instantly lost the right to work and very soon after that the killings began. It was the events which followed that brought about the term 'ethnic cleansing'.

Those responsible for the murders were groups of men with very little military training or discipline, equipped and run like little private armies. They gave themselves intimidating names like the 'Tigers' and the 'Avengers' and turned the town into a modern-day depiction of Pieter Bruegel's *The Triumph of Death*.

The epicentre of the daily killings in Višegrad was the bridge over the Drina river, where every day men, women and children were marched to the middle to became the playthings of the paramilitary; some were beheaded and thrown into the river, children were flung into the air and shot at as they fell to the water. The women and girls, of course, were brutally raped, *and then* killed. The killings spread out into the many surrounding villages, where on a number of occasions Bozniak civilians were rounded up into barns and outbuildings, grenades tossed inside and buildings set on fire to burn those still alive.

It was a blessed relief when the front-door bell rang, pulling Boyd out of the grim reading material based on the eyewitness accounts collated by the UN.

He walked down the hallway and pulled the door open to find Okeke standing on the step. She was wearing her usual work clothes: sensible flats, dark trousers, a white blouse and an almost-matching dark suit jacket.

'You been on shift today?' said Boyd. 'I thought you –'

'Fucking annoying, fucking patronising old bitch!' Okeke snapped.

'And lovely to see you too,' Boyd replied.

She didn't wait for an invitation and pushed past him into the hallway. 'Williams has been riding me like –'

'Desert Orchid?' he supplied.

'What?'

'Desert Orchid. He's a race horse. I thought you were going to say "horse".'

'I was.' She shook her head and pulled a WTF face. 'Riding me like I'm her little bitch… since she clapped eyes on me.' She stomped down the hall towards the dining room, leaving Boyd alone to close the front door.

He looked down at Ozzie. 'I think she wants a beer, don't you?'

Boyd joined her in the dining room where she was sitting, drumming her nails on the dining table. She looked like someone planning a hit and run. Boyd pulled a couple of fresh beers out of the fridge and beckoned at the open back door. 'Step into my office, Okeke.'

She followed him outside, grabbed a garden seat and one of the beers. 'She's picking on me because I'm a black woman.'

'Um... I'm no expert on these things, but isn't she also a black woman?' Boyd sat down on his lounger and adjusted it so the back was up while Ozzie curled up in a doughnut on the ground. 'So, why would she do that?'

'I don't know why! But the point is that she pissing well is!'

He raised his brows. 'Is it possible she just doesn't like you?'

Okeke dead-eyed him. 'And that's meant to make me feel better how?'

'My point being,' he began, 'that maybe it's personal. As opposed to...'

'Skin colour and gender?'

He nodded.

'Pfft. That's *exactly* what it is.' Okeke took a swig of her beer.

'Hold on... Has someone just turned two pages over at once? Why would she be racist and sexist against –'

'She's doing the West Indies mum thing,' Okeke cut in. *'You got to be twice better than t'em white men, chil', or you go on home!'*

'Maybe it's coming from a good place,' offered Boyd. 'She wants you to shine.'

'Well, she needs to stop bloody shooting me down every time I open my mouth, then.'

'Tough love.'

'Yeah, right,' Okeke mumbled, and took another chug of beer.

'How's the investigation going?' he asked, trying to change the subject. 'I saw on the news there was a big raid in Brighton last night. That discreet little operation *was* something to do with the hijacker, I'm guessing?'

The Brighton student protests at Stonecross Road had run into Saturday morning and shaky smartphone footage of several cuffed bleary-eyed students being bundled into police cars had propagated across Facebook and Twitter over the last eighteen hours.

'Williams and her two minions seem sure that this guy didn't act alone now,' Okeke said.

Boyd smiled 'Minions?'

'Ughh... she's brought over two baby-faced nerds from CTPSE who think they know everything.'

'Baby-faced? You mean, Warren's age?'

'Probably. Only, get this – they're both DIs.'

'*What?*'

She shrugged. 'I know. Five or ten years ago I could have been babysitting either of them. They look like they've come straight out of school. Anyway... Williams and her rug rats are becoming increasingly sure he might have been part of a cell. Or radicalised by some cleric or a returned ISIS fighter acting as a recruiter.'

Boyd was surprised at that. The man he'd interacted with on the train didn't seem to have the *focus* of a radical – that steely-eyed determination of a zealot with a mission.

'His housemates were interviewed this morning. One of them mentioned seeing Rizmet Hadzic with an older man in a coffee shop. He said he went over to say hi and asked, "Who's your friend?" Hadzic claimed he was an uncle and pretty much shooed him away.'

Boyd sat up. 'So his name *was* Hadzic, then?'

She nodded. 'An Albanian according to his passport.'

'And this older bloke?' Maybe he'd got it wrong? Maybe Riz was part of something more organised. 'Did you guys get a decent description?'

'Older, fifties maybe. Thinning hair on top, greyish beard. Not Middle Eastern; maybe Mediterranean in appearance, maybe Eastern European.'

'A name?'

'Just an uncle.'

'What's Williams' plan?'

'To track this "uncle" down, obviously. They're hoping to get something off Hadzic's laptop.'

'What about his phone? He had one, right?'

She nodded. 'They opened it, but there was nothing useful. Some calls to pizza places, Ubers. No incriminating search history.'

'So he's been very careful.'

'With his phone, yeah.'

Which, again, leant towards the theory that Hadzic had had some training or mentoring.

Boyd was aware the world of covert communications had turned full circle. The old-style whispered conversations had become dangerous, requiring parties to actually meet up, and things had moved on accordingly. Recent exchanges had been mostly online, through encrypted chatrooms. Although a digital breadcrumb trail was as good as dropping a signal flare when it came to getting caught these days, the old-school whispering in dark corners was becoming more popular once again.

'So the investigation's all about this "uncle" now?'

She nodded. 'Williams isn't interested in anything else.'

'But is there anything else?' Boyd asked.

Okeke shrugged. 'I had something I thought was worth looking at.'

'What?'

'Hadzic had a tattoo done on his arm, not that long before the train hijacking.'

'So?'

She looked at him as though he was an idiot. 'Well, if you're getting ready for martyrdom, would getting tatts be right at the top of your bucket list?'

Boyd had no idea what he'd want to do if he knew he was going to die next week. A trip to Las Vegas to gamble everything on one number maybe.

'I think,' she added, 'it was important to him.'

'What was this tattoo of?'

'A scorpion. That or a badly drawn lobster. I saw the post-mortem picture. It's a very, very fresh tattoo.'

Then she held her empty bottle up. 'Do I help myself, or are you going to be a gentleman?'

39

Boyd spent Sunday trying to turf his deforested back garden. The slash-and-burn barbecue earlier in the summer had been a success in terms of reducing the unruly jungle to an apocalyptic landscape of soil and ash, but weeds had begun to grab a toehold and flourished in bloody-minded clusters. He spent several hours digging out the worst of them to the soothing soundtrack of potty language being lobbed over the fence by Fergie the parrot and Ozzie's indignant and loud comebacks. The turf had arrived in the afternoon on a pallet on the back of a flatbed truck. It had taken him a couple of hours to carry it from where it had been dumped at the front, two rolls at a time, through to the back yard.

Having done a total amount of zero research, he began to unroll the lengths of turf and stamp them down against the underlying bed of soil. He was halfway through the job before he realised that a) he should have soaked the turf and rolled it flat first, and b) his area calculation was woefully off and he'd only bought enough to cover one third of the garden.

'Marvellous,' he muttered as he and Ozzie reviewed the

lumpy floor of grass. It was all probably going to wither and go brown in a few days anyway and then he'd have to get someone in who knew what they were doing to do the job properly. He decided to hose down what he'd done and call it a day.

He checked his phone on the way to get a shower. There was nothing from Sunny yet. He'd emailed him a photo of Okeke's scribbled sketch of the tattoo. It looked like a prawn waving a pair of maracas around, so he'd explained in the email that it was supposed to be a scorpion.

He'd also had a quick chat with Charlotte this morning. She'd sounded harried. She was working at the White Rock theatre today; there was a Sunday evening performance by the Veteran's Wives Choral Society, which required all hands on deck to prep the stage for fifty singers.

As he showered the muck and sweat off, he thought ahead to his 'date' with Lucas Pesic that evening. He wasn't sure whether it was going to be awkward or weird. It'd probably end up being a five-minute drink followed by a 'see you around, mate'. He'd been drunk the only time they'd chatted and still in shock as they'd exchanged farewells. They didn't have anything in common other than having been through the same traumatic experience and being one half of an impromptu Batman and Robin act.

He caught up with Emma over teatime. She didn't linger on the phone; she was pulling a double shift with Patrick because one of the hotel's reception staff had called in sick.

'You going to be late?' asked Emma.

'Hopefully not.'

'Don't forget to get his autograph,' she said, grinning.

Boyd rolled his eyes.

At six-thirty he left Ozzie guarding their kingdom from his perch in the bay window as he began his amble downhill to the old town.

The Old Pump House was as quiet as he'd assured Ruth Cadwell it would be. Bonnie Tyler was quietly singing 'Total Eclipse of the Heart' and the pub's one-armed bandit was chirruping away to itself in the corner beside the fireplace. He was ten minutes early and decided to get a pint of Caffrey's in.

He waited at the bar for a minute before Daniel appeared, looking morose.

'All right, Boyd?' he said gloomily.

'Hey, Dan. How's things?' Boyd asked.

Daniel pulled a fake smile. 'Okay, I guess.'

'What's up?'

He shrugged in reply. 'It doesn't matter. Caffrey's, isn't it?'

Boyd nodded. 'I've not seen much of you recently,' he said as he watched Daniel pull the pint.

Daniel's brows bounced limply. 'Uh-huh.'

'Have you and Emma fallen out or something?'

'Not exactly...' He sighed as he jerked the pump a couple of times to froth up the head. 'She just doesn't seem that interested any more.'

'Well, she's busy. She's working hard,' Boyd said cheerily.

'I know, I know. That's what she keeps telling me.' Daniel set the pint on the bar and took Boyd's money. It's just...' He pressed his lips together, paused for a few seconds and finally came out with it. 'Is she seeing someone else?'

Boyd shook his head in surprise, beginning to wish he'd left well alone. 'I shouldn't think so! She's either at the hotel or she's home with me. She usually too knackered to do anything.'

'Right.' The reply seemed to have lifted Daniel's mood slightly.

'Do you want me to ask?' added Boyd.

'Christ, no! Just... No, no, it's all good.'

'Talk to her,' Boyd said, picking up his pint. 'Give her a call.'

The Last Train

He offered the lad a fatherly smile. 'Sometimes it's okay *not* to play it cool, if you know what I mean?'

'I *have* called her. Several times,' Daniel said, looking downcast again. 'She just says she's too busy to talk.'

'Oh,' Boyd said, momentarily stuck for words. 'Maybe you need to give her a bit of room, then.'

'So I *should* play it cool?'

'Right. Maybe.' Boyd had a suspicion he wasn't helping much. 'I'll try and catch her between shifts and see what's what, eh?' he said, clutching his pint and beating a hasty retreat.

He took the narrow steps up to the back of the pub to find it perfectly deserted.

He was a couple of sips into his pint and ruminating on the abortive mess that was his lumpy back-garden lawn when a man clambered up the three steps to the rear lounge with a pint in his hand. He was wearing a baseball cap, sunglasses, a leather jacket and brand-new trainers. He looked disconcertingly like an old Radio 1 DJ.

The man grinned and raised a hand. 'Boyd!'

'Lucas?'

Lucas came over to the table and sat down opposite him. 'My agent give me money to buy new clothes and disguise.' He peeled the leather jacket off. 'Is nice gear, eh?'

'You been shopping in Priory Meadow?' Boyd asked.

'Da. In disguise,' Lucas said, peering over the top of his sunglasses.

'As the Fonz?'

Lucas grinned. 'Ah! *Happy Days*?' He did the thumb and the 'hey-y-y.'

'That's the fella.' Boyd lifted his pint glass and Lucas did likewise.

'*Zdravica za dug život i mrinu smrt!*'

Boyd nodded and smiled. 'And up yours too.' They clinked,

both took a slug, then set down their drinks. 'So, how've you been coping, Lucas?'

'Crazy life. Crazy.' Lucas wiped the beer suds from around his mouth. 'You see me in the newspaper?'

'Oh, yeah.' Boyd grinned. 'In pretty much *every* paper. I think you're doing a good job of charming the entire country.'

'My agent say this nation love a "plucky hero".' Lucas shrugged. 'So I play along, eh?'

'Why not,' replied Boyd. 'Is this getting you some money?'

He nodded. 'Thousands. I am becoming rich.'

'Good. Just make sure no one's ripping you off.'

'My agent take good care of me.'

'That's this Ruth Cadwell, is it?'

Lucas nodded.

Boyd wondered how large her commission was. 'So she said that you wanted to talk with me? About what happened?'

Lucas nodded, his chirpy smile fading away. He removed his sunglasses. 'I have very bad memories. They come to me. I get nightmares.'

'Yeah, me too.' Boyd had shared some of the train incident with his therapist, but not much. Talking about it put him right back there, stoked up the adrenaline and made him feel sick. 'It's called PTSD, Lucas – the flashbacks, the memories. I've been told the best way to deal with it is to just talk it all out.'

Lucas had a haunted look about him, the face of a man dragging chains of memories behind him like a ship's snagged anchor. 'I get flashes. When I think about what happen.'

'Me too,' conceded Boyd.

'My memories... confused,' said Lucas. 'Feelings... are angry and frightened.' He glanced up from his pint. 'Hate.'

'I think that's pretty normal.'

'I am not brave man,' Lucas muttered. 'I am coward.'

'Well, the evidence suggests otherwise, Lucas. I'd say you've got a big swinging pair of balls to have got up like that and charged him down.'

'It was fear make me do that. Not a hero.' He sipped his beer. 'I am scared the people see what is real me.'

'I think that's just the point,' said Boyd. 'In a situation like that, everyone's frightened. What marks people out as special is what they do despite being afraid.'

Peisc nodded absently, lost in his own thoughts for a while. At last he looked up at Boyd. 'Will you come on TV with me? It is on Friday with Greg Norman.'

Boyd shook his head. 'No. That's not really my thing. Look, I don't think anyone wants to hear about me.' He shrugged. 'I'm the guy who was the *second* one to make a move. You're the bloke they all want to hear from.'

'I am scared, Boyd.'

'Scared of what? Going on TV?'

Lucas hesitated, then nodded. 'I think... I do not want this much fame.'

'It opens doors, mate.' Boyd tried to lighten the mood. 'You'll never have to buy your own pint again, that's for sure.'

Lucas smiled. 'This is true.'

'You got anyone back in Albania who might recognise you on the news?'

He shook his head. 'No.'

'No one?'

'Parents dead. No brother or sister.'

'A wife? Child? Friends?'

Lucas shook his head to each of those. 'All dead now.'

Christ, no wonder he was so bloody chatty on the train. Lonely bugger.

Lucas looked at Boyd. 'What about you? Family?'

'Just a daughter. And some parents who seemed determined to barbecue and pickle themselves on the Costa del Sol.'

Lucas frowned.

'They're in Spain,' explained Boyd. 'They're busy getting pissed in the sun on their pensions.' That was something that still bothered him a little. They'd come over for the funerals obviously, and lingered for a couple of weeks afterwards, but it had been his daughter who'd been there to prop him up. Not his folks. 'You mind me asking what happened to your family, Lucas?'

Lucas frowned deeply. 'They all killed.'

'Shit. How?'

Lucas pressed his lips together and puffed out his cheeks. Finally he sighed. 'I tell you big secret?'

'Do you really want to?'

Lucas nodded. 'The war,' he replied. He tapped the side of his head. 'I have some memories. Very bad. Mess up with my head. So I remember nothing now.' He took another chug of his beer. 'I tell newspaper I am Albanian. I am not. Easier to say this. But –' he took a deep, steadying breath – 'I am Bosnian.'

'Christ.' The research reading Boyd had done yesterday on the war had given him only some semblance of the horror. 'Lucas,' he said, 'you don't have to say more.'

Lucas nodded; there was a brief flicker of gratitude. 'You are right.'

'I lost family too…' said Boyd. 'I'm not sure how helpful it is to drag it out and talk about it.'

Lucas nodded. 'I try to forget.'

Boyd couldn't agree with that. He remembered every day. He sometimes pictured Julia and Noah existing in a parallel universe that faintly overlapped with this one. That they'd all moved down to Hastings together, and every now and then he imagined he glimpsed their ghostly outlines – Julia getting up from the sofa and throwing a log on the fire, Noah lining up soldiers on the carpet, only to knock them down again with faint pew-pew sounds.

Lucas shrugged.

'So I am Pesic, from Albania.' His hangdog forehead rumples vanished as he threw on a cheerful smile. 'Maybe Lucas Pesic from Great Britain soon, eh?'

Boyd had seen the *UK Daily*'s funding campaign. The signatures were already rolling in, in their thousands. 'You deserve to be,' he said.

40

DI Matthew Connor had the floor in the Incident Room. Okeke looked at DCI Williams, who had the appearance of a proud mum at a primary school Christmas concert.

'...Rizmet Hadzic's iPhone has been a pretty poor source of intel, but –' Connor, pointed at the projected image on the whiteboard and his second slide came up – 'I sourced the records from his service provider, which gave us the ping history from the 5G masts in the area. That gives us a pretty good record of his movements in the weeks and days leading up to the hijacking.'

The slide showed a map of Brighton with pin-markers clustered in the centre and several others up to the right where his houseshare was located in Moulsecoomb.

'His housemate Rani said he saw Hadzic with an older man in Costa Coffee in the city centre...' DI Connor moved on to the next slide – which was zoomed in on Churchill Square shopping centre. There was pin-marker in the middle. 'But what we didn't have from Rani was a precise time. He wasn't even sure which day it was. Consulting the mast pings puts Hadzic right here in the Costa mentioned for just over an hour, starting at ten seventeen, on the fifth of September.'

'Good work, Matt,' said Williams.

Okeke managed to control the urge to stick a finger down her throat. *For God's sake. He's hardly Sherlock fucking Holmes.* Even numbnuts O'Neal could have collated that kind of intel. Connor's laborious 'this is how we do it' mansplaining was beginning to get on her nerves.

'So, this precise time window gave me and Hermione a chance to inspect Costa's internal CCTV, and we got this...'

Slide four was a shot from behind the counter over the barista's head: Rizmet Hadzic, clear as day, standing beside an older, taller man with a silvering beard.

'Excellent work, you two,' said Williams.

So that's how you two spent Sunday, was it? Okeke tried not to grind her teeth too loudly. If Boyd had been running this operation, he'd have *shared* his thoughts with her rather than hero-grabbing. He'd have asked her if she wanted to take a trip over to Brighton on a day off and she'd have jumped at it.

'Good job,' added Williams, for good measure.

'Oh, it gets better.' Connor grinned at his SIO. Her beaming smile only broadened.

Christ, get a room, already.

'The older man really slipped up here,' he continued. 'He tried paying with cash but he didn't have enough to pay for both coffees and sandwich wraps. So he used his plastic.'

The next slide was a close-up photograph of the till roll. 'And this is the transaction. I had the store manager take a photo and text it to me. You can see that the transaction matches the CCTV timestamp to within a minute. Now, as I'm sure some of you will know, the vendor can't store any personal details but can create a "token" number, which is assigned to a card number, and that token number they *can* store. This is how retailers can tell on the till whether a customer is a repeat customer. The good news is that our man is a regular customer. His token shows very regular mid-morning visits.' Matthew turned to Williams. 'That's what we have. Ma'am?'

Williams stood up. 'Thank you. So... we have the so-called uncle,' she began. 'This man could very well be our recruiter. He could be the first significant high-value link in a previously undetected terror network, which is why this operation is going to scale up.'

She looked at DI Smith. 'Hermione, next slide.'

The whiteboard now displayed the zoomed-in map of the shopping centre.

'We're going to stake out this coffee shop,' Smith announced. 'When that customer token is triggered again, we'll have him.'

'And make the arrest?' asked DI Abbott.

She speared him with a look of incredulity. 'Please tell me you're joking.'

By the look on his face, Okeke guessed he hadn't been.

'We will follow him, DI Abbott,' Smith said matter-of-factly. 'We need to know who his contacts are and if there are any more recruits in his cell. We need to watch his interactions. Get his ID. His address. We'll obtain a full suite of warrants and put him under surveillance. Then –' she glanced back at Abbott – 'when we've got everything we can on him... *then* we'll arrest him.'

41

Boyd brought the coffees over to Emma, who was holding Ozzie between her knees. He set them down on the bench table and sucked in a deep breath of salt-tinged air.

'So how was your date with a hairy old Albanian man?' she asked.

'Longer than I thought it would be,' Boyd said. This morning he'd awoken with an aching back (from the failed turfing) and an aching head.

'How are you feeling?' she asked.

'Better, but not yet brilliant,' he replied. The fresh air on the pier was clearing his head nicely. The pint with Lucas had turned into three, and they'd spent the last hour before closing time debating which Pink Floyd album was the band's finest hour. He'd briefly met Ruth Cadwell. The woman definitely seemed to have adopted the role of manager-stroke-mother.

'So it seems like it wasn't the stilted, awkward drink date you've been worrying about, then?' Emma grinned. 'Quite the contrary.'

'He's a nice guy,' said Boyd. 'Fun. Funny.'

'The picture in the paper makes him look like Pumbaa,' she said, chuckling.

'Huh?'

'From *The Lion King*? The funny warthog. You remember... "Hakuna Matata"?'

Boyd nodded. They'd taken her to see the musical in the West End and that song had been a relentless earworm in the Boyd household for the next few weeks.

'Right. Yeah, I guess he does a bit.'

She peeled the plastic lid from her coffee. 'I heard he's going to be on *The Greg Norman Show* on Friday.'

'How do you know that?' Boyd asked her. He didn't remember having said anything to her about that.

She looked at him as though he'd just climbed down from the Stupid Tree. 'Errr. The internet?'

'Of course,' Boyd said, rolling his eyes. He took Ozzie's lead from her and gestured. 'Shall we?'

Emma grabbed her coffee and got up. They headed along the promenade and down a few steps to the beach.

'So how're things with you and Daniel?' he asked. 'I've not seen much of him lately.'

Emma shrugged. 'I've been busy.'

'He said.'

She looked at him, surprised.

'He was working at the Pump House last night.'

'Did he say anything else?' she asked, a slight edge to her voice.

'*That's three pounds seventy-five, Mr Boyd...*'

'Dad,' Emma groaned, and elbowed him for good measure.

'No,' Boyd lied. He didn't want to drop the lad into hot water – she was her mother's daughter when it came to arguing. 'I just realised I hadn't seen him for a while.'

'Well, he's been gigging and I've been working. Anyway, I

thought you wanted me to get on with things? You know, get a career going....?'

'Working the reception in a hotel isn't exactly a career, Ems.' They were halfway down the shingle and close to the water's edge now. He let Ozzie off his lead and laughed as Ozzie raced straight into the water without a backwards glance.

'At least I'm not skulking around the house, which is what you said you wanted, wasn't it?' she replied.

'I want you to be happy is all, Ems. That's it. You were out at gigs and rehearsals with Daniel almost every night before. I thought you liked that.'

'I need to earn some money,' she replied. 'And I need to start somewhere.'

'Well, what about going to college?' he said. 'It's not too late to consider that, is it?'

'Dad, not this again.'

'I just want you to... to launch your life properly.'

'Launch? Charming.' She gave him heavy flickering eyelids. 'I'm not a bloody oil tanker.'

He laughed. 'Perhaps something more flattering... A yacht, then.'

They watched Ozzie splashing around in the cold water and snapping at the gentle waves that buffeted him.

'I just want you to see beyond the horizon,' he added.

She cocked a brow. 'Are we still on the nautical metaphor?'

'You promised me in London, once we got settled here... you'd focus on yourself,' he replied, 'and stop fussing over me.'

'I have,' she replied. 'I'm enjoying the job. But I've only been doing it for five minutes! And these days it's more like you fussing over me – gimme a break!' Emma stopped and looked up at him. 'My generation have different expectations out of life.'

'Like what?' he asked.

'Well, we've figured out that not everyone's going to have or want a career, a home, several cars, two and a half children and a pension.'

'Christ, that's not very realistic. How are you going to live?'

'It's perfectly realistic,' she countered. Then she rolled her eyes. 'Relax. I'm not going all emo on you. It's just that when I look at the world, the rising temperatures, the wildfires... to me, there are more important things than how many holiday homes I could own. Materialistically, not every generation has to do better than their parents. And that's okay.'

'Right,' Boyd said, feeling well and truly put in his place.

'Life's about people, Dad... not things.' With that, she called after Ozzie, who was making great headway towards France.

Boyd watched his daughter trying to coax their dog back to the shallows and realised how incredibly wise his little girl was.

42

DCI Williams had given Okeke the 'short straw' job of sitting in Costa and waiting for their mystery man to turn up.

The encrypted data – the client-transaction ID numbers, or tokens – indicated that their target came in here most weekdays between eleven and three and ordered the same thing: a black Americano (medium) and a hummus wrap. Occasionally, seemingly as a treat, he'd push the boat out and have a Danish pastry too. The team had only had yesterday afternoon to attempt to extract any inferences from that information. DI Hermione Smith, the expert young profiler with the degree in criminal psychology, had put together some thoughts...

Their man worked in Brighton but didn't necessarily live there. The flexibility of the hours (between eleven and three) signalled that he wasn't locked down to a fixed lunch-break window, so it was likely that he was either self-employed or non-office-based. Hummus suggested that he was possibly a vegetarian. And the black Americano, Smith had informed the team, meant that he was health conscious, having no sugar or milk.

She'd offered up those brushstrokes as if they were genius pieces of deduction, but to be honest, thought Okeke, they were easy guesses that anyone with or without a degree would be able to throw together. The flexibility of his lunch break could have been down to a lunchtime rota. The black coffee – dairy intolerance. Honestly, there were any number of deductions that could have been made from timing and drink and sandwich choices.

Okeke had always thought there was something of the fairground palm-reader about profilers, all smoke and mirrors and dressing up the Bloody Obvious to sound frightfully clever. In the Costa, she lifted her coffee cup and pretended to sip it. It had become tepid in the last hour and the chocolate-chip cookie on her plate had been absently mined for all its chocolate chips, leaving just a plate full of crumbs.

At least she was inside.

Outside Churchill Square Shopping Centre, it was pissing down steadily. Williams and her growing team of CTP officers were sitting in a couple of unmarked vans just outside the shopping centre's southern entrance on Russell Road. A pair of officers were stationed just inside. From her seat, Okeke could see them sitting in the main concourse, a man and a woman, attempting to look like a couple, bored with each other's company and swiping away on their phones. Neither of them were doing a very good job, as they kept looking up from their screens and studying the shoppers walking past.

Williams' plan was thus: when the customer ID token was triggered, it would flash up on the Costa manager's office screen. As soon as that happened, he'd emerge from his office and approach Okeke's table, ostensibly to clear her plate away. The customer waiting to pay right in front of the till would be their man, and Okeke would call in a head-to-toe description to Williams and her team inside the van. As soon as he stepped out of the Costa, he'd be inside what was called 'the box' – a diamond-shaped area with a surveillance officer at each corner. One either side of him, one ahead, one behind – all four of them in constant voice-coms with each other.

The trick, obviously, was to keep the target in this box at all times, with one officer trailing the target, giving a running commentary so that the others wouldn't have to keep looking back over their shoulders to know which way to go or how fast to walk. They were specially trained for this, all eight of them: the two sitting outside, the two ready to join them and the other four-man team ready to replace the first team as and when required.

Keeping the target in the box was their only job. It was, apparently, a completely infallible system passed down to them by MI5.

43

The morning did not look promising as far as walks on the beach were concerned.

'I'm sorry, Ozzie, old boy,' said Boyd. 'Much as I love you, there's no bloody way I'm stepping out into that.'

Ozzie's hopeful head drooped onto the back of the armchair and he resumed watching the raindrops racing each other down the bay windows.

Boyd had nothing planned for this morning. Literally nothing. While there was much to be done to the garden, he had finished all the Must-Do jobs inside his vast Victorian house weeks ago. Apart from walking Ozzie, with the possibility of bumping into Charlotte during her lunch break, there was little to do beyond switching on the telly and watching endless property shows and antique-hunting roadshows.

This option definitely didn't appeal to him. He was someone who felt guilty watching any TV once he'd grabbed the headlines over breakfast. Daytime TV was a slippery slope as far as he was concerned, and back in London he'd started to slide down it.

Now, Boyd sipped his coffee and watched the raindrops

with Ozzie, pondering whether or not he could ask Google for some hobby that would keep him busy until Hatcher considered him fit enough to return to work.

As his mind flitted through the possibilities – building a wooden sailing ship, picking up the guitar again, or even picking up a book to read – he was mercifully rescued by the phone ringing. He reached over Ozzie's back and grabbed it.

'Boyd.'

'Hey, Boyd – thought I might have caught you old-man napping.'

It was Sunny. Boyd smiled and settled back for a chat.

'Up yours,' he replied. 'Anyway, they're called "power breaks"... until you turn sixty.'

'Whatever you say, old-timer. Anyway, I've got something for you.'

Boyd swung his legs off the couch and sat up straight. 'Let's have it.'

'That scribbled scorpion logo you sent me?'

'Go on...'

'Where did you get it from?'

Boyd was reluctant to mention that it had come from Okeke – it was technically an actionable infraction, revealing sensitive details about the case. DCI Williams sounded as though she was actively on the hunt for something to beat Okeke with.

'It was something I spotted on that hijacker's arm,' said Boyd. 'A tattoo.'

Sunny made a sceptical 'huh-huh' noise. 'Of course you did. Well, it kind of fits the picture.'

'What picture?'

'Well, like I'd said, Hadzic is a common Bozniak name around Višegrad. And I've found that one of the Serbian paramilitary groups active there was called Scorpians. No surprise, they've been implicated in war crimes in that area – a lot of those fucktards actually had scorpion designs tattooed all over them, like neo-Nazis have swastikas.'

'But that doesn't make sense, Sunny,' Boyd interjected. 'If this guy Riz was a Muslim, why would he be part of a group like that?'

'Maybe he *wasn't* a Muslim,' Sunny offered.

'But he looked like –'

'Seriously, mate?' Sunny cut him off. 'A beard and a backpack? Is that all it takes to ID one of us?'

Boyd closed his eyes. 'Sorry. That was bloody idiotic of me.'

Sunny sighed. 'I'll let you off this time, you dumb kefir.'

'So, which one was he, Sunny? Was Riz Hadzic a Serb nationalist or a Bosnian Muslim?'

'Err... the name says Bosnian Muslim, the tattoo says Serbian nationalist. But obviously, mate, he can't be both.'

'Maybe Riz was trying to stir something up?' suggested Boyd.

An unsettling thought had occurred to him. Could this be false-flag terrorism? Pretending to be 'the enemy' and committing some ghastly act in their name? What if Riz had been some crazy Anders Breivik type, attempting to stir up anti-Muslim, anti-immigrant outrage? If so... then he'd been incredibly successful. Quite a few of the tabloids – and leading the charge was *UK Daily* – had been banging on about the government going soft on border control over the last week.

'Sunny, let me do some thinking about this,' Boyd said.

'Okay, mate. It's yours to play with.'

'Thanks again for all the digging.'

'Salam, big man.' Sunny was teasing him.

'Salam right back.'

Boyd put the phone down and watched the rain pelting against the sash window.

Who the fuck were you, Riz?

44

Okeke was pretty sure the man who'd just entered Costa was the same man captured by the CCTV camera over the counter. He was slim, in his fifties, with a clipped beard dashed with silver and grey. He was wearing a green baseball cap, a dark-blue anorak with the hood up and loose jeans that were wet from the knees down to his trainers. In one hand he held a burgundy Thermos flask, in the other a dripping black umbrella. On his back was a small dark-grey backpack.

She surreptitiously watched him as he joined the queue. The place was getting pretty busy now that it had gone twelve – the beginning of the lunchtime rush. The man's back was to her as he studied the savoury pastries under the display glass. She debated whether to text DCI Williams that she had a possible eyes-on. Fuck it.

Possible sighting of target. Want a descrip?

She kept one eye on the man in the queue, the other on her phone. Three ellipses appeared on the screen and danced a Mexican wave until Williams' reply came back:

NO. Not until target confirmed!

Wrong descrip will lead to confusion.

'Oh, piss off,' Okeke muttered to herself.

She turned her attention back to the man at the counter; he was next but one to be served. He took another step towards the till. She pondered her description. The Thermos flask and the umbrella were going to be the most helpful items to mention. But, also, Williams had cautioned on the way over this morning that such items were not to be relied upon. Things like hats, bags, gloves, jackets could be ditched in the blink of an eye. If their target was experienced at working covertly, or at an elevated level of caution and awareness in the wake of the train incident, accessories like those might be things he was carrying specifically to discard if he felt spooked by anything.

Okeke started to thumb the description into her phone...

Slim, mid-50s, Middle-Eastern or Mediterranean. Dark anorak, backpack, green baseball cap, jeans, trainers. Holding black umbrella, burgundy flask.

It was the man's turn to be served now. He handed the flask over the counter to be filled up. Her eyes darted across to the manager's office door, waiting for any sign of him.

Hold fire. He hasn't paid. The token won't have been triggered yet.

She waited anxiously for the Thermos to be handed back, thumb poised above the 'send' icon.

Come on. Come on.

At last the flask came back filled, and the man reached into his back pocket and pulled out a wallet.

Here we go.

He took out a card and Okeke let out a sigh of relief. He tapped it on the card machine and her eyes shot back to the office door, certain now that this was their guy.

Come on. Hurry up.

Their target moved aside to let the barista serve the next person in the queue. He walked to the end of the counter, where he grabbed a couple of sachets of sweetener and pocketed them.

He's not drinking in. He's leaving. She desperately wanted to press send, but Williams had been absolutely clear – not until the manager emerged and came over to Okeke's table.

She watched him stash the Thermos flask in his backpack. She quickly deleted the flask from her ready-to-go text message.

Now he was swinging the backpack onto his back, grabbing his umbrella and heading for the exit.

Shit. Come on!

Finally the staff door opened just as the man stepped outside, onto the shopping centre concourse.

The idiot manager met her eyes and sent an indiscreet thumbs-up her way.

Okeke typed 'EXITING NOW!' at the end of her message and sent it. She looked out of the window at the 'disinterested couple' sitting on the bench outside. A couple of seconds passed and they both casually stood up, put away their phones and began to make their way towards the Russell Road exit to box in their target.

Okeke's phone buzzed. She looked down at the message.

Eyes on target. Exiting shopping centre.

Good job. U can stand down now.

She heaved a sigh of relief. Her part had been completed without any fuck-ups; it was Williams and her highly trained team of Tweenies who were carrying the ball now.

Just as Okeke was about to get up to leave, the office door opened again. The manager stuck his head out, then, about as subtly as Mr Bean, wandered over to her table, trying to look nonchalant. He leant down and cupped his mouth like some badly acted butler in an am-dram whodunnit. 'Is the coast clear?' he whispered hoarsely.

Okeke nodded quickly. 'It's done,' she said. 'Thank you for your cooperation.'

He grinned. 'This'll be on the news or something, right?'

She skewered him with a hard stare. 'It had better not be.'

'Oh, right.' He nodded. 'Understood. So, uh, what happens now? You guys gonna tail him?'

She nodded just once. That's all he was getting from her.

He smiled. 'Good. Hard to lose him, eh?'

She almost let that go... then: 'Sorry?' she queried.

'The guy with the shoulder bag.'

'Backpack,' she clarified.

'No. The shoulder bag. With the white strap,' he said.

'White strap? Are you sure?'

He nodded.

Okeke all but dragged him by the ear through the office door and over to his desk. 'Replay the CCTV. Now.'

Clearly surprised by Okeke's reaction, the Costa manager sat down, clicked his mouse on the CCTV window and scrolled back over the last few minutes. He stopped and pointed at the screen. 'That guy.'

Okeke peered at the static image. Clearly in shot was the man she'd had her eye on, the slim one with the umbrella. But the manager wasn't pointing at him. It was the man *before him*. A similar-looking man but a fraction taller, his beard more pronounced.

'*He's* the one?' said Okeke.

The manager nodded.

'Why the hell didn't you come out immediately?!' She didn't know how she didn't scream that into his gormless face.

'I-I th-thought I was meant to wait until he was away from the counter...'

'NO! You were meant to –' Okeke stopped. It was Williams who'd briefed him. But she'd been very clear. She'd said *immediately*.

Shit.

Okeke pulled her phone out but the signal here at the back of the shop was non-existent. She hurried out into the main customer area and checked her screen again. One bar. Enough for a text. She was furiously pecking out a message when she felt the manager nudging her arm.

'Jesus! I'm trying to type a fucking –'

'Look, there's your guy,' he said, pointing through the window at the mall's concourse.

Okeke followed his gaze and saw the man with the shoulder bag peering at the Waterstones display opposite.

45

Okeke emerged from Costa just as the man stepped into Waterstones. She dared not take her eyes off him until she was sure he was staying in the shop. She hurried across the concourse and then slowed down to a casual saunter as she walked in after him.

She spotted him quickly; he was picking his way through some of the books stacked on one of the centre tables. She made a mental note of the books that caught his attention. She turned to the staff member at the till.

'Can I grab one of your plastic bags? I forgot to bring one.'

'Sure, I'm afraid it's ten pence when you pay,' she replied.

'That's fine,' said Okeke, dropping a quid on the counter. 'Pop the change in the charity box.'

The staff member tore one from the hook by the till. 'Fill it up with wisdom and goodness.'

'Thanks.' Okeke wandered over to a neighbouring table and faked interest in a Jeremy Clarkson book while she studied the man. *He* was the one in the CCTV image beside Rizmet Hadzic. He was in his mid-fifties, slim, with a greying beard and dark hair, silvering at the temples, with a pronounced widow's peak.

The Last Train

The man put down the book he was looking at and wandered towards the back of the shop. Okeke went over, picked up the book and carefully placed it in her bag, mindful not to smear her fingerprints over the cover.

She watched as he headed over to the Computers and Technology shelves and browsed the books there for five minutes or so, before suddenly turning and heading straight towards her. Their eyes met for a moment and a polite smile flickered across his face as he sidestepped past her and walked towards the front of the shop and the exit.

Okeke turned to follow him, wary in case he looked back as he stepped outside. She saw him turn right, heading further into the mall – instead of out onto Russell Road. Okeke hurried towards the shop's exit and past the till. The young girl who'd given her the bag called out. 'Excuse me...'

Okeke passed it over the counter and handed it to her. 'Can you keep this safe? I'll be back to get it.'

'Uh, sure, okay.'

'And don't touch it,' she cautioned. 'It's police evidence.' She flashed her warrant card.

'Huh?'

'Don't touch it! I'll be back.' Then Okeke dashed out of the shop.

The man was heading further into the shopping centre; he didn't seem to be in a particular hurry, but he wasn't dawdling to look in shop windows either.

Okeke glanced down at her phone in the vain hope that a viable signal might have miraculously returned, but now she was down to Wi-Fi, which, while free, would almost certainly involve entering email addresses and passwords.

It's just you, girl. Williams with her vans and her teams of expert surveillance types were all wasting their time following an innocent mark. On her say so.

She picked up the pace to narrow the distance between

herself and the actual mark – mindful not to get too close to him. As she watched his back, she evaluated what she knew so far about him. His English was good enough to browse the blurb of a crime novel and several other books. He seemed to have an interest in computers, or programming.

Okeke stayed in his wake as he casually made his way through the shopping centre to the exit on the far side, which opened onto a pedestrian area surrounded by crescent steps. He pulled his anorak hood up and hurried out into the torrential rain and onto the main street beyond.

She reached the glass doors and watched to see which way he was heading. He went left. She glanced back down at her phone and saw that she finally had a signal strong enough to make a call. As she pushed the door open, she dialled Williams.

DCI Williams answered on the third ring. 'What is it?'

'You're following the wrong man,' Okeke blurted out.

'What?!'

'It's the wrong man. The manager fucked up; you're following the wrong man.'

She heard the DCI curse under her breath. Then: 'Please tell me you have eyes on the *right* man.'

'I do,' Okeke confirmed. She clocked a sign on the side of a building to her left. 'I've got the Prince of Wales pub to my left and Western Road directly ahead of me. He's just turned left onto Western Road.'

'Dammit! We're all on the other side.' Okeke heard her barking instructions through a radio. 'All units abandon target and converge on the north entrance to the shopping centre!' She was back on the phone: 'Okeke, you still eyes on?'

'Yes, ma'am.'

'Stay on him at all costs. We're on our way over.'

'Yes, ma'am.'

'And don't let him see you on a phone. If he gets a whiff he's being tailed, we're done.'

'Got it.' Okeke ended the call and hurried up the crescent steps after him. The rain had driven most of the pedestrian traffic away and, apart from a few hardy shoppers in raincoats and a couple huddled at a bus shelter nearby, it was almost deserted.

She spotted her man further up the road. He was on the far side now, passing by Poundland. He'd picked up his pace, but she suspected – well, hoped– his haste was motivated by wanting to get out of the rain rather than out of any suspicion that he was being followed.

Okeke opted to stay on her side of the road and matched his pace from a discreet distance. It was probably the wrong thing to do in the eyes of Williams' Surveillance Tweenies – but if he crossed back again a moment later it was going to be blindingly obvious that she was following him.

Maybe he's sussed me already? Crossing the road could have been Test Number One. Test Number Two might be reversing direction, taking some unnecessary detour, or even turning round and heading straight back towards her.

Suddenly he *did* stop and Okeke almost yelped. He veered towards a Co-Op Bank cash machine, reached into his shoulder bag and pulled out his wallet.

It took every ounce of Okeke willpower not to punch the air and scream 'Gotcha!' as he slotted the card into the ATM and tapped in his PIN. Instead she strode past on the other side of Western Road for another fifty yards before stepping into a newsagent's.

She lingered at the doorway, peering through the shop window and not daring to take her eyes off him as she fumbled in her jacket for her phone.

She called Williams again, who this time answered on the first ring. 'Still with him?'

'Yes,' confirmed Okeke. 'I'm on Western Road. There's a Co-

Op cash machine between the bank and Poundland. He's using it right now.'

'Yes!' Williams gasped.

'How far away are you?'

'A couple of minutes, Okeke. Keep him in sight. My foot team are exiting the shopping centre now. As soon as he's back in the box, get that cash machine put out of service.' Williams actually sounded pleased with her, for the first time ever.

'Yes, ma'am.'

'Are you in his line of sight?'

'I'm inside a newsagent's. He can't see me calling.'

She heard Williams draw a breath. 'Good work, Okeke.'

'Thanks, ma'am.'

As she hung up, the man had finished withdrawing his money. He stuffed the card and cash into his wallet, then placed his wallet back in his bag.

Then he looked up and waved right at her.

What? Shit.

He slung his bag over one shoulder and dashed across the road towards the newsagent's, still waving.

No. Wait. He was flagging down a bus that was about to pull away from its stop. He ran right past the newsagent's open doorway, so close that she could have grabbed him, and hopped aboard the bus as its brakes hissed and the door rattled shut.

Okeke could do little more than quickly step out into the rain and take a photograph with her phone of the rear of the bus as it rolled away up Western Road.

'Fuck,' she muttered through gritted teeth.

She jogged across the road, narrowly dodging a wall of rainwater kicked up by a passing delivery truck, and planted herself beside the cash machine as she waited anxiously for Williams' foot team to arrive.

A man in a donkey jacket hurried over towards the machine. 'You using it, love?' he asked.

'You can't use it,' she replied.

He peered at the screen. 'It's fine. Out the way, sweet'eart.'

'You can't use it,' she said more forcefully.

His face flashed with irritation and, before he could say something that he was going to regret, she pulled out her warrant card for the second time that morning and flashed it in front of his face. 'It's out of use. Now piss off and use another one.'

She spotted the leading point of the surveillance box a moment later – the 'husband' of the mall couple – walking briskly towards her. He was out of breath and panting. When he reached her, he practically doubled over as he tried to get his breath back.

'Where is he?' he managed to get out after several wheezy gasps.

'Bus,' Okeke replied grimly.

'Oh, for fu–'

46

'The cash machine was the big win from this morning,' said DCI Williams. She picked out Okeke in the room and gave her a crisp appreciative nod. Then she turned to DI Connor: 'Matthew, can we have an update on that, please?'

Connor stood up. 'We have the sixteen-digit number from the machine's log at the precise time our suspect used it...' He looked at Okeke. 'Thanks for noting the time as well.'

Okeke smiled. 'No problem.'

'The first six digits give us the bank... which in this case is an internet one favoured by foreign workers: GoPayGo. They're headquartered in Dublin and obviously operate under European laws. So we're going to have to apply through the Europol/Border Force interface to get a warrant in order for them to release the customer data. But that could take a few days, maybe a week.'

'They won't just hand it over?' asked Minter. 'Given that it's a counter-terrorism case.'

Connor shook his head. 'It's one of their corporate mantras:

customer privacy and all that... particularly in dealing with the UK.'

The door to the Incident Room opened and a familiar voice broke the silence. 'DCI Williams?'

Okeke twisted in her seat, surprised. She hadn't been expecting to hear his voice in the station for a while.

'Can I have a word in private?'

∼

'WHAT CAN I HELP YOU WITH?' asked Williams.

Boyd and Williams were sitting in the small interview room that looked across the corridor onto the Incident Room – the very same room in which he'd interviewed Okeke just nine months ago on his first morning with Sussex Police.

'I know I'm meant to be on leave,' he began, 'but I've had time to review what I remembered from the train hijacking. Specifically what Riz was saying to me as he died. He was saying *Hadzic*. It's a Bosniak name. Bosnian Muslim. Possibly his name.' Boyd shrugged. 'Or it could be someone he was after. I think our man on the train might have been some sort of right-wing activist *posing* as a jihadi.'

Williams frowned sceptically.

'Just listen,' said Boyd. 'I think whatever was going on may have roots back to the Bosnian war. He –'

'That was, what, thirty years ago, Boyd?' interjected Williams. 'According to his *Albanian* passport, Hadzic would have been a child back then.'

'And do you know that passport is genuine?' Boyd asked.

Williams shrugged. 'We don't have confirmation of that yet,' she conceded. 'Where are you going with this, Boyd?'

'I... I'm just not sure this is what it appears to be.'

Williams' patience looked as though it was wearing thin.

'Do you have a specific theory for me? Or is this just a patronising piece of advice to keep my mind open?'

'He racially selected hostages,' said Boyd. 'White hostages. He was overtly presenting himself to look like he was a Muslim radical. The beard, the suicide bomb, the ritualistic bit with removing that bloke's clothes...'

'But?'

'But I don't think it was as it seemed.'

'So what was it then?'

Boyd took a deep breath. 'What if it was some kind of false-flag act? What if he was *pretending* to be Muslim? Picking out white faces to execute.'

'And why would he do that, Boyd?'

'Why do you think? To stir things up.'

She settled back in her seat. 'To provoke anti-Muslim sentiment in the UK?'

He nodded. 'Not that it needs any stirring up in some places.'

'And this theory is all on the back of what? Him saying his name, or some Bosnian Muslim name, as he died?'

Boyd shook his head. 'No... It's based on the fact that he had a Bosniak name and the logo of a Serbian paramilitary group tattooed on his arm. A scorpion.'

Williams' face hardened. 'That's a confidential detail from the pathologist's report. How would you know about that?'

Boyd realised he was in danger of dropping Okeke in it. 'I saw the tattoo. The scorpion.'

'Rubbish,' she countered. 'That would have been in your original statement. Who leaked that detail to you? As if I can't guess.' She clearly wasn't going to indulge him.

'Look,' he tried again. 'The point is that this group, the Scorpions, were a particularly vile bunch who carried out a whole string of massacres during the Bosnian War. Most of those bastards had that tattoo on them somewhere.'

Williams shook her head. 'That's a huge leap based on one potentially misheard word and a tattoo, Boyd. You actually want me to repurpose this investigation to look into... what? A tit-for-tat act of revenge from a thirty-year-old war?' She shook her head. 'No. I'm sorry. This is a load of nonsense.'

'The tattoo is something you will *have* to be able to explain in your inquiry.' Boyd said. 'He had that done just a few days before the hijacking. It meant something to him. It was important to him.'

'Ah, so it *was* Okeke who leaked to you, then?' Williams said, a tight smile on her face.

Bollocks. There was always going to be a risk that he'd end up getting her into trouble.

'She's concerned,' he said, 'as am I... that we're sidestepping a piece of evidence that doesn't fit the story.'

'Well, I'm *not* concerned,' Williams replied. 'The tattoo is a piece of... of camouflage. A deflection. Frankly it's an irrelevance.'

'He had it done right before he hijacked a train,' Boyd said. 'You can't just write it off.'

'Boyd...' Williams pulled out her tablet and swiped her way into the action log. 'I'll show you the damned thing.' She picked her way through several files before selecting a thumbnail image. She expanded it to fill the screen and turned the tablet round.

He was looking at a photograph of the tattoo, taken by the forensic pathologist.

'Yes, you're quite right, Boyd,' she said. 'It *is* a tattoo of a scorpion. But why don't you look more closely at it? DI Connor has already identified that as a computer-game logo.'

47

'For God's sake, Lucas. What's the bloody problem now?'

Ruth had moved her troublesome client out of the Premiere Inn because, as she suspected it would, the word had got out and the press had turned up like wasps around an overfilled bin. Currently he was installed in an Airbnb cottage far away from anywhere remotely interesting. The place looked as though it served no other purpose than the occasional holiday booking. There were no telltale signs that anyone lived there when it wasn't being used by a holidaymaker, no photos in frames, no curious family knick-knacks nor laundry stashed away in bench cupboards.

Ruth had given a moment's consideration to taking one of the bedrooms for herself so that she could continue to keep a permanent watch on Lucas, but, since it literally was in the middle of nowhere and the rain was lashing down steadily, there was little chance of him wandering off, getting into trouble and attracting attention.

Also, she didn't want him getting any funny ideas. She was his agent and minder, nothing more. He might be Britain's Hero of the Week, but that didn't necessarily mean he was going to behave like the perfect gentleman.

Ruth's sister lived twenty minutes away in Godalming; she'd decided to crash with her until this TV show was done. After that? Well... her instincts were telling her that his newsworthiness would begin to wear off within the next week. The exclusives on him would be done in a couple of days and the remaining offers for interviews after that would start to taper off in value. She suspected after the weekend he'd be good for a couple more weeks of radio interviews at best, then his short-lived fame would be done.

Come Monday next week, Ruth planned to move onto something else. One of the contestants in *Love Resort*, Gina, had been having a meltdown all week and was almost certainly about to be booted off the reality show on Saturday night. Ruth wanted hers to be the first shoulder available for Gina to cry on.

Lucas would have his nice pot of money (minus her lucrative commission, of course) with which to restart his life in Britain and he'd have a solicitor working on his behalf – paid for by *UK Daily*'s crowdfunder – to sort out his legal status. The chances of the current Home Secretary rejecting Lucas's case were pretty slim since the government wanted to ride a popularity bounce in the polls.

The continued hand-holding for Lucas would have to become someone else's problem. Maybe that Hastings detective Boyd would take him under his wing. He seemed to have a soft spot for the crazy bastard.

He won't be my problem for long, though.

'Where is beer?' Lucas called. 'You said there is beer in this place!'

She found him in the kitchen staring into the open fridge, his face registering deep disappointment.

'No booze, I'm afraid, Lucas. I want you clear-headed for the next few days.'

He stood up straight and swung the fridge door shut. 'I have no drink for two days?'

'Nope. But you have plenty of food in the freezer, milk in the fridge, and you have the internet. I notice there's a computer in the corner of the lounge and there's a games console beneath the TV. You'll be fine here.'

She was about to step out of the small kitchen when he raised his arm to block her way. 'What is happen after the TV show?'

'What do you mean?'

'I mean... what is next?'

She'd been hoping to avoid this conversation until the weekend. She'd noticed he was prone to sulking when he didn't get what he wanted.

'Let's just focus on *The Greg Norman Show*, huh?' she said.

'Yes, but what is happen next after show?'

'Do you mind, Lucas?' Ruth looked meaningfully at his arm, which was blocking her way. 'I have to be somewhere.'

'Where?' His voice had a slight edge to it.

'That's my business, Lucas. Now move!'

'Is not business time now, Ruth.' He looked out of the kitchen window. It was getting dark.

'I'm visiting my sister,' she replied firmly. 'She's expecting me.'

Ruth glared at him. That was something else she'd picked up about him. He couldn't hold eye contact for long. Lucas looked away after a few seconds, and let his arm drop to his side. Ruth stepped past him into the cottage's lounge area and grabbed her bag from the coffee table.

'You won't leave me, will you?' He sounded almost childlike.

Ruth stopped beside the front door. 'No, of course not,' she lied. She switched on a professional smile. 'We've got so much more work to do.'

His face slackened with relief. 'Good. This is good.'

'Just relax, Lucas. I'll call you later this evening, all right?'

He nodded and looked at the console. 'I play *Mario Karts*.'

'Good idea.' She opened the door and stepped outside. 'Speak to you later.'

He acknowledged her with a little wave and she closed the door. As it clicked shut, she let out a deep breath and realised she'd been holding her car keys tightly with the metal protruding from her knuckles, the way they teach you in self-defence classes.

48

Safan Salmani let himself quietly into the house. He could hear music playing in the kitchen, something cheerful and catchy that Ness was obviously familiar with – he could hear her singing along loudly.

To his right, through the open room he could see that the front room was filled with the saturated glow of the new 42-inch TV that he'd fixed to their wall just last week. Ness's three girls were watching, squawking and giggling at something on Disney+ that seemed to involve lots of talking cars.

Right now he wanted to savour this moment. A household full of happiness and contentment. The four lovely ladies in this modest little terraced home had allowed him to become an irreplaceable part of it. They'd welcomed him in – without questions or doubts – as a partner and as a father.

Safan was old enough and wise enough to recognise his good fortune at having a second chance at happiness. The chaotic soundtrack of a noisy, happy home was a thing to be relished. He really couldn't understand those men who came home from work and insisted on peace and quiet. Who sent their kids upstairs, turned their wife's music off, and switched the TV to a sports channel. Or worse, men who delayed their homecoming until they'd had a couple of spirit-sapping pints of lager.

Not wanting to break the magical spell, he tiptoed up the hallway and peered into the kitchen. Ness was busy making dinner for the girls, her iPhone on the small kitchen table, music pumping through the speaker next to it – another device he'd brought home from work for her. She was swinging her hips to the beat, stirring the pan in time, fudging the lyrics loudly and out of tune (she really couldn't sing despite what she claimed) but to his ears it was a perfect delight.

She turned away from the cooker to pick something up from the table and spotted him lingering in the doorway.

'Oh, hello, lovely! I didn't hear you come in. How was work today?'

Busted – he stepped into the kitchen and took a seat at the table. 'Very good. I sold another two of the gaming PCs today.' Over the past five years, his little electronics workshop, which he'd started in a bedroom, had expanded first into a garage and then into a proper retail unit on Western Terrace. The business of upcycling old PCs and repairing and reselling thrown-out big-ticket electrical products had proved to be a modest winner during the Covid crisis. Where restaurants and high-street retailers had struggled to hang on to their retail units, businesses like his had happily filled the gaps.

Ness finished rinsing a bowl, then shimmied over, cupped his bristly grey jaw in her hand and planted a kiss on his lips. 'Proud of you,' she said.

The age gap between them spanned two decades, he was in his mid-fifties and she in her thirties, but some couples just looked right together. Safan had a Jean Baptiste air to him, according to her. And, in kind, he would say that she was his younger Sophia Loren. The first time he'd said that she'd been baffled – due to the age gap, of course.

'I will spoil you and the girls this weekend, yes?' he said, smiling.

Her face lit up.

'I think maybe the Lego place?' he suggested.

'Oh, Saffy... the girls would love that.'

He kissed her again, then got up. 'It is a deal.' He left the bag of shopping she'd asked for on the table and opened the back door. 'How long is dinner?'

'Half an hour?'

He nodded. 'I will finish some work.'

'All right, my love. I'll give you a shout.'

Safan made his way down the narrow back garden to the shed at the bottom. When he'd moved in three years ago it had been rammed full of random garden tools, cardboard boxes and spiders, but now it served as his workshop-at-home. He spun the combination on the padlock and pulled the shed door open. He flipped a switch on the door fame. The desk lamp on his workbench blinked on; the computer's hard drive whirred to life as the machine sluggishly began to boot up.

He eased himself down into his cushioned office seat and moved aside some of the clutter that had accumulated on his desk: empty popcorn bags (the sweet 'n' salty kind), enough stacked takeaway coffee cups to make a tall tower, and a sectioned tray of electronic components and circuit boards.

As he watched his Linux PC flicker to life, his mind shifted gear from the pleasant present to a dark past, like some multi-dimensional traveller stepping between parallel worlds.

The two very different lives of Safan Salmani.

This second life was all that he could have hoped for at his age. A second love, a second family, a second chance for happiness to carry him all the way to those autumn years and whatever lay beyond... but there was the life that had come before this one. A life that had featured another love – a first love – another family and another home that he'd also thought would be his until he died a very old man. But this first life had been savagely torn to pieces by the ghouls that had arrived one day in his village. They'd arrived without warning like demons erupting from the depths of hell. Ghouls that wore black berets, some with ski-masks, some without, but all of them carrying Russian-made guns provided by the recently mothballed Yugoslavian army.

The Day They Came was the door that separated his two lives.

Ness knew nothing of this, of course. She knew he'd come to Britain twenty years ago because of unpleasant memories, but that was *all* she knew.

And that's how he planned to keep it.

The nightmare would stay in its sealed box. In actual fact, the nightmare stayed in this shed. His computer had fully awoken, its Linux-powered system a Ferrari compared to the cumbersome shambles of Windows, and infinitely more convenient when delving into the flipside world of the Dark Web.

49

Boyd opened the front door to find Okeke standing on his front doorstep yet again, this time in the spattering rain. She looked even more pissed off than before, if that were possible.

'What the actual fuck, Boyd?'

'What's up?' he asked guiltily.

'You! Your *What's up!*' she fumed. 'Williams dismissed me from her team this afternoon!'

She stepped inside, once again without an invitation, turned left into his study and waited for him there. He closed the door and tried to marshal his defence. Yes, he'd talked to Williams earlier. Yes, she'd guessed they'd spoken; and no, Williams hadn't said anything about reprimanding Okeke, or, for that matter, kicking her off the team.

He followed Okeke into the study, mouth open ready to explain himself.

'She said you blabbed on about that tattoo,' Okeke said, glaring at him.

'I had to. I thought it was evidence she was deliberately ignoring. I was supporting you.'

'Well, great. Thanks very much. But it's on *my* performance record now. It's on my record that I *leaked evidence*.'

'I'll talk to Sutherland about it when I come back to work. I'll explain it came from a good place. You were concerned something important was being overlooked.'

She dropped down heavily into his office chair. 'And right after I'd finally got on her good side as well.'

'Good side? She has one? What did you do?'

She explained about how the surveillance operation had misfired in her favour. 'They've got his full card number and we should be getting his details when... if the bank rolls over.'

'They're not cooperating?' he asked quickly, keen to distract her from any further bollocking.

'The bank's based in Dublin. They're not obliged to cooperate. Anyway...' She got back to the point. 'Thanks for completely dropping me in the shit!'

He pulled a taut smile. 'Sorry.'

'Knob,' she grunted.

'Coffee?'

'Beer. And not the cheap own-brand crap that you usually give out either.'

'Deal.' He went off to the kitchen and came back a minute later with two beers and a bottle opener. 'So what's the bottom line?'

'I'm off the case and back on general duties.'

'That's not so bad,' said Boyd. 'That's the lightest reprimand Sutherland can give you.' He smiled. 'Which suggests he's not a big fan of hers either.' He uncapped a bottle and handed it to her. 'She's a bit of a dragon, isn't she?'

Okeke took a couple of slugs and wiped her lips. 'She's a black woman in a white boy's club. What do you expect? I imagine she's had to fight like a bastard all the way to DCI.'

'Hold on. You were moaning about her a second ago.'

'No. I was moaning about you!' she replied sourly. 'Anyway. It is what it is.'

Boyd sipped his beer and let a moment or two pass. 'She still seems to think she's on the trail of a terrorist cell operating out of Brighton?'

Okeke nodded. 'The man I was tailing looked significantly older than Hadzic. She thinks he could be the leader, or a recruiter. We got his fingerprints... There's nothing on LEDS, though.'

'So he's clean, then.' Boyd nodded. 'That's how they operate, isn't it? One step removed. Keep a clean slate, head down, don't attract attention?'

'Uh-huh... according to Wonder Girl.'

'Huh?'

'One of the genius foetuses from Thames Valley.'

'Williams showed me the pathologist's photo of the tattoo by the way,' said Boyd.

Okeke looked surprised. 'She did? Why?'

'She's convinced it doesn't mean anything significant.' He shrugged. 'It did look a little computer gamey, to be fair.'

'And for some reason Hadzic insisted on having it done just days before doing what he did. That didn't strike her as a bit odd at all?'

Boyd shook his head. 'She said he might have had a personal reason to get it done. But that it was probably inconsequential. She said, "Jihadi-Johns do actually have PlayStations or some such crap."'

Okeke pulled a face.

'Sam, I think there's something very different going on here. You know Hadzic is a Bosnian Muslim name?'

She raised her eyebrows. 'Bosnian? He had an Albanian passport. But that could be fake.'

'Could be,' he agreed. 'If he was Bozniak, this could possibly have something to do with the Bosnian War.'

'That was ages ago, wasn't it?'

'Ninety-two to ninety-five. Three decades ago.'

'The passport put him in his thirties,' she replied. 'He's too young.'

'*If* the passport's legit,' said Boyd. 'But the point is, he doesn't have to be old enough to have fought. The name Hadzic got me started on this. I worked out it was what he was saying to me on the train. I wasn't sure what I'd heard initially... but also, Sam, the way he was behaving on the train just didn't seem to fit the profile of a guy hellbent on taking out as many kefir as possible.'

'And you know all this... because?'

'I've been doing a little digging myself,' he admitted.

'Hang on. Aren't you meant to be chilling out on Her Madge's orders?' she asked.

He shook his head. 'I've been running that Friday night through in my head. Running it and rerunning it. I think he was searching for something.'

'Searching for what?'

'I don't know. A person maybe. I mean he was *really* studying us as he made his way up the train before it all kicked off. Taking his time... like somebody doing an identity parade.'

'Or he could have been scoping out potential hostages, guv,' said Okeke.

'But the hostages all looked the same,' Boyd said.

'What? You don't look anything like... that Albanian meercat,' replied Okeke. 'He's short and... Mind you, I'm not gonna lie – you're both a little podgy, no offence.'

'None taken,' Boyd muttered.

'You deserve that,' Okeke grunted.

He leant forward. 'Look, we weren't alike-alike as such, but we were of a *type* – we were all white, males over fifty years old. We were all somebody basically who could have actually been a participant in that war.'

Boyd explained the history, or the broad strokes of it taken from his Wiki cut-'n'-paste research on the subject, focusing particularly on the early days of the war and the Višegrad massacres. He mentioned the various paramilitary groups, including the Scorpions, and described some of the atrocities... not even the worst.

'God,' uttered Okeke finally. 'That's horrific. I can't believe that actually happened in...'

'Our lifetime?' Boyd nodded. 'And in Europe. Not some far-flung war-torn piece of jungle, but Yugoslavia. Well, as it was.'

'Shit.' She looked down at the bottle in her hands. 'So, you think the train hijacker was in the war?'

'That's what I thought. Except that he looked far too young. And...'

'What?'

'The picture Williams showed me earlier of the tattoo indicates it really was recently inked.'

'So what? You think he was some twisted fucker *inspired* by them?'

'No. I think we're dealing with something quite different.'

'You keep saying that, guv. What exactly are you thinking?'

He grabbed a piece of paper from his desk and tried to draw a scorpion. Like Okeke's effort it was crap. He drew the circle round it. 'I looked very closely at the photo, Okeke. That wasn't just a circle around it...' He drew a cross over the top. 'It was a cross-hair.'

She took in a sharp breath. 'Fuck.' She stared down at the drawing. 'Shit... you're saying...?'

'I'm saying maybe it wasn't some gaming logo... but some emblem of vigilantism. Maybe Rizmet Hadzic was hunting down a war criminal.'

50

Boyd had been right: the steady drizzle had driven away the last of the summer holidaymakers, and the shingle beach was pleasantly deserted and – for the first time in months – free of the detritus they left behind.

Walking through Pelham Arcade on the way back was a little depressing, though. Absent of sun and over-sugared kids, it was a moribund and cheerless place. The few rides that were still open were dripping wet and looked uninviting, despite the flickering arcade lights and pumped disco music. Even the gulls had figured out the season for easy dive-bombed chips and 99 flakes was over.

Ozzie spent twenty minutes on the beach chasing Mia, while Boyd and Charlotte walked side by side from Pelham Arcade to the pier.

'He reminds me of Ernest Borgnine,' she said. 'At least that picture of him eating the doughnut does.'

The name rang a bell for Boyd. A faint one.

'Ernest Borgnine, the actor?' She pulled a face. 'Or are you too young to remember him?'

He chuckled. 'You're four years older than me. That's not a you're-too-young thing. I know Ernest Borgnine.'

'Four years would have been enough of an age gap for me to bully a little first-year squib like you if we'd been in school together,' she said, laughing.

Boyd smiled. She was more right than she realised. His growth spurt had arrived relatively late.

'You're rather taken with that Albanian chap, aren't you?' asked Charlotte.

Actually not Albanian. Bosnian. Lucas had shared that with Boyd and then asked him to keep it to himself. He didn't want anyone probing into what his life had been like during 'those troubling times'. And Boyd had sympathised with that. Lucas had come to the UK for a new life, to close the door on what must have been a horrifically traumatic past.

'I feel sorry for him,' he said. 'It's easy to forget that these people we see on the news – being pulled out of the back of freight containers or crammed into inflatables – are more often than not fleeing war zones.'

Charlotte nodded. 'We look at old black-and-white footage of Jews fleeing the Nazis and feel pity. Rightfully. Why do we not feel the same when we see the exact same story played out in full colour? ... My mother was World War Two refugee, you know?' she added.

'Wow. Right. Uh... Jewish?'

Charlotte shook her head. 'My granddad – Mum's dad – was a socialist. A proper one, not a National Socialist.'

'German?'

'French actually. Bellefeuille.'

Boyd liked the way she said it. 'Well now, there's another thing I didn't know about you.'

He watched her as she gazed at the gulls hovering opportunistically off the end of the pier. There was actually quite a lot he didn't know about her, and each piece of her past had been handed to him sparingly. Getting her accidentally stoned (along with everyone else) in his back garden had yielded little about her backstory, other than she once went to college, once played a flute, and might once have been a bit of a party girl.

'You speak any French?' he asked, curious.

She snorted. 'Just about enough to order a croissant. A pity really. I'd have loved to have spoken to them more. Particularly Grandad... I didn't get to see them in their last ten years.'

'Why not?' he asked.

Charlotte was silent for a moment, then she nodded at the bank of clouds to their right. 'Apparently, according to ITV Weather, the late summer's definitely over.' She turned the other way to look at the shingle beach stretching up to Rock-a-Nore in the distance. 'At least the bucket-and-spade brigade have gone again until next year.'

'Good,' replied Boyd, letting the dropped question go. He looked down at Ozzie and ruffled the fur on his head. 'We'll have the beach all to ourselves again, eh, mate?'

She smiled. 'Still got to pick up that poop, even if no one's around to see.'

He raised his hands in surrender. 'I've been properly schooled on that, one – I promise.'

She narrowed her eyes at him, then smiled. 'That's what I like about you, Boyd.'

'What?' he fished.

'You take it on the chin,' she said, laughing. 'Any way... my lunch break's over. Got to get back. Thanks for the company.'

'No problem,' he replied.

He watched Charlotte and Mia cross the road and enter the theatre, then he and Ozzie made their way back home.

THE PHONE WAS RINGING as Boyd entered the house, and he let Ozzie trot off to the kitchen with his lead still attached while he headed into the lounge to pick it up before it rang off.

'Boyd,' he answered.

'It's Sunny again, mate.'

'You do know I'm not paying you for this?' began Boyd. 'Or is this a social call?'

'It's all right, mate. It's on the house. I think I came across something thanks to that scorpion logo. There's a forum on one of the Dark-Web/Onion offsprings.'

'Sorry, dark-onion-what-what?'

Sunny chuckled. 'Shit, it's like talking to my Uncle Assad: *What the bloody is a dark spring-onion web?*'

Boyd laughed. Sunny did the first-generation Anglo-Bangladeshi accent pretty well.

'The Onion bit is the name for the various encrypted chat servers. Then you go and find whatever niche community you're into,' Sunny explained.

'Right. Makes perfect sense,' Boyd lied.

'You need the Tor browser to view it because it's on the Dark Web, but then when you get to the forum the messages are all encrypted, so you're getting pages and pages of alpha-numeric gobbledygook.'

'Yeah, right,' said Boyd, still a bit baffled. 'You said something about a forum somewhere in there, I think?'

Sunny laughed. 'Yeah. Anyway, so I did an image search based on your description and – to cut a long and very tedious story short – your scorpion is the logo for a particular Dark Web forum.'

'Well now you're talking my language, Sunny. Can I view this forum?' Boyd asked.

'Not unless I come round and fiddle with your computer. I'd need to install a whole bunch of stuff, unless you're savvy enough to do it yourself – which, going on this conversation, is pretty unlikely...'

'Ha ha – yeah, maybe not. I'll end up bricking my computer, probably.'

'Want me to come down and sort it? Tonight if you like,' Sunny offered.

'Can you?'

'If you put me up, take me out. Wine me and dine me. Sure. You can have another go at convincing me to move out to Hicksville, if you like.'

'Central London losing its charm, is it?' Boyd laughed.

'The property prices aren't plummeting like I was hoping yet. All that dirty money waiting to be laundered is keeping the prices up, I'm guessing.'

Ozzie, who had been busy shlopping from his water bowl, wandered up and shoved his dripping wet muzzle into Boyd's thigh. Boyd stroked his head absentmindedly 'All right. That's good of you, mate.'

'No sweat. I got a taste of the seaside vibe with Brighton, see?'

'Yeah, well, Hastings isn't exactly Brighton.'

Sunny laughed. 'Oh, so now I'm coming down to check it out, you're backpedalling on the hard sell?'

'Just... yeah, don't expect sun, sea and sangria.'

51

'What's up, Saffy?' asked Ness. 'You seem like you're a million miles away, lovely.'

Safan was. Not a million, just a few thousand miles away... and thirty years ago. He was twenty-seven again, young, handsome, a science teacher. The woman and girls in the school used to call him 'Tom Cruise' because, supposedly, he looked a little like the American actor, had a motorbike and he could speak a bit of English.

But his heart-throb days were behind him. He had his leading lady – Nastasja – and she was carrying his little boy. Both he and his wife were still haggling over what his name would be. Nastasja wanted a more traditional name for him, whereas Saf wanted a more western-sounding one.

'What if he wants to move abroad? Move to England? Isn't it better he has a name that fits in more easily?' That was his logic. Something like Stefan.

He'd once overheard someone ask the question: if your life was broken into episodes, which would be your favourite? If Safan was asked that, his true answer would have been back then: in his late twenties, finding the love of his life, teaching at the school he used to go to and awaiting their first baby. If Ness asked him that same question today, he would say his mid-fifties and finding her and the girls. For her. It wasn't true. It had been a good episode but not his happiest.

Those hot summer nights lying out on beds of brown pine needles, drinking cold beer and listening to Led Zeppelin and Deep Purple cassettes, and the freedom he had on his bike to race through the mountains. That had been a golden time.

It had been short-lived.

Safan sometimes permitted his memory to wander into that good time, but he stayed well away from the edges. The borders of his memory were marked with warning flagpoles that bore fluttering blood-red banners, decaled with leering skulls, tigers claws, scorpions... signs that cautioned 'Monsters Lie Beyond'.

Past those flagpoles, and a few steps into the dark landscape beyond, existed Dante's Hell.

His mind's eye stayed well away from there, because stepping too closely to the border gave him sudden, shocking freeze-frame images of the Day They Came. Stills of horror: those men in their black berets... their guns... their bayonets... Nastasja... his mother... his father... his unborn son – to quote Shakespeare – 'untimely ripped'.

And blood. There had been so much of it.

Safan had witnessed it all while awaiting his turn to die. But somehow – and he was still unclear how – he'd managed to escape into the woods. And he'd run. And run. And run.

The question, Saffy, is... will you do it? Will you?

Nastasja was asking him that. *Will you do it, then come and join me, and Stefan?*

52

'Fuck me, Boyd – it's a bloody mansion!' said Sunny after he'd had the tour upstairs and down.

'That's what coming out of London gets you,' replied Boyd. 'Have I convinced you yet?'

Sunny sat down at the dining table, admiring the high ceiling and tall window. 'I'm halfway there, mate.'

Boyd checked his watch, 'My colleague Okeke will be here in a sec–'

Perfectly timed, the doorbell rang and Ozzie let loose a volley of window-rattling barks.

'Jesus!' Sunny called out after him. 'Is he normally this loud?'

Boyd headed up the hall, opened the door and waved her in. 'Sucky day at work?'

'Very,' she replied. 'I'm back on the floor with Warren. Sutherland's got us entering archive cases onto LEDS.'

'When I get back, I'll have a word with him,' Boyd reassured her.

'Oh, he's just going through the motions for William's benefit.' She looked up at Boyd. 'He's made it pretty obvious he thinks she's a knob too.'

Boyd led her down the hall into the dining room. 'Okeke, this is Sunil Chandra, all-round computer whizz and wannabe property speculator. Sunny, this is Samantha Okeke, my...'

'My what?' queried Okeke. 'Pain-in-the-arse colleague?'

'My most promising junior detective... but I'm more than happy to go with your bio as you can be a bit of a pain in the arse,' he finished.

'Knobhead,' she replied, laughing.

Sunny offered her a hand and she shook it firmly. 'Good to meet you,' he said. 'He says mostly good things about you, and I do love an eighties insult!'

'Beer anyone?' Boyd cut in.

They both nodded. Boyd stepped into the kitchen, grabbed three beers from the fridge and a bag of spicy masala nuts. He sat back down, uncapped the beers, passed them round and opened their informal team meeting.

'Right. So... while DCI Williams and her merry men continue their hunt for some Islamic terror cell based in Brighton, we're exploring a different theory: that Rizmet Hadzic is in fact part of some vigilante group attempting to track down Serbian war criminals who escaped the UN's efforts to bring them to justice.'

'Very much like the Simon Wiesenthal Foundation,' said Sunny. 'They tracked down the Nazis that escaped the Nuremburg trials. They also collated eyewitness accounts of the Holocaust, creating an archive of evidence to counteract any future Holocaust deniers.'

'The difference with these people is that they don't have any support or recognition,' added Boyd. 'They're operating on their own. They're survivors of the ethnic cleansing that happened in and around Višegrad.'

'And they're largely Muslims,' said Sunny. 'Which means keeping their heads down. Especially after what's going on in Afghanistan.' He pulled out his laptop, opened it up and turned it round. 'There's a group who meet on the Dark Web. They have a name that I'm not going to try and pronounce, but it translates to Bosniak War Crimes Investigation and Retribution. Not the catchiest of names, but their logo's pretty cool.'

He pulled up the image that resembled Hadzic's: a scorpion caught in the cross-hair of a sniper's rifle.

'That's it!' said Okeke. 'That's the tattoo!'

'Precisely,' said Boyd. 'I think it's possible that Hadzic could have been a member.'

Sunny pointed at the screen of his laptop. 'This is their chat space. Their hangout place.'

Okeke leant forward and peered at the text. 'It's gibberish.'

'It's encrypted,' Sunny explained. 'It's quite a common form of encryption using a numerical value that's part key number, part VPN number. If you get invited into the forum and become a trusted member, you get the key and the forum's contents become readable. When you log out, it gets flushed from the computer's cache memory.'

'If Sunny can hack the encryption, we can read what's in here,' said Boyd.

'Oh, I won't be able to hack it, mate. This isn't an episode of *Spooks*.'

Bord turned to him. 'I thought...'

Sunny shook his head. 'You'd need serious brute force computing to crack that.'

'So what's the plan, then?' asked Okeke.

Sunny sat back. 'We're going to get ourselves invited in,' he said.

'Well, how's *that* going to happen?' she asked.

Sunny tossed a couple of the masala nuts into his mouth. 'We ask nicely, I guess. But first, we have to identify the admin.'

'Please tell me you have a way of doing that,' said Boyd.

'It's guesswork. Chances are it's one of the more prolific posters here. Hang on...' Sunny scrolled back to the top of the forum and nodded. 'Duh... obviously.' He pointed at the screen. 'That comment is pinned to the top. It probably contains rules for the forum.' His finger slid to the left and settled on an avatar, a cartoon picture of what looked like a Dungeons and Dragons spell book. Beneath it was a string of letters and numbers.

'It's more than likely this guy.' He scrolled down the page again, pointing at various posts made by the same person. 'He seems quite prolific. If he's not the admin, then he's at least a moderator.'

'How are we going to reach him?' asked Boyd.

'I can have a go at identifying who the VPN service provider is. There's a database for that. If it's one of the free VPN providers, the chances are they're logging and selling information to third parties. We might get lucky there. Failing that we use a thing called Deep Packet Inspection, which allows us to analyse the structure of data packets and identify what *kind* of information is being sent, just not what it is... if you get my drift?'

Boyd sighed. 'You lost me at "I can have a go"'

Okeke rolled her eyes. 'You're such a cave man.'

Boyd pulled a face at her. 'Because, obviously, you're getting what he's on about, right?'

'Actually, most of it, yeah.'

'Look, leave it with me,' said Sunny. 'In the meantime... where's good to eat in Hastings? You owe me a fancy meal, Boyd.'

53

Boyd chose the Lansdowne Hotel's restaurant. Partly because he'd never tried it, mostly because he hoped there might be a discount seeing as how Emma worked there.

'Three to four pounds a starter?' said Sunny, checking the menu. 'Christ, it's like eating out twenty years ago.'

'Hastings prices,' replied Boyd. 'Look at the drinks menu.'

Sunny did and let out a low whistle. 'Bloody hell, mate. You can afford a whole bottle, then. Let's have the Cabernet,' he said before Boyd could suggest a slightly less expensive bottle of red.

The waiter took their order and returned a few minutes later with their twenty-nine-pound bottle and two glasses. Sunny tasted it, then nodded at the waiter to pour.

He lifted his glass. 'Very fucking civilised, this is, Boyd.'

'I forgot – you're more used to doner kebabs and KFC these days, right?' Boyd raised his glass too and took a sip of what was actually a very nice red.

Sunny grinned. 'All halal obviously.'

He talked about the less ambitious properties he was eyeing up that were outside central London. The property crash in the

City that he'd been waiting on hadn't materialised so far, so he'd decided to look further afield. As Sunny chatted away, Boyd realised he'd been placed in a seat that gave him a glimpse of the hotel's reception desk, which was on the far side of the entrance foyer. He couldn't help a small smile when he caught sight of Emma behind the counter dealing with someone checking in.

He felt as though he'd hardly seen her recently. She tended to cross paths with him briefly in the mornings and evenings, depending on which shifts she'd just come back from or was rushing to get to. He knew one of her colleagues was providing lifts on occasion – the elusive Patrick, but he'd yet to meet him.

'Earth to Boyd!' Sunny's dulcet tones brought him back to the present.

'Sorry? What was that?'

'I said, any romantic entanglements yet?'

'Not really...'

'Not really is not a no.' Sunny's brow's arced comically. 'That sounds promising. Details please.'

'It's a bit of a wait-and-see situation,' Boyd said uncomfortably.

'Does this "situation"' have a name?' He narrowed his eyes. 'It's not Okeke, is it?'

'Oh God, no! Sunny! She's closer to Emma's age than mine. Anyway... you don't make your bed where you work. Or eat where you sleep... or something like that.'

'Okay, okay!' Sunny backed off. 'But there is someone, right?'

'Maybe.'

'This "maybe" is down to you, or down to her?'

'It's down to timing,' Boyd replied. 'I'm not sure if –' he shrugged – 'whether I'm ready to put Julia into the past.'

You can't hide away forever, Bill, she whispered.

'You can't hide away forever, mate,' Sunny said.

'Well, technically, you can actually. There's no law against being single. *You* are, for Chrissake.'

'Yeah, well, that's because I'm a dick. I like to play around. But you...' Sunny smiled. 'You were born to be a good husband, Boyd. A solid family guy.'

'Speaking of family...' Boyd said. 'I'd better let Emma know you're staying over tonight.'

'Where is she?' Sunny asked. 'I haven't seen her since she was knee-high. She was obsessed with friendship bracelets, right? I wore that bloody pink-and-silver one for days – forgot it was there!'

Boyd laughed. 'She's here. She works on reception,' he said, glancing her way. She wasn't busy. She was laughing at something with a young man lounging against the desk. He was very close to her and she didn't seem to mind. The man's blond hair was quiffed up like a restrained version of Jedward's and he had a face that was perfect to model knitwear in a catalogue. He placed a hand on her shoulder. He had some sort of tattoo on his forearm. Boyd noticed that Emma didn't shake his hand off.

Ahh...So, this is Patrick, then.

Boyd disliked him immediately. He stared at them for a moment longer. There was something about that tattoo that was bothering him.

He stroked the tip of his nose absently. 'Sunny,' he said slowly. 'What are the chances of there being two unrelated Bosnians, pretending to be Albanian, on the same train back to Hastings on a Friday night?'

Sunny turned from surveilling the two women at the next table to look at him. 'What's that, mate?'

'I'm just saying...Boyd said. 'Do you know if there's a sizeable Bosnian community in Hastings or Brighton?'

'No idea, mate...' Sunny stopped mid-sentence. 'What are you thinking?'

Boyd took a deep breath. 'I think Hadzic might have been hunting Pesic.'

'Shit, man! You said you had a pint with the bloke, right? Are you suggesting Pesic is some Serbian war criminal-in-hiding?'

Boyd nodded slowly. 'It's a theory that fits.'

The more he thought about it, the more sense it made. It explained Riz's odd behaviour on the train: the scrutiny of everyone's faces, the selection of candidates. The hesitancy and uncertainty – not the behaviour of a brainwashed young zealot on the fast-track to martyrdom, but someone wanting...

... to be absolutely sure.

'Christ, Sunny.' He felt the blood drain from his face. 'I think that's it.'

54

Safan logged into the forum, typed his key number and hit enter. The text on the screen refreshed and become a legible wall of exchanges between members of the group.

The newest and most active thread was the one entitled 'Is this LP?!' There was a link to the website for *Denevni-Ava*, Bosnia's most popular newspaper; the main headline was about the looming mayoral election in Sarajevo and rumours of Serbian interference in it. However, at the bottom of the site, under international news, was an article about the train hijack in England and the hero who'd brought it to a premature end – one Lucas Pesic.

The photos in the article showed Pesic with an arm in a sling, emerging from a hotel with a woman leading him to a car. The comments beneath the link had been piling up since it had been posted a few days ago.

I*t*'*s the same name.* **Plus he's the right age. He doesn't look much like his army photo, though.**

It HAS to be. He is claiming to be Albanian, but with a Serbian fucking name? Is anyone in the UK not even noticing that?! WTF!?

They wouldn't know. Or care. They're dumb and British. Probably don't even know how to say that name. OMFG

This is the bastard that Avenger9 and Fragginz were after, isn't it? Does anyone know if either of them were involved in the UK train thing?

Neither have posted for a while I notice. I really hope this wasn't their work.

The article says the hijacker was a jihadi called Rizmet Hadzic. There was a Hadzic family before the war. They were among the dead.

Rizmet Hadzic could be one of us. This will bring attention.

It could just be a coincidence that there was someone called Pesic on the train. We don't need to panic.

Sure, don't panic. But IF it was Avenger or Fragginz who did the train, then that could lead police to this forum and to the rest of us. They'll brand us a terrorist group!

SAFAN WAS TEMPTED to step in and say something to reassure them, that armed police weren't going to be kicking down their doors any time soon. But then his Minecraft pickaxe avatar would be prominently displayed beside his name – Avenger9 – and he'd be besieged with replies from the rest of the group. He'd dropped out of commenting two months ago when he and Fragginz had committed to going ahead with their plan. He'd been a lurker ever since. It had been the sensible thing to do… The moderator, Damocles, had been on the verge of kicking him and Fragginz out of the group completely. Their regular exchanges about Pesic, and the fact that his name had been flagged up in the UK, had begun to concern Damocles. Safan and Riz had exchanged specific details on how they could find him – their conversation in the forum had started to sound like a real plan of action, and Damocles got twitchy that Europol were going to descend on them.

That was when Safan and Riz had taken their conversation away from the forum and onto Telegram, the encrypted messaging app. That was also when the idea of hunting Pesic down had graduated from an idea to a plan.

On Telegram, developing a relationship, developing trust, they'd switched from forum nicknames to actual names: Safan and Riz, two very different men of very different ages. There was a generation between them, but they were two men united by the shared flash-frame images of a similar nightmare. And the centrepiece of that nightmare was a stocky Serbian corporal with the name L. PESIC stencilled roughly onto the water bottle dangling from his army webbing. The corporal had worn the same ragged black balaclava over his face during both of their gruesome ordeals.

Safan's unguarded mind allowed a memory to escape its locked box – the stocky corporal with a bloody bayonet in one hand and the head of Safan's father in the other... and those manic eyes, wild with exhilaration.

Rizmet's nightmare had come from the exact same day. Pesic's paramilitary unit had moved out from Višegrad to sweep the surrounding villages and L. Pesic had randomly picked the Hadzic household to visit. Rizmet had been very young. Only a small boy and had managed to hide and survive, but he too had seen that same water bottle and remembered the letters stencilled across it.

Safan wondered again whether to post something on the forum now – something to reassure the others that everything would be okay. But then all the questions would come: why have you been quiet for so long? Where have you been? If this Rizmet Hadzic isn't Fragginz, why isn't he posting here too?

The questions would create traffic, and traffic, particularly the same name or words repeated over and over, could attract the attention of software, even if they were an encrypted sequence of letters and numbers.

Better not to post at all.

Not even to bid them farewell.

55

Boyd got out of bed when Ozzie decided it was time. Both of them had got into the habit of lying in until gone nine thirty, but the sound of the fridge being opened and closed pulled the spaniel out of his deep slumber to full alertness within a matter of seconds. He jumped down onto the floor, nosed the bedroom door open and shot down the stairs.

Boyd followed him to find Emma in the kitchen preparing her lunch box. He slapped the kettle on. 'Saw you last night, Ems,' he said.

'Huh?'

'At work. At the Lansdowne.'

She looked surprised. 'You... came to the hotel?'

'We ate in the restaurant. Very nice.'

'Ooh!' She grinned conspiratorially at him. 'Did you take Charlotte?'

'Nope, Sunny.'

'Ah... that's who's in the spare room? He snores incredibly loudly,' she added. 'I had to put headphones in to get some sleep.'

Boyd laughed. Maybe *that* was why Sunny was permanently single. 'I spotted you doing your reception job,' he said.

She nodded. 'Uh-huh.' She focused intently on the task of rolling her hummus wraps into a foil sausage.

'So the guy on reception with you... I'm guessing that's Patrick?'

'Uh-huh.'

He could see pink blossoming on her cheeks. 'I had a view from my table. What's the deal with Patrick, Ems?'

'What do you mean? He's just a guy I work with,' she said, not looking at him. She stuffed her lunch box into a bag.

'Does Daniel know about you and him?' Boyd asked.

Emma pushed her way past him, out of the kitchen.

'Ems!' He followed her down the hallway. 'What about Daniel? You can't mess him around like this.'

She stopped halfway to the front door. 'Dad, there's no me and Patrick, all right?'

'You'd better tell Patrick, then, because I don't think he realises that.'

'For fuck's sake, Dad... Patrick's just flirting. He flirts with everyone. That's how he is. Don't worry and butt out, okay?'

Her face was almost scarlet now – more embarrassed than angry. He wondered if she was worried he'd seen more than he had. She continued towards the door and all but tripped over Ozzie, who was standing behind her.

'For fuck's sake, Ozzie!' she snapped at him. She grabbed the front door and turned back to look at Boyd. 'And don't spy on me like that at work again!'

She yanked the door open, and heard her say, 'Oh, morning... He's inside,' and then she was gone.

Okeke stepped in and peered down the hallway. 'Bad time, guv?'

He was still barefoot and wearing his bedtime T-shirt and jocks.

'And what're *you* doing here?' he asked.

'Nice to see you too. I pulled a sickie,' she said, grinning.

'Um, word to the wise... That's not the kind of thing you openly admit to your boss,' he said.

Okeke looked him up and down.

'I'll make the coffee if you go get dressed,' she said, and pushed past him into the house.

Boyd came back downstairs five minutes later in jeans and a sweatshirt. Looking out of the window at the spitting rain, it seemed his summer shorts and flip-flops were going to be retired from service until next year's week of summer.

He found Okeke sitting at the dining table with a mug of coffee and half a digestive in her mouth. She was fondling Ozzie's ears while he optimistically rested his muzzle in her lap.

'Last I heard, the point of taking a sickie is *not* working,' he said to her, sitting down.

'Williams has got her head in the sand about this, that's for sure,' Okeke said. 'She's seeing some kind of ISIS terror cell setting up camp in Brighton and she's got her talented toddlers and the rest of her idiots trawling through social media for terror-related keywords. She's got Minter, O'Neal and Abbott doing back-to-back interviews with everyone Rizmet Hadzic might have spoken to since he arrived in the UK. She's asked Sutherland for more CID boots for door-to-doors in Brighton.' She let out a heavy sigh.

'She's going full speed in the wrong direction,' Boyd agreed. 'Well, that can happen sometimes with specialists. When you become a hammer, you see everything as a nail.'

Okeke tilted her head and looked at him questioningly.

'It's from some shite SYFY channel film, I think. It's depressing the crap you find yourself watching when you're off work.'

He heard the ceiling above them creak as Sunny started moving around in the guest bedroom.

'Christ, you really want her to fail, don't you?' Boyd said, looking at Okeke.

'No, guv. Absolutely not. But I want *you* to succeed,' she replied. 'I want the bad guys taken down. But I want Sussex Police CID to be the ones to do it. Not the Tweenies from Thames Valley.'

The stairs creaked noisily and Ozzie, intrigued that there appeared to be yet another human in his house, padded off into the hallway to investigate.

'Good boy,' they heard Sunny muttering. 'Yeah, yeah, slobber, slobber... Now back the fuck off, big boy.'

He wandered into the dining room, dressed but dishevelled. His dark hair was sticking up and his work shirt was only half tucked in. He was carrying his laptop in both hands; it was open and on.

Okeke smiled. 'Good night last night?'

'Oh, hello again,' Sunny said, putting his laptop down and quickly buttoning his shirt at the bottom to hide his hairy belly.

He sat down opposite Boyd. 'Don't worry. I've not been lying in, Boyd. I've been, you know, actually working.' He spun the laptop round so that Boyd and Okeke could see the screen. 'It looks like I have an identity for that forum's admin.'

'Seriously?'

Sunny nodded. 'Easy-peasy. Hey, Boyd, have you told Okeke about our theory?'

'Theory?' Okeke looked at Boyd. 'What theory?'

He opened his mouth to speak as she spread her hands and asked, 'So... do I get to hear it?'

Sunny jumped in. 'Hadzic was hunting down Pesic,' he said, 'who's a potential war criminal.'

56

'I have to go somewhere today,' said Safan.

Ness looked up from her notepad on the kitchen table. She had a list of things to get for the girls (things she'd forgotten) now that they were back at school. The last few weeks – until that bloody rain hit – they'd spent most of their time barefoot and in the garden. Now it was all school shoes, socks, uniforms, stationery and packed lunches.

Safan was clean shaven. Occasionally he did that if he wanted to make a good impression. He'd done that when they'd first started dating, and again when she'd arranged for him to meet her parents.

She stroked his chin to indicate she approved of the look. 'Where are you going? Who are you seeing?' she asked, smiling.

'I have a big job.'

Saffy occasionally carried out IT installations: a lot of running cables around obstacles and making sure all the computers and printers linked up correctly.

'Where?'

'In Hammersmith. London. It's a TV place over at Riverbank.' He smiled. 'It will pay very well.'

'TV? London?' She was surprised. Saffy's usual IT jobs were local, hooking up shops and small business. That explained the clean-shaven look. Best first impressions for a new London client. 'Wow. This sounds big. Good for you.'

'Thank you, my love.' He kissed her cheek tenderly – not a perfunctory peck of gratitude but something more meaningful.

Ness turned to look at him. 'Is everything okay?' She noticed his eyes were a little red. 'Saff?'

'I am fine,' he muttered in that brushed-off way that meant he was keeping something from her. That was the only thing about him that she wished she could change. In every other way he was perfect. She just wished he had a latch on the side of his head so that she could open it up and see what was going on inside.

He shook his head. 'I am fine,' he repeated.

Those three words were his barricade. It was no use probing him any further. He was one of those men who kept everything inside. A fortress of masculine brooding – attractive of course, very, but frustrating too.

She had known from the beginning that Safan came with emotional baggage. He'd come from a country with a troubled past. He'd left behind some dark memories twenty years ago for a fresh start over here. It was an early unspoken agreement at the start of their relationship that he didn't have to talk about. It was too painful for him. What happened before he arrived in England was something they just didn't discuss.

'What time do you think you'll be back?' she asked, letting it go.

'I don't know. It will be late,' he said.

He kissed her again – this time on the mouth, no bristles prickling the bottom of her nose. He pulled back. 'I love you, Ness.'

'Love you too, baby.'

'And the girls,' he added. He stood up straight and shouldered his work bag.

He's not right, was all she could think.

'I can stay up,' she said. 'We can have dinner together when you get back?'

He shook his head. 'No. You should eat with the girls. Then get some sleep, my love.' He squeezed her hand and left the kitchen.

The last thing she heard him say as the front door shut behind him was not his usual 'see you later'.

It was 'goodbye'.

57

'So it turns out he's was using one of those free VPN servers.' Sunny looked at Boyd and Okeke and tapped the side of his nose. 'And they're not as safe and secure as most people like to think they are.'

'You got an IP address?' asked Okeke.

Sully nodded. 'And that was the tricky bit, but once you've got an IP number there's any number of databases you can use to find out who owns it.' He rapidly typed out a URL and a website popped up. It showed a picture of a beautifully green river valley flanked by rolling hills and beneath it a photo of an ancient-looking stone bridge crossing an almost-turquoise river. Beneath those two photographs was the caption: Villa Brajovanic.

'The admin runs a B and B in Višegrad,' said Sunny.

'Jesus.' Boyd looked at the photo of the bridge. 'Is that the bridge where...'

Sunny nodded. 'That's the River Drina. Eyewitnesses say it was stained red with blood on the worst of the days.'

There were a few more thumbnails on a sliding gallery. The

town looked beautiful, green hill tops towering over villas and plazas. The streets were lined with open air cafés and bars.

'So,' said Okeke, 'this admin runs this place?'

Sunny nodded. 'Runs it or works there. The computer that's used to log into the forum is located there anyway.'

'So how do we get hold of the right person?' asked Boyd.

Sunny shrugged. 'I dunno. Ring and ask?'

Okeke blew across her coffee. 'Right, because having gone to so much trouble setting something up on the Dark Web and encrypting it... they're gonna answer, *"Bastard-Busters here – how can I help you?"* Plus,' she added, 'there's another issue. Do any of us speak Bosnian?'

'They probably speak a little English,' said Boyd. 'Being a tourist town now. Mind if I...' He looked at Sunny as he reached for the touchpad.

'Knock yourself out,' said Sunny, sliding the laptop towards him. 'By the way... can I have a coffee too?'

'Sorry, mate,' said Boyd, remembering that Sunny had only got up a few minutes ago. 'There's a cafetiere just in the kitchen there. Help yourself.'

He clicked on the main menu of the website and found the contact tab. There was a phone number and an email address. He looked at Okeke. 'What do you reckon?'

She pressed her lips together. 'If you call, you'll get an unguarded response?'

'Right.' He stroked his chin thoughtfully. 'If I call...'

'Where're the mugs, Boyd?' called Sunny.

'Cupboard above the kettle!' Boyd looked at Okeke again. 'If I call and spook this admin, that whole forum could come down in minutes.'

Okeke nodded. 'So here's an idea: don't spook them.'

'Great. No really, thanks. That's helpful.'

'Do you want me to do it?' she asked. 'With my best friendly female voice? I might be a little less threatening than you growling down the phone?'

'Okay,' he replied. 'But softly-softly, okay?'

'Softly-softly,' she echoed, tapping the number into her phone. 'What's the international code for Bosnia?'

He quickly looked it up on the laptop. 'Plus-387. You drop the first zero, then add the –'

'I know, I know.' Okeke cut off his mansplaining and finished dialling. 'What's the time over there?'

Boyd had no idea. At a guess they'd be a couple of hours ahead. 'Midday, maybe?'

Okeke put her phone on speaker mode, and they listened to the ringtone bleat once, pause and bleat again. Sunny stood beside the table to listen, coffee in hand.

'Just be *really* careful,' whispered Boyd.

She flashed her eyes at him to shut up. The ringtone stopped and a woman answered in fluent but heavily accented English.

'Villa Brajovanic? Can I help you?'

'Uh, hello,' Okeke began, with her most pleasant telephone voice. She even smiled as she spoke. 'Would it be possible for me to make a booking?'

'Yes. Of course. One moment...' They heard the rustle of movement and classical music playing in the background. Then the woman came back onto the call. 'When would you like to visit, please?'

'I have a few questions first,' replied Okeke. 'Do you have internet there?'

'Yes, of course. We have the hotel Wi-Fi. Guests may use this.'

'Is there a computer that guests can use? I don't want to have to bring mine along,' she asked.

A pause. 'You have a smartphone, perhaps?'

'No, I'm afraid. I... prefer old-fashioned phones.' Okeke looked at Boyd. 'I find them more secure.'

Another pause.

'Yes. I understand. I am sorry there is no internet terminal here. Only the Wi-Fi that can be used in the hotel.'

'Ah, I see, *discretion is very important to me*,' said Okeke pointedly, ' but I'll still make a booking if that's okay?'

'Yes. Of course. May I start by taking your name?'

Okeke looked up at Boyd again. He suspected where she was going with this. *Carefully!* he mouthed silently.

'My name is... Hadzic.'

This time the pause stretched out for several seconds. But the woman hadn't hung up. They could still hear the music in the background.

Then: 'Who are you?' the woman asked coolly.

Boyd nodded at Okeke, hoping she'd understand. *Tell her the truth... but very gently.*

'My name's Samantha,' she replied. 'Or Sam. Look, I'm a UK police officer investigating a hijacking incident that happened on a train over here.'

There was another long pause, then: 'Why have you called this number?'

It was the moment of truth. Boyd couldn't help wincing.

'I know about your forum,' said Okeke.

The music stopped. The call suddenly ended with a clack and a protracted *brrrrr*.

'Crap,' she uttereed. 'Sorry, guv. I think I...'

'No, you did fine,' Boyd said. 'You did it the way I would have done.'

Sunny sat down. 'Well, it proves you've found the right person,' he said cheerily. 'That's something. So Damocles is definitely a *she*, not a *h*.'

'So what do we do now?' asked Okeke.

Boyd had no idea. This was in no way *official* police business. Taking this any further while claiming to be officers on the case was going to put them in breach of the code of conduct and possibly even the law.

Okeke's phone buzzed on the table. The screen showed UNKNOWN CALLER. She looked at Boyd, touched the speakerphone icon and answered it. 'Samantha Okeke.'

'You are British police?'

'Yes... yes I am.'

'How did you get this number?'

Boyd nodded again at her to give her the truth. 'We know about your group. We know that what you're doing is... is about getting justice. Not terrorism. We need your help.'

58

Safan gazed out of the train window at green countryside rushing past, drizzle streaking almost horizontally across the glass. He hadn't yet stepped over the line. When the train pulled into London Bridge Station, he could always buy a ticket and take the next train back to Brighton and the world would be none the wiser. Ness would never know what he had intended to do. Life would go on as before for them all.

And Pesic will continue to be this country's hero.

That's what Safan knew he couldn't let go. Seeing that man's grinning face on TV telling the world how he was nothing special really – and knowing that only made him more of a legend in the eyes of these blind, easily-fooled British people.

Safan had to do this. When he'd met Rizmet that first time, Safan had quizzed the younger man on his resolve to do it. To kill Pesic.

'You understand you will also likely be killed?' Safan had said. 'They will see a terrorist – not someone seeking justice.'

Riz had nodded and said that he was already dead. That

witnessing the murder of his father, the raping and murder of his mother and sister, had killed him thirty years ago.

'This is not living,' Riz had replied. 'This is just waiting.'

'Waiting?'

'To see them again.'

The younger man had had the strength that came from his faith. A certainty that a reunion awaited him on the other side. As far as he was concerned, death was a welcome inevitability, provided that it came *after* he'd successfully brought justice to Corporal L. Pesic.

Safan didn't have that: faith. He had a hope, at best a *suspicion*, that there might be some form of 'continuance' after death. When they'd met in the coffee shop to discuss the how and the when, Riz had been ready to go. Mentally, his bags were already packed and all that mattered to Riz was that Pesic should be dispatched first.

Safan wasn't sure whether it was Riz's conviction that had rekindled his lapsed childhood faith, stoked it back to life from slumbering embers, or whether it was the anger that had done it. The endless misguided hero worship of this vile monster – stoked by the foolish newspaper *UK Daily* – had convinced Safan to finish the task that Rizmet had set out to do.

If I die... I will find out. If Safan didn't and he ended his days in prison, even if he failed and Pesic was unharmed, then at least the people of this country would understand the truth about the monster they'd embraced as the embodiment of their values – as the very Best of British.

59

'Avenger9 and Fragginz are two members of our group who wanted to pursue Pesic, even though he is located in the UK,' said 'Damocles'. 'The rest of the group, including myself, we argued against this.'

Okeke peered at Boyd's scrawl on the notepad in front of her. '*Why?*'

'Why?' The woman laughed at the stupidity of the question. 'We would be branded terrorists. Your government would pressure our government to arrest us. And there will need to be very little pressure. The Serbians in our government deny much of what has happened.'

'But the war crimes are documented,' replied Okeke.

The woman laughed again. 'As they are also for the Second World War ... but each year those who deny the crimes increase in number, yes? So, to answer your earlier question... yes. I warned them, *no more talk of seeking Pesic in the UK.*'

'So they left your group?'

'They have not posted again,' was her response.

'Do you think they continued to communicate privately?' asked Okeke.

'Yes, I am sure of this. They were very determined.'

'And you believe they acted on this alone?'

'Yes. The train hijacking in your country – I have seen this on the BBC news – I believe that is them, yes.'

Boyd quickly scribbled some more notes and turned the notepad round so Okeke could try to decipher his scrawl: *Check Riz's name. Genuine? Can we get her to name other guy?*

'So,' said Okeke, 'Rizmet Hadzic, that was his actual name?'

'Yes. Fragginz's name was Rizmet Hadzic.'

'You're sure about that?'

'I knew him.' The woman's voice thickened with emotion. She cleared her throat. 'I knew his family very well. Pesic was the man who killed them all. Riz was there. He witnessed it. You know he was just a boy?'

'Yes,' said Okeke. 'We understand he was young back then.' Boyd watched her as she calmly noted everything down. 'And how did you know the family?'

'Riz went to the same school as my boy. They were friends. In the same class. He often came to play in my home with...' The woman's voice faltered.

Get Avenger9's name! Boyd scribbled, then tapped the notepad with his index finger for emphasis.

Okeke frowned at him.

'I'm very sorry to be asking you these difficult questions,' she continued on the phone. 'Was your boy...'

'Yes, my Bilal was killed by them also. He was seven,' the woman replied sharply. 'He was shot in the head and thrown in the Drina river.'

Boyd suddenly felt queasy at the thought that he'd spent an evening with Pesic. *I drank with that bastard. I got drunk with him!*

'Was it Pesic who did that?' pressed Okeke.

'I do not know which of the men were doing the executions on the bridge on that day.' The woman cleared her throat again.

'Most of the men committed war crimes, you know? But only... few.... only very few were ever brought to justice.'

'I appreciate your help,' said Okeke, trying to suppress her anger at the brutal bastards. 'We know that Fragginz was Rizmet Hadzic, and we know what happened to him. So we very much need to identify Avenger9, because we're concerned he may attempt something else.'

'He came over to your country twenty years ago.' A cryptic response.

'And is he from Višegrad too?' Okeke asked.

'Yes, of course. I knew him also.'

Boyd tapped the notepad with his finger again.

Okeke nodded. 'Will you tell me who is Avenger9?'

'You understand... he wishes only to bring justice?'

'I know,' said Okeke. 'But we can do that. We can arrest Pesic and start the process of investigating his involvement in war crimes. We're concerned that Riz's friend might do something...'

They heard 'Damocles' take a deep breath. 'He was a teacher in the school. Computer sciences.'

'His name,' urged Okeke, 'please?'

'Safan,' the woman muttered. 'His name is Safan Salmani.'

60

Safan emerged from London Bridge Station to get some fresh air and a few moments of peace. He'd done his research. The Greg Norman television show was recorded on Thursday nights at a place called Riverbank Studios in Hammersmith.

He studied the Tube map on his phone and wondered how anyone could make any sense of the multicoloured spaghetti strands. He'd visited London once before, about fourteen years ago in 2006 and got completely lost in the system, travelling in loops beneath the city for over an hour before eventually pleading with one of the staff to help him find his way out.

Today, Safan typed 'London Bridge to Hammersmith' into his smartphone and waited for his maps app to calculate his route. It wasn't as difficult as he'd first thought it might be. There were only two changes. The black line, change to the red one, then change to the dark-blue one.

The rain stopped at last and the London sky offered him a reassuring glimpse of feathered blue through tears in the grey clouds. A shard of sunlight speared down in front of Safan. He grasped that as a good omen. A portent. Perhaps – if he allowed himself to be fanciful – it was Riz, showing him the way.

61

Sunny's laptop screen displayed Safan Salmani's business website: Salmani Computers and Electronics. There was a picture of his shopfront, a large sign above it, and Salmani himself standing outside the shop door.

'That's him,' said Okeke. 'That's definitely the guy I tailed.'

'Well, it's not like he's been hiding behind an alias, then,' said Sunny.

'He's not been hiding at all,' said Okeke. 'I mean, his name's right out there.'

The website indicated that Salmani had a retail unit in Brighton where he took in PCs and TVs for repair. He also did location-based IT work on the side.

Boyd looked at Okeke. 'So, what do you think Williams would make of this? If we took it to her, I mean. He looks like he's too invested in his life to throw it all away on a cause. And Damocles didn't say anything about Salmani or Hadzic being radicalised. Their goal was personal. An act of revenge.'

'Their goal is justice,' said Okeke.

'It sounds like what your boss wants to hear is that this guy is a cleric at some local mosque or works for some dodgy-looking Hamas-funded "outreach" project. He's a terrorist and has his very own Blue Peter ISIS badge to prove it,' said Sunny.

'That's it in a nutshell,' said Okeke.

'This is personal,' Boyd repeated. 'Which means it's not terrorism. She'll have to see it.'

'I don't agree,' Okeke said, chewing her lip. 'If we take this to her... she'll sideline it. If she admits that it's not terrorism, she'll have to hand the case over to us.'

'You have Damocles?' said Sunny. 'Could you explain to her your investigative route? Let Williams speak to her? Would that help Williams to see sense?'

Boyd considered that. Okeke had made assurances to Damocles that Interpol or, worse, some standard-issue Bosnian Secret Police boots weren't going to kick her front door in.

'We need something else,' he said finally. 'He's not a radical. He was a science teacher. That's what she said, right?'

'He might have been a science teacher,' Sunny pointed out, 'but if there's one thing that's going to radicalise you, mate, it's witnessing your family being butchered.'

'Why don't you call him? As a customer?' suggested Okeke. 'Arrange a shop visit or something?'

Boyd nodded. 'That's what I'm considering. But I think it'll have to be you again, Okeke. I'm pretty sure my mugshot has been used in some of the papers.'

She bit her lip for a moment. 'Okay. So what's my script?' she asked.

'You've got a knackered old PC and want to bring it in to upgrade it,' he replied.

'He'll ask you what it is,' said Sunny. 'What version of Windows, what CPU, what memory it's got... and what do you want, blah, blah.'

'So I'll just act super-dumb,' Okeke said. 'Like I'm just bringing it in for my boyfriend.' She looked at the screen. 'Which number? The mobile or the shop line?'

'Mobile,' said Boyd.

She began to tap the number into her phone.

'Just set up a time to bring in the computer,' said Boyd. 'Nothing more than that, all right?'

Okeke nodded and lifted the phone to her ear. She held perfectly still for a few moments, then she blew her cheeks out and sighed. 'Straight to voicemail.'

'Hang up.'

She ended the call. 'Shall I try the landline?'

'Yup. But put it on speakerphone this time, you muppet,' Boyd reminded her.

She dead-eyed him and raised a brow, then tapped in the second number; this time they all listened to the electronic *brrrrrr* of the ringtone together.

Several rings later a woman answered. 'Salmani Electronics?' She sounded as if she'd been running.

'Ah, hello,' began Okeke, her best posh voice conjured up again. 'I've got an old PC that's in desperate need of upgrading.'

'Safan's not here right now,' the woman said. 'Have you tried his mobile number?'

'Uh, yes. But it went straight to voicemail.'

She sighed. 'He does that on call-outs. You can drop the PC at our home if you like? He's got a workshop in the back garden. Or... I can take a name and number so he can get back to you?'

'No, that's...' Okeke bit her lip again. 'Look, when's he back? Maybe I can call later?'

'He's got a big job in London today,' the woman replied. 'I don't think he'll be home until late.'

Boyd scribbled a word on his pad. <u>Where?</u>

'Oh really? London?' Okeke said in her best 'casually chatty' voice. 'Whereabouts?'

'Umm, Hammersmith, I think. So anyw–'

'I know Hammersmith!' Okeke cut in again. 'I used to live there.'

'Right. That's... anyway, so if you want to try calling back tomorrow?' The woman was clearly keen to end the call.

'Where in Hammersmith?' Okeke pressed.

The woman hesitated. 'Sorry? I... Look, I'm really sorry – I've got three kids here who are clamouring for sandwiches and crisps. Can you please try calling back tomorrow?'

Shit. We're going to lose her. Boyd leant forward. 'Hello? Mrs Salmani? This is DCI Boyd, East Sussex CID.'

A pause.

'The police,' he added for clarity. 'We urgently need to speak with your husband.'

'We're not married.' The pause lengthened. In the background they could hear a TV set and the sound of youngsters squabbling with each other.

'You said you're the police?' she said eventually, her voice suddenly pitched a little higher with concern. 'Has something happened to him?'

'Nothing's happened,' Boyd said. 'But we're concerned for his safety. Do you know where *precisely* he said he was going?'

There was another pause. As this new pause lengthened, he decided to give her a measured-out version of the truth.

'Your partner, Safan...' he said. 'We're concerned he may be after someone and may attempt to hurt them.'

'*What?*' she exclaimed. 'No... Saffy's not... What the hell're you on about?'

'You know Safan's a Bosnian war-crime victim, don't you?'

'I... no that's not right. He's Albanian.' She sounded confused.

Pesic had done the same thing – camouflaged where he'd come from. Even used the same country. 'He's Bosnian Muslim.' Boyd confirmed.

'I know he's Muslim, but he... he said he was from Albania.'

'He's a survivor and a witness of some very brutal war crimes,' Boyd told her. 'I believe he's suffering – *been* suffering –

PTSD for the last thirty years. We know he's been trying to trace the man who killed his family, and we think he's finally managed to locate him.'

'Oh god,' the woman whispered. 'That...' They heard her voice break, then heard in the background one of her kids asking her what was wrong.

Okeke cut in. 'This is DC Samantha Okeke speaking. I'm sorry for lying about the PC. What's your name, love?'

'Ness.'

'Look, Ness, we want to find him before he does something stupid.'

'But he's not a violent man!' Ness whispered. 'He's so gentle. So kind. He's not –'

'I know. And we don't want him to go to prison, or worse. Please... did he say anything more specific about where he was going?'

'Worse?' Ness breathed.

'Ness, if he has a weapon and attacks someone in London? Look, the Metropolitan Police are on a far higher level of alert for acts of terrorism than down here. We need –'

'Terrorism! Oh my God! He's not a terrorist!' Ness gasped.

'We know, we know!' Boyd interjected. 'But *they* don't. And there's a lot of armed officers around tourist locations, public places... the South Bank –'

'Bank! Wait... Riverbank!' said Ness. 'He said he had a job at a TV place. He said it was called Riverbank!'

Boyd turned to Sunny, who was already tapping on his keyboard. He turned his laptop round and Boyd took in the glossy website: Riverbank Television Studios. Beneath the header was a list of upcoming events looking for studio audiences. Right at the top of the list was *The Greg Norman Show* and beside it *'ticket applications closed'*.

'Shit,' he whispered. Pesic said the show was on Friday night.

'Listen, Ness,' said Okeke. 'We tried his mobile but it's sending us to voicemail. If he calls you, tell him we know who he is. Tell him we know exactly who he's after. And we *are* going to arrest that person. That man will face justice.'

'Who? Who's... he *after*?'

'I can't say,' said Okeke. She looked at Boyd for a steer. He nodded. 'Just tell him he's to tell you where he is and stay right there. Then call us.'

Boyd leant forward. 'Listen to me, Ness. It's really important that he doesn't do anything that endangers himself. Did he take anything with him? Backpack? Equipment bag?'

'Y-yes.'

'Right. If you get through to him, tell him if he's approached by any police wanting to question him... to set his bag down and to put his hands up. To cooperate. Tell him we're coming.'

62

3.15 p.m.

Ruth Cadwell watched her client pacing up and down in his dressing room like a circus tiger in a holding pen. He was cradling his lower back.

'Are you okay, Lucas? Have you hurt yourself?'

'What?'

She nodded at the way he was holding his back.

'Ache,' he said, tapping his hip lightly. 'When I get the stress.'

'Lucas, you're going to be fine. It'll be just like having a chat with an old friend. Greg's a lovely bloke. He'll make you feel comfortable.'

She'd decided to bring him into the studio centre earlier than planned because he'd been prowling the cottage and threatening to cancel the whole thing. Stage fright was really getting to him badly. Along with this new back pain, he'd claimed he had stomach pains and felt sick.

'Just sit down and relax,' she said reassuringly. 'I'll walk you through some breathing exercises to calm you down.'

He sat down carefully on the chair opposite her. 'I do not want to do this any more.'

Time to get firm with him.

'Lucas. You have to. You've accepted the money and they've planned this week's show around you, so I'm afraid you're just going to have to step up. Now...' It was quarter past three in the afternoon and they'd let him have his dressing room early. 'The first thing you should probably do is tidy yourself up a little.'

The beard and moustache he'd been growing over the last week had gone from a suggestion of five-o-clock shadow to full-on thatch almost before her eyes. His thick dark bristles seemed to be growing at the same rate as kerbside nettles.

'I like this look,' he said, glancing at the mirror. 'Like a pirate, huh?'

'Yes, you do. But the point is you look quite a lot different to the cheeky chap who saved a train full of people a fortnight ago.'

'I normally have beard,' he replied.

'Well, that's as maybe, but everyone knows you without the beard. So perhaps we should have a go at shaving that awful thing off?'

His thick brows knitted. 'No! Is my beard, my face!'

Shit. The producer had already had a word with her about 'smartening him up a little'. And she was quite right: Pesic was starting to look more like a manic Bob Hoskins than Sergei the Meerkat... and the latter look was the one that everyone had found so endearing.

'No one will recognise you, Lucas. They'll be going, *Who the hell's this?*' She said that with a smile in an attempt to lighten the mood.

He nodded. 'I surprise them, then.'

'No, but seriously... Lucas, come on.' She looked at the suite of make-up and grooming equipment set out tidily beside the mirror. 'Let's get those clippers and have a little go, shall we?'

She reached out for the shaver, charging in its dock, and suddenly he leant forward and grabbed her wrist firmly.

'Ow! Let go!'

'No shave!' he hissed at her, compressing her wrist painfully in his big hand. 'You do what I say. I am boss, not you!'

'Lucas, let me go!'

He flexed his fingers, grinding her wrist bones painfully against each other. 'After this, we do what I want from now on. Da?'

Ruth wanted to tell him that after this he could go fuck himself. She'd have her commission and she'd be done with this petulant, overgrown child.

She looked him in the eye. 'Let me go right now, or...'

His beard parted showing a surprisingly white and tidy row of little teeth. It was a smile, but not a particularly pleasant one. 'Or?'

Not for the first time since adopting him as a wayward and bemused-looking stray, she felt a little frightened of him. When he'd blocked her exit with his arm back at the cottage – she'd passed it off as a bad mood and a bit of clumsy body language. But this... was a direction of travel that she didn't want to know anything more about.

She managed to return a smile. 'Well, fine... if you want to look like Blackbeard...'

63

3.45 p.m.

Safan arrived at the television studio far earlier than he'd thought he would. The notice on the main entrance announced that show-ticket holders would be admitted at 5 p.m. and no sooner. Already, though, a couple of dozen people were standing outside with takeaway coffees and chatting excitedly about tonight's guest list: a Hollywood leading man, an anarchic stand-up comedian, an on-the-up music act... and, of course, the Have-A-Go Hero – Lucas Pesic.

He found a Pret nearby that had a clear view of the television centre's front entrance. He was surprised at how hungry he felt and ordered a vegetarian sausage roll along with his coffee, then he picked a stool that faced the front window, which had a narrow counter for customers.

A final supper.

Perhaps.

So there it was – his first serious acknowledgement that tonight *could* end with him facing the same fate as Riz.

On the train up he'd been shaking. On the Tube too. But

sitting here now, with his coffee and food, he wasn't trembling any more. The nerves had gone and a calm determination had settled on him. He took a hearty bite out of his sausage roll as he watched the queue of ticket holders steadily lengthen.

It would be a lie to say he'd been waiting for this moment for thirty years. Because he hadn't. For most of the time since he'd come to England, he'd been focused on building a new life. Which was no small achievement given that he'd arrived here with a slender grasp of the English language, gleaned from listening to bootleg rock music and watching fuzzy episodes of *The X-Files* on pirated VHS tapes.

And then the internet had come along, with its blogs, forums and other watering holes for people to gather around. And with those things came ways to find lost childhood friends and ex-colleagues: Friends Reunited, Myspace. He'd dabbled with those and found pitifully few people he'd known from childhood. And not because the folks of Bosnia–Herzegovina didn't do the internet, but because so many of them lay in mass graves, some of them unmarked, never to be discovered.

Safan's past, his loved ones, his friends, his old colleagues, his cheeky students and all the memories that were baked into those relationships had been almost completely edited out by men in masks and berets. No, not men... Monsters. Ghouls

He'd eventually stumbled across Katarina via Facebook in 2013. She had been a colleague from his school who he'd barely known back then, the school's librarian.

Katarina had spent the intervening years more bravely than he had. She'd not tried to escape the past and her own scarred recollection of those weeks, but had embraced them. She'd treated them as a puzzle to be put together with the single goal of identifying those vile men, those creatures, who'd scuttled away into the long dry grass after the war had ended.

Those Scorpions.

Some had been local men, known in the town; others had

come from afar. All of them so casual and assured in their daily barbarism that they'd unknowingly left seedlings of evidence in their wake.

Katarina had taken her labours to the dark side of the internet, because too many authority figures in their country preferred certain parts of the past to be forgotten. And it came as no great surprise that the ones who championed that were not Bozniaks but Serbian Bosnians.

Katarina had established her secret group of scarred survivors away from prying eyes – she'd created a safe space for them to gather and curate testimonies and evidence that might, in the future, see the light of day.

Katarina had given herself the name of Damocles.

The truth would one day plunge like a spike into the skulls of men like Pesic, men who thought the past was buried and forgotten.

64

4 p.m.

'Okay, I think we've done enough,' said Boyd. 'This is Williams' case. She needs to know what we've got. Right now.'

Okeke sighed. 'For fuck's sake… but you're right.'

'You got the number for the Incident Room?' he asked.

Okeke picked up her phone. 'Better than that. I've got Williams' number. It's one of the last numbers I called.' She passed her phone to him and opened her 'recent calls' log.

'This one?'

She shook her head. 'That's Jay's nightclub. The one below.'

Boyd tapped the number and waited for half a dozen rings until Williams' answerphone kicked in.

'This is DCI Boyd,' he said. 'I'm on Okeke's phone. I need you to call me back on this number as soon as you get this.' He hung up.

'What now?' asked Sunny. 'Do we call the Met?'

Boyd shook his head. Out of professional courtesy he didn't

want to jump straight over Williams' head. 'Let's give her a moment; she might have just nipped to the loo or something.'

'Whoa. Hold on. Are you talking about the Met's CT unit?' Okeke turned to Sunny. 'You know what they're like.'

Both Boyd and Sunny *did* know. The CT FTOs were fast, fearless and professional but always set off anticipating the worst possible contact scenario. It was par for the course in London. But Okeke had made a promise to Ness that they'd make sure everyone was well aware that Safan wasn't a terrorist. She was still hoping it was true that he'd just gone to London for an IT job – although, she had to admit, that wasn't the most likely reason.

If the Met got involved, any possible nuances would be quickly lost as the 'possible terror threat' alert was sent down a long chain of command.

Boyd picked up Okeke's phone and dialled DCI William's number again.

4.15 p.m

Williams stared at the name on her phone. *For God's sake. What does she want now?*

Actually, she had a pretty fair idea. Detective Constable Okeke wanted to plead her case – she wanted to be put back on the team. But it was done. Williams had absolutely no time at all for tattletales. Even though DC Okeke had displayed initiative and coolness in tailing the suspect from the coffee shop by herself after the surveillance op had veered off piste, she'd stepped over a line by taking critical evidence to Boyd, who was outside the team.

In an operation like this, where a single misstep could lead to alerting or losing a target, there just wasn't room for someone she couldn't trust.

She let the phone buzz softly on her notepad until the

name disappeared from the screen and sighed with relief. She was nursing a bugger of a headache that had been threatening to escalate to a migraine all morning. The last thing she needed right now was to have a heated row with a disgruntled junior detective.

'Ma'am?'

DI Connor had got up from his desk and was heading over. She smiled. 'What've you got for me, Matt? Please make it some good news.'

'I think so, ma'am. It looks like we might have a winner.'

Williams had set Connor the task of collating data from the Costa's Wi-Fi access history against a number of 5G providers in the area of the coffee shop. 'I've got a repeat user ID number that matches with our man's regular visits and transaction token timestamps,' he told her.

'Good work. Have we got a reliable candidate?'

'Yes, ma'am. Can I go ahead and call his service provider to request a live feed on the mast hits?'

'Yes, of course. Let's get that happening right away.'

'I'm on it,' he said, jogging back to his desk.

Williams got up. 'Oh, Matthew?' she called. 'I'm just nipping out to get something. My head's killing me. Do you need anything?'

'I'm fine, ma'am.'

Williams picked out Minter. 'Sergeant, which way's closer for a pharmacy? Uphill or down?'

'Downhill, Ma'am. Are you after a Boots or something?' he asked.

'Just someone who sells paracetamol,' she said.

'Downhill, then. Take the right onto Magadalen Road. There are some corner shops along there that should be able to sort you out.'

4.45 p.m

'Oh, fuck this for a game of soldiers! Let's just drive over to the station,' said Boyd.

'She's not answering your calls because you're using my phone,' said Okeke. 'She probably thinks it's me phoning to have it out with her.'

'Right, well, that's all the more reason to go face to face.' Boyd picked up his car keys from the dining-room table. 'Both of you are coming. Sunny, bring your laptop. We'll show her this vigilante group and see what she says to that.'

'Uh, Boyd... Strictly speaking, I'm breaking some data protection rules here,' Sully reminded him.

'I'm pretty sure she won't charge you,' Boyd told him. 'Come on.'

He led them out of the house with a hopeful Ozzie bringing up the rear. Boyd blocked his way at the front doorstep. 'Sorry, mate. We'll do a walk later – I promise, buddy.'

He drove them along the seafront and turned right at the White Rock Theatre. He caught a glimpse of Charlotte, sitting at her desk, the office blinds pulled back to make the most out of the grey daylight, then uphill on Bohemia Road, past the Travelodge and the fire station.

'Guv!' Okeke pointed. 'There she is!'

Boyd spotted Williams slogging her way back uphill, looking out of breath and irritable. He quickly indicated, pulled up ahead of her at a crowded bus stop and jumped out.

'Williams!' he shouted.

Heads turned as he hurried downhill to meet the DCI, Okeke following in his wake.

'Am I staying with the car?!' Sunny called out from the back seat.

65

5.02 p.m.

Safan approached the main entrance and joined the queue filing through the double doors into the Riverbank Television Centre. He could see a security guard casually glancing at tickets as they were waved in front of him. He wasn't exactly giving the job his A game.

Safan lifted the lanyard around his neck and held it out. 'Salmani Computers. I am here about the faulty guest Wi-Fi router?'

The security guard barely made eye contact with him as he waved him inside. Safan stepped into the brightly lit reception area, punctuated with billboards featuring titles for this evening's recorded shows: *Osman's House of Games*, *The Hello Show* and *The Greg Norman Show*. To his right was a café with a curved wall of floor-to-ceiling glass that looked out across the Thames. With the overcast sky making it prematurely darker, lights were already winking on along the riverbank, making London look Christmas-lights pretty.

The area was busy. All three shows taking place in Studios One to Three, were, it appeared, getting ready to call in their audiences for pre-recording sound checks. Safan could see kiosks being set up outside each studio with production assistants, wearing radio mics and carrying iPad tablets in the crooks of their arms, fussing around them. He noticed a couple of uniformed security guards lingering alongside each kiosk, getting ready to welcome the guests.

It looked as though security entering the studios was a little tighter. On the tablets, presumably, were the names of those attending each recording.

Safan spotted a sign for the toilets and headed over to it, feeling desperately conspicuous with his holdall in one hand. A guard watched him cross the floor with passing interest. Safan wondered whether pulling out his phone and pretending to use it would make him look nonchalant, or even more on edge and suspicious.

He pushed the door to the gents open. Most of the urinals were occupied by ticket holders taking their last chance to have a pee before being locked inside the studio for the duration of the show. He found a vacant cubicle and stepped inside. He closed the door, locked it and only then allowed himself to let out a long sigh of relief. He flipped down the toilet lid and slumped down, taking several more gasps.

You can still turn round go home.

It was Thursday night – games night. Ness usually ordered a pizza for the girls and they all played *SingStar* on the PlayStation. He could be back with them in a couple of hours and he could always tell Ness the job got cancelled.

He dearly wanted to, but...

That bastard's right here. In this building.

The man who'd murdered his wife and unborn child thirty years ago had the stronger gravitational pull and Safan stayed where he was.

The Last Train

He opened his holdall and pulled out the things he was going to need.

66

There was a knock on the dressing-room door and it was pushed open before she had time to reply. Ruth Cadwell got up off her chair, a big smile plastered across her face. 'Oh my goodness!'

Greg Norman stepped in and closed the door behind himself. He was a tall and slim man, with a mop of curly hair on top of buzzcut sides and comically protruding ears. He wore thick rimmed glasses that were an essential part of his image in a less over-the-top way than the likes of Harry Hill.

He strode over and offered his hand to Pesic. 'It's an absolute honour to have you on my show, Lucas!'

Pesic took his hand and shook it warily. 'You are Greg Norman?' he asked.

The host laughed self-consciously. 'Obviously not the global name I thought I was!'

Pesic nodded as Greg continued to pump his hand up and down.

'What's with all the face fungus?' Greg said, gesturing at Lucas' beard. 'I nearly didn't recognise you.'

'You like it?'

Greg pulled one of his comedy faces and made a long sceptical *hmmmm* sound.

'I said he should have shaved before the show,' said Ruth, approaching him with her hand outstretched. 'Ruth Cadwell.'

'Ahh!' He wagged a finger at her. 'So *you're* the one my producer was moaning about.'

'Moaning?'

'For driving such a hard bargain on this one here,' he said, indicating Lucas.

She nodded. 'We're just making hay while the sun shines,' she replied. 'Right, Lucas?'

Greg turned back to Pesic. 'You'll be the third guest on tonight. You look nervous. Are you nervous?'

Pesic nodded.

'Well, don't be, Lucas. We're going to chat a little about what happened a couple of weeks ago. Nothing too heavy. We're going to be sensitive about the train driver who died, of course, but also, I think, be very upbeat about how bloody brave you were to take that terrorist down. How good's your English? I heard it's pretty good.'

Pesic nodded. 'I can speak it well.'

Greg turned to Ruth and winked. 'Just love that accent.'

'I wanted Boyd to come on this show with me,' said Pesic. 'But Ruth said no.'

Greg frowned. 'Boyd?'

'The off-duty policeman who helped him,' explained Ruth. 'I said that's not who you wanted.'

'Quite right,' said Greg. 'He was brave and utterly professional, I'm sure, but you know how coppers speak – like bloody train station announcers. He'd have the audience asleep in minutes.' He turned back to Pesic. 'Okay, so... we'll talk a little about how you tackled the bad guy. If it gets at all uncomfortable for you, I'll pick up on that and move things along, all right?'

Lucas nodded.

'We're going to talk about the Fund This Now campaign and the legal appeal that's being lodged to review your settled status – you okay with that?'

He nodded again.

'And then we'll end on what you want to do once everything's sorted. Dreams? Ambitions? That kind of thing. Sound good?'

Pesic managed a smile. 'Yes. Thank you very much, Greg Norman.'

'Greg!' he said, howling with laughter. 'Okay? Just Greg.'

67

5.20 p.m.

'I will absolutely raise a complaint once this is over,' said Williams as she led the way up the stairs the to the first floor and the CID area.

'Well, that's fine,' replied Boyd. 'I really don't care, but you can leave DC Okeke out of it. This is my call.'

'She leaked case details to you, for God's sake!' Williams pointed out.

'A detail,' Boyd conceded. 'One you weren't going to do anything with – and one that actually turned out to give us the man's identity!'

Williams strode down the corridor, setting the pace for both of them, then pushed open the door to the Incident Room. 'You have both overstepped the mark and I'm going to write it up whether it turns out you've got something or not!'

Minter looked up from his desk. 'Boss? What're you doing in?'

'I got bored with gardening,' Boyd replied. 'Where're Sutherland and Hatcher?'

'Still in, I think. Want me to go get them?'

'Yeah.' Boyd glanced at Williams. 'If Salmani's partner is right, he could be scoping out an opportunity right now.'

Minter looked to Williams. She conceded and nodded. As Minter got to the door, Okeke and Sunny stepped into the room. 'Okeke? What's going on? Aren't you supposed to be off to–'

'I got bored watching the telly,' Okeke interrupted, flashing him a grin as she and Sunny wandered over to join Boyd.

Williams peeled a couple of paracetamol out of a foil packet and popped them into her mouth. 'Everyone!' she called to the others in the room. 'Team briefing. Now!'

∞

SAFAN PULLED the fake suicide jacket out of his holdall. Like Riz's, at first glance it looked the part, but any closer inspection would reveal it to be nothing more than soap-bar-sized blocks of modelling clay wrapped in cling film and linked by red wires. He lifted his sweatshirt and wrapped it tightly round his waist, then lowered his shirt.

If he was picked by security and frisked, then it would be over. He'd have to decide whether to turn and run or pull out his gun and try to find Pesic that way. He had no idea if any of the guards in this complex carried guns, but he wouldn't be surprised if someone did, given the general heightened awareness of terror threats in the last year.

Safan was taking a calculated risk – but he figured being able to lift his shirt and flash the vest bomb might buy him additional cooperation from those nearby if he needed it.

The other thing he pulled out of his bag definitely *wasn't* fake. He'd got the design from another website on the Dark Web and printed it on his 3D printer a couple of days ago. The gun looked like a badly made toy. He'd sprayed it black to make it look a little more convincing because there was no point threatening someone with a gun if the wretchedly cumbersome thing looked like kid's peashooter.

He tucked it into his armpit and reached down for some electrical tape to secure it there. The six bullets and the firing pin, the only metal components, he tucked into his socks. He'd never seen any security guard bother to wave a metal detector all the way down to the ground.

The last thing he pulled out of his bag was a utility belt, the one he normally wore when he was doing networking jobs. It had a holster for a power drill, a pouch with a voltmeter in it, and pouches for a variety of clips and wire strippers. It might just, together with the lanyard, get him into the studio without the need for drama.

And if it didn't?

Well – he'd have to make that decision when it came to it.

Safan zipped up the holdall. There was nothing else in it, just a few empty crisp packets and usual random detritus that accumulates in a scruffy work bag. He picked it up, opened the cubicle door and went to look in the mirror beside the hand basins. He shrugged his shoulders and twisted his torso slightly to see if the small packages of the vest were showing through his sweatshirt.

He emerged from the gents to find that the audience for Studio One had been called and the ticket holders had formed a high-spirited and noisy queue, waiting to show their tickets to the production assistant at the kiosk and head into the studio.

I am the IT technician, he told himself. *I am here to fix the guest Wi-Fi.*

He even had a bogus job email that he could show the woman if she queried him – though it would mean turning his phone on, something he didn't want to do unless he had to.

I am the IT technician, he said to himself again as he crossed the busy floor towards the kiosk and walked past the noisy queue to the front. The woman with the iPad was alone. The security guards were a short distance away, chatting to each other and paying absolutely no attention to anything going on around them.

Safan took that as a sign that this was meant to be. Not God's will – that's where Rizmet had drawn his resolve from. For Safan it came from a more earthly place: a simple desire for justice to be done.

He was standing beside the kiosk now and the young woman turned to look at him. 'Yeah?'

'I am the IT technician,' Safan said calmly.

68

5.35 p.m.

'His name is Safan Salmani,' said Boyd. He turned to Sunny and nodded at him to put the image up on the projector screen. 'This was taken by his partner a few of days ago. She says he's wearing the sweatshirt and jeans you see in this picture today.'

The image showed Salmani in the couple's back garden; he was holding a little girl in one arm and a BBQ spatula in the other. He had an apron round his waist that boldly claimed he was the World's Best Chef.

Boyd continued. 'He's Bozniak, a Bosnian Muslim. A survivor of the ethnic cleansing that occurred during the Bosnian War. We believe he and the train hijacker were working together to locate a Serbian-Bosnian paramilitary soldier called...'

And here we go...

'Lucas Pesic.'

The name took most of the team by surprise, except

Williams. Boyd had given her the highlights on the way up to the station.

'Shit. That's the have-a-go-hero!' said DI Abbott, looking at Boyd, slack-jawed.

'We've got some very strong intel that suggests Salmani is casing out a location today with a plan he intends to carry out tomorrow night. Which... is, we suspect, to kill Lucas Pesic live on TV,' Boyd said.

Williams reinforced his statement with a resigned nod. 'The intel does seem solid,' she agreed.

Sutherland's eyes rounded behind his glasses. 'Blimey!'

Hatcher, who was sitting next to him raised a hand to her mouth. 'Where?' she asked. 'Where is this happening?'

'Lucas Pesic told me he's a guest on *The Greg Norman Show* tomorrow night. It broadcasts from the Riverbank TV Studio in Hammersmith. Salmani's partner said he's at the studio today to do a job. We suspect he's scoping it out for tomorrow.'

'We'll need a warrant, ma'am, to raid his home and his business,' Williams said to Hatcher. 'We need to know for certain that his motive is a targeted assassination and not an act of terror on random targets.'

'It's not,' Boyd cut in. 'He wants Pesic, and only Pesic.'

'Rizmet's motive was supposedly the same,' Willams added. 'Yet he ended up killing the train driver and almost murdered another passenger. We need to know what weapons he's got on him and whether he's determined to kill only Pesic, or if he's prepared to take out innocent people alongside him too.'

'Why does he want this chap Pesic?' asked Sutherland.

'Because of the Bosnian War. Pesic is a war criminal,' Boyd answered. 'The train hijacking was a first attempt on his life; we think Salmani is going to finish the job.'

'He's a *suspected* war criminal,' Williams corrected him. 'We don't know this for sure.'

'We need to alert the Met,' said Hatcher. 'Do you think this

Salmani intends to go home today and return to the studio to carry this out tomorrow?'

Boyd shook his head. 'His partner said he left with a large bag. And that he was acting strangely.'

'Did she say in what way his behaviour was strange?' Hatcher asked.

'She said that, looking back, it felt like more of a goodbye. She didn't think he'd be back,' Boyd told her. 'Maybe he'll try to find some place in this Riverbank complex to hide overnight. He could be in the studios right now.'

'Well, surely we need to mobilise someone right now?' said Okeke.

'We need to know what we're dealing with here,' said Williams. 'The suicide vest and the gun were both fake on the train – this time it could be different. We need to search his home and his business premises right away. My team needs to know what they're facing,' she looked at Okeke. 'It'll define their engagement orders.'

'Shoot to kill?' ventured Hatcher.

Williams nodded. 'Of course, ma'am.'

Hatcher steepled fingers beneath her chin as she processed what had been laid out to her in the last few minutes.

∽

THE WOMAN WAVED Safan through without a second thought, and he walked past the kiosk and into the corridor. There was a rope cordon halfway down it and a sign on a stand that declared *'Greg's THIS way, folks!'* with an arrow pointing to an open door on the left. He could hear upbeat music and the murmur of voices spilling out from the space beyond.

On the other side of the rope cordon, the corridor continued down to a door marked 'Green Room'. A man who looked large and stern enough to be some celeb's personal security guard was standing in front of it. Safan decided his ruse would probably hit the wall if he tried to get past him. The problem was that he now stood out, looking more like a contractor than a member of the audience. But he had no time to do anything about that, worrying that if he paused any longer he'd alert the security guard to his presence.

He turned left and headed into the studio.

The space was showbiz-lit with coloured spots on the set and dusky crimson lighting on the seats. It was large and busy with audience members shuffling along seat rows and offering '*excuse me*'s to those having to stand up to let them past. The seating area was set on a stepped scaffold that left a dark void beneath. Wandering towards the back of it, Safan undid his utility belt and tossed both it and the holdall into the darkness.

'Hey!'

He looked round to see a young man with a clipboard in one hand and a radio mic in the other, hurrying towards him. Safan felt his resolve begin to waver as fight-or-flight adrenaline surged into his bloodstream.

The crewman pulled up short and for a second Safan thought he was going to ask him what the hell he'd just tossed under the seats...

'Sorry, mate,' the crewman said apologetically. 'Health and safety. There's trip hazards and electrical flex everywhere back here.' He smiled. 'We do studio tours during the day if back-of-set stuff is your thing?'

Safan managed a smile. 'I... am interested in these things, yes.'

'Cool. Well, ask about the tours at reception on your way out; meanwhile I'm going to have to ask you to find a seat quickly and sit down. We're about to start.'

'Ma'am?' Boyd prompted. 'We need to act now.'

'All right,' said Hatcher. 'I want raids on his home and business premises on my authority. Boyd, I want you on that.'

She looked at Williams. 'I presume you've got a straight-through relationship with the Met's CTU?'

'Yes, ma'am.'

'Then call who you need to call. Let's get boots in transit ASAP. And, from this point on, I'm acting as the SIO on this operation.'

Williams nodded, her phone already in her hand.

Boyd was about to make a call too when Okeke parked herself in front of him. 'Let me go over to his home with family liaison,' she said.

'It's an hour and a bit's drive, Sam,' Boyd said. 'The police will get there first.'

'I know,' she replied. 'But they'll tear through the house and scare the crap out of Ness and her girls. Let me just get over there to reassure her. I want to let her know we're going to try to bring Safan home alive.'

Boyd nodded. 'All right. Go.'

He pulled up the number for Brighton police station's CID, hoping he'd catch their DSI before he clocked off for the day.

69

6.05 p.m.

'Good evening, everyone! I'm Helen, the floor manager – and I'm also the boss while we're recording, despite what Greg might think!'

The studio filled with a ripple of good-natured laughter.

'I have a bit of housekeeping for you all before we get going. First things first... phones off, please. And I mean properly off,' she added. 'Not on sleep mode or vibrate. The boom mics you see swinging around above you are incredibly sensitive.'

There was a rustle of activity as the entire studio audience, some two hundred of them, reached into their bags and pockets for their phones.

'Now that the doors are closed for recording,' continued Helen, 'we're going to take you through a few volume tests to make sure we've got our levels right. So... I'm going to count from three down to zero and then I want you all to imagine that Tom Cruise or Ed Sheeran has just stepped out – and if neither of those do it for you, then just imagine Greg coming on in his birthday suit! Okay.... are you ready to make as much noise as you can?'

The adult audience replied like a theatre full of sugared-up kids at a Christmas panto. 'YEAH!!!!'

'Excellent!' Helen smiled. 'Right then.... Three... two... one...'

Safan, seated on the second row back, cheered and clapped along with everyone else.

~

Lucas Pesic had been led through from his dressing room to the Green Room. He had no idea why it was called that. It wasn't even remotely green. Ruth had invited herself along even though the production assistant had very clearly said it was for 'talent only'.

Pesic shook his head with disgust as she spent time with everyone except him. She was chatting, laughing, flirting with the famous American actor, and handing out her business cards like sweets.

He was starting to suspect that she was going to drop him like a hot brimstone the moment she got her share of his money.

He sipped at the cup of punch he'd helped himself to. It was very orange, sweet and almost completely – but not quite – hiding the subtle taste of vodka.

He glared over at Ruth. A horsefly. That's what she was. Another summer horsefly landing on his skin and sucking away at him. Only now she was looking for someone else to pretend to care about.

70

The crimson audience lights dimmed to total darkness, leaving the set – a pink sofa, a swivel chair, and a coffee table on which was a jug full of water and a model of a Kawasaki Z1000 – garishly decorated with swirling multi-coloured spotlights.

Loud music suddenly filled the studio theatre, and the production boss Helen walked between the audience and the stage, clapping her hands above her head. The audience responded as they had during the sound-check, whistling, clapping and hooting. Safan did his best to join in with the rest of them.

And then Greg Norman appeared, emerging from between two green-screen partitions, all smiles, glasses, big ears and curly hair. He paraded back and forth across the low stage, offering the audience a friendly wave before holding both hands up in the air to settle them down.

'Wow. Thank you! Thank you! This is too much! You're all too much!'

Safan found his gaze resting on the model motorbike, the Kawasaki. He'd had one of those a long time ago. One of the old ones made in the early 80s. He'd been 'the Man' riding it about town with its crackling broken exhaust.

Look! There goes Safan!!

He was smiling now, not at Greg Norman's show-opening gags, but at all the good memories that jangled in the wake of that old bike like the tin-can tail of a wedding car.

His other life. His better life.

The Z1000 had taken him up into the mountains, forded streams, carved lines across freshly turned fields and weaved through orchards. It had been their matchmaker, the one that had brought Nastasja and him together as a result of those first words that had tumbled from her mouth and won his heart.

You really think that noisy thing makes you super-sexy, don't you?

6.32 p.m

Boyd and Minter watched the vest-cam footage that was being streamed from Brighton. The team heading to Salmani's shop were lagging behind the one that had gone to his home address. He was glad Okeke was in a patrol car, on her way over with PS Gale Brown, and that she hadn't witnessed the heavy-handed way in which those boots had entered the poor woman's terraced house.

Ness and her girls were huddled in the front room, all of them sobbing, terrified. Ness was screaming at everyone to get out of her house, and no one seemed to be trying to either comfort her or calm things down.

'Tell them that Salmani has a workshop in the back garden,' said Boyd. 'That's what we need to look at first... Forget about pulling the poor woman's home apart.'

His message was relayed down the chain and finally he was looking at jerky, bouncing chest-cam footage showing the back door being yanked open. The officer stepped outside. A torch snapped on and caught the reflection of a pane of glass at the end of the garden.

'That must be it,' said Boyd. 'That's the shed. That's his workshop.'

The officer hurried down the yard, past a rain-soaked trampoline, a hula hoop and a discarded pink bike with stabilisers.

Boyd watched as gloved hands wrestled with the door before cupping a padlock. 'Shed's locked.'

'Well, kick it in for fuck's sake!' snapped Boyd.

It took about ten seconds for his suggestion to work its way back to the officer. The toe of a boot came into view and kicked out hard, just below the padlock. The flimsy door rattled inwards without any further effort, and they were now looking into the dark space beyond.

The officer panned his torch around.

Blurry details whipped by on the screen, giving Boyd the general impression of a computer-nerd's man cave: gutted PC cases, CPU fans and crowded circuit boards cluttered the workbench.

The torch panned along the equipment.

Something caught Boyd's eye, something that he registered the moment it swung out of view.

'Go back!' he said. 'What's that glass-box thing?'

It took several frustratingly long seconds for the object to come back into view. It was a glass or Perspex container with what looked like a fairground grabber-claw suspended in the middle of it.

'Looks like a 3D printer, boss,' said Minter, peering over his shoulder.

It took a moment for Boyd's mind to catch up with the implications of that. 'Oh shit. Fuck. Fuck.'

71

6.37 p.m.

Safan had copied the audience, laughing when they laughed, clapping when they clapped, but his mind had been far, far away.

But now it seemed that the American actor and stand-up comedian were done, and Greg Norman had begun introducing his final guest.

'Now, if there was a *Guinness Book of Records* entry for the largest pair of free-swinging testicles...'

Much laughter.

'... it would have to go to my last guest. As I'm sure you'll all recall, it was two weeks tonight that an armed terrorist held a train full of innocent passengers captive for several hours through the night...'

Riz was not a terrorist. Safan shook his head. *And not everyone on the train was innocent.*

'Armed police were called, negotiators, the whole deal. And there was a campsite right beside the track, full of holidaymakers.' Greg's delivery had changed gear from laddish comedy to something more restrained. 'It could have been disastrous had the terrorist's bomb been real. But what *was real*, ladies and gents, was the courage this man displayed in tackling the terrorist – not bare-handed, but with his hands *tied behind his back*! Please will you put *your* hands together and make one helluva lot of noise for our very own caped crusader... Mr Lucas Pesic!'

∽

ON THE OTHER side of the Incident Room, Williams, Hatcher and Sutherland were crowded around another monitor with a direct link to the CT-SFO squad, who were huddled in the back of the van, waiting for further instructions.

They could hear the murmur of voices and the rustle of the handset being passed. 'This is Sergeant Dale speaking... I've got a DSI Drummond here as acting Silver.'

'Let me speak to him,' Hatcher said.

'DSI Drummond here. Who am I speaking to?'

'Detective Chief Inspector Hatcher, Sussex Force. I'm acting Gold. What's the sit-rep?'

'Ma'am... we're parked just outside the studio complex. So far we've kept low-key. No blues and twos. No one inside is aware we're here. We contacted the studio's security and they say there are three shows in three different studios being recorded right now. *The Greg Norman Show* is in Studio One. That's the largest studio, ma'am.'

'Sorry, repeat that last. Did you say the shows are being recorded now?'

'Yes, ma'am. For broadcast tomorrow.'

∽

BOYD all but kicked his chair across the room as he jumped up and hurried over to his senior officers, nearly losing his footing in the process.

'I think there's a *real* gun this time!' he barked. 'I think he's 3D-printed one!'

Hatcher turned to look at him. 'And we've just found out they're recording the show *right now*. It's not a live broadcast, as we thought.'

'Ma'am,' said Williams. 'we're on a GSB protocol now. We need your approval as Gold to authorise a shoot-on-sight.'

Boyd leant into the huddle. 'Ma'am... Salmani is there for one person only. He's not a random shooter. Can we get word into the studio – discreetly – and have Pesic pulled out from the show? Have someone announce he's ill or something? If they've got a back door, we could walk him out quietly.' He looked at Williams. 'What do you think?'

'I think that we'll still have an armed man, potentially wearing a bomb, in a crowded space,' she said. 'We need to act swiftly and take Salmani out now.'

'The bomb's probably fake,' said Boyd. 'Hadzic wore one as a way to keep control of people in the carriage.'

'And this one might not be,' countered Williams.

'I'm telling you – this is a *targeted* hit,' Boyd argued. 'Salmani's there for one man only. We get Pesic pulled; Salmani will have to walk out with everyone else when they finish and we can pick him up then.'

Hatcher rubbed her tired eyes. 'I've got a man in a crowded interior space, with a gun we *know* is real and a bomb that *might* be real,' she said. Hatcher looked up at Boyd. 'I hear what you're saying, but I can't soft-pedal this. You're asking us to hope he doesn't just suddenly snap and go for it?'

'I don't think Salmani wants to take down innocent people,' Boyd replied. 'That's not his goal!'

'There are too many thinks, Boyd,' replied Hatcher. 'But...'

'At least stall Pesic's interview. Get them to fake a credible reason as to why he's not ready to come on yet,' Boyd said.

'Fine. But in the meantime we should get the SFOs into the building,' added Williams. 'If Salmani does suddenly kick off, we'll need them ready to go straight into the studio.'

Hatcher nodded. 'All right, send them in.' She looked around the room. 'Will someone get me a fucking phone number for the studio. Now!'

∼

SAFAN WATCHED the man walk onto the stage to the sound of whistling, clapping and cheering. The people around him were exhorting – *celebrating* – a monster. Pesic waved and smiled at the audience, accepting Greg Norman's proffered hand and shaking it politely.

The applause showed no signs of dying down.

Safan felt rage stirring up inside him. Rage at them all for being so blind. And so stupid for simply seeing Rizmet and Pesic wrongly, as terrorist and hero.

Enough.

He reached for his gun and stood up.

The audience member in the next seat looked up at him, grinning and clapping like a circus monkey, and he stood up too. Others around them began to do the same.

Safan couldn't stop himself. The rage was unbearable.

He pulled the trigger.

72

'**M**a'am,' said DI Connor. 'I've got the show's producer on the line.' He handed his phone to Hatcher.

'Hello? Who am I speaking to?'

'Helen Raddon, floor manager, Studio One. Who's this?'

Over the phone, Hatcher could hear the racket the audience were making. It sounded like a football match.

'This is the police,' she replied. 'Listen to me very carefully, Helen –'

'Sorry, it's noisy... Who did you say?' Helen was shouting over the noise, her voice distorting the speaker.

'*The police!*' Hatcher shouted back.

'Police?'

'Yes! Now listen to me –'

BANG! The single gunshot produced an almost instant silence.

Then the screaming began.

'Shit!' Hatcher hissed. She leant into the desk mic. 'This is Gold. Shots fired. You have authorization to enter and shoot on sight!'

SAFAN WAVED HIS GUN. 'MOVE! OUT OF MY WAY!'

The seats around him cleared within seconds and he dashed to the low stage, keeping his gun arm straight as he approached the guests' sofa.

The funny host with his big ears and mop of hair wasn't so funny now. He was curled up in his seat, hands raised above his head. The all-American action hero with his tanned skin and shiny evening suit was doing the same, cringing back into the upholstery, legs up to protect himself, almost tucked into a foetal position. The comedian was frozen in place with a bemused expression locked on his face.

Pesic, however, had the look of someone who'd been expecting this day for more than half his life.

Safan fired into the air for a second time.

'SHUT UP!' he screamed, as he tried to quell the panic in his mind, vaguely remembering that the print instructions had cautioned that the weapon could become unreliable after three shots. He just needed to get that third shot right.

The studio fell silent.

'You can go,' Safan said to the other guests cowering on the sofa. The American actor got to his feet, hands raised, and quickly backed away; the comedian and Greg Norman followed suit and retreated at speed off stage.

Safan glanced over his shoulder at the audience. In the glare of the spotlights, he could barely see them, but he could hear them: whispers, whimpers, the rustling of movement.

He turned back to Pesic. 'You know who I am?'

Pesic shook his head vigorously.

'I know you,' said Safan.

'Is m-mistake...' uttered Pesic. 'We have n-never... Please...'

'Thirty years I have waited for this,' continued Safan, 'for you to be the one who is begging for mercy.' He took a step closer. 'You people came to my town. You came to the villages. You raped and murdered. Men, boys, girls, women.'

'No! Is not me! I am...'

'You! You came to my home... You also came to Rizmet's home.' Safan turned to the unseen audience and raised his voice for them to hear. 'Your *hero* rapes girls! Your *hero* put a knife to my wife's belly and cut out my son in front of me!'

'I am not this man!' Pesic pleaded. 'Please... this is not me.'

Safan turned back to him. 'Rizmet saw your tattoo – as you raped his mother and sister.'

'I rape no one!'

'He said it was on your right hip. Lift your shirt.'

Pesic directed his plea to the hushed audience. 'Please help! Please!'

Safan took a step closer. 'LIFT YOUR SHIRT!'

'There is nothing. Nothing. Please!'

'LIFT YOUR FUCKING SHIRT!!!'

Pesic shook his head frantically, tears of desperation spilling down his round face.

'Then we are done with this,' said Safan softly. 'This is for Nastasja...'

He squeezed the trigger. The shot was much louder this time as the gun exploded into jagged shards of plastic. A puff of blue-grey cordite, stained red by the blood from his disintegrated hand, hung in the air above the ragged end of his wrist.

Safan Salmani stared at the damage to himself, a look of incomprehension matched with incomprehensible grief. His gaze settled on Pesic, in the vain hope that the bullet had found its target. There was a hole in the couch and a plume of stuffing floating down beside the man. He had missed.

Safan let loose a pitiful wordless wail of grief.

And then the studio's reinforced and soundproofed doors swung inwards. A single muted gunshot cracked dully in the acoustically treated studio. The green screen just behind Greg

Norman's chair was suddenly decorated with a ragged crescent of blood.

In the silent second or two after the shot, Safan dropped to his knees. He flopped forward onto the glass coffee table sending the jug of water, the plastic flowers and the model motorbike crashing to the floor.

73

Like that old 80s band the Boomtown Rats, DC Samantha Okeke wasn't that keen on Mondays either. Especially damp and grey ones.

She lingered by the entrance, not so close to the double doors that she was puffing smoke into the faces of those coming and going, but close enough that she was still protected from the tapping rain by the entrance portico.

She wasn't feeling quite ready to go inside and risk a chance encounter with DCI Williams. Rumour had it that she and her Tweenies were packing up and pissing off today, back to Thames Valley HQ. If Okeke could have taken a day's holiday in order to avoid any possible encounters on the CID's floor, she bloody well would have.

Okeke had been at Ness's house when the news arrived that her partner had been shot dead. The idiot sergeant who'd received the message from control about an hour after it happened had just blurted it out right in front of the poor woman and her daughters. And that had come just after Okeke had been doing her very best to reassure them that the police knew Saffy wasn't out to hurt anyone else. That they were planning to talk him down, not shoot him dead.

The doors banged open and the last person in the world she wanted to see emerged with a vape in her hands.

'DC Okeke,' said Williams cordially.

'Ma'am,' she replied icily.

The DCI took a deep pull on her vape and let out a voluminous cloud of steam. 'I presume you know about Pesic?'

Okeke did. He'd been rushed to hospital Thursday night. A thick shard of plastic from the printed gun had wedged itself in his throat. His carotid artery had been nicked and he'd lost a lot of blood. The paramedics had stabilised him and got him to hospital, but it hadn't looked promising. The Sunday papers had revealed that he'd died in the early hours of Friday morning.

But what was new information was the dressing discovered by the paramedics. Apparently Pesic had performed some impromptu surgery on himself days earlier, a ham-fisted operation to cut away an uneven triangle of skin on his lower back.

'You were right to flag up that tattoo,' said Williams. 'It seems he was worried that Hadzic had been checking for tattoos on the train, and Pesic wanted to get rid of his in case anyone else came knocking.'

'Yeah.' Oh, Okeke very much wanted to say, *I bloody well told you so*. But that would have cheapened this moment and devalued her little victory.

Williams took another pull on her vape. 'I'm sorry if I was too hard on you.'

'You were shitty with me, ma'am.' Okeke said with a shrug. 'Sorry, but there's no other way of putting it.' She finished her fag and flicked the butt away. 'Was there any particular reason why?'

Williams turned to look at her. 'Why the hell are you still a detective constable?'

Okeke glared at her. 'Why don't you have a wild guess?'

Williams shook her head. There was a look of disappointment on her face. 'That's not good enough, Okeke. You have to *make them* notice you or you go home... and I don't just mean Boyd.' She wagged a finger at her. 'You're going to have to stand head and shoulders above everyone else... or you're just wasting your time. That's how I did it.' She tucked her vape into her jacket pocket and gave Okeke a tight nod, the ghost of a smile on her lips. 'Maybe I'll see you around.'

74

'Really? Oh my, that's great news!' said Charlotte. 'When?'

'Tomorrow, Wednesday maybe,' said Boyd. 'Dr Munroe said he'd be signing off on me today and sending an email to Hatcher.' He shrugged. 'Apparently I'm not as fucked in the head as I should be.'

Charlotte winced at his language. 'I'm almost certain that wouldn't have been the diagnosis label.'

Boyd smiled and bent down to pick up the tennis ball that Mia had dropped at his feet. Ozzie failed to see what the hell was so fascinating about a fuzzy green ball, but Charlotte's dog for some reason couldn't take her eyes off it. He tossed it as far as he could along the shingle and she shot after it like a rocket, Ozzie chasing after her like a bat out of hell.

'So was he guilty, then?' Charlotte asked. 'That Lucas chap?'

'I don't know,' Boyd replied. 'Guilty maybe of belonging to one of those paramilitary units.'

'But we'll never know?'

'I think the paramilitary thing's a given. He tried to cut out his tattoo... but whether or not he committed the specific crimes that Salmani and Hadzic claimed he did…' Boyd shook his head. 'The man had a mask on. They both identified him from the name stencilled on a piece of army kit. I don't know if that would have been enough for a guilty verdict.'

Boyd had been doing some more reading over the weekend about the war and the aftermath. If Pesic had lived and a court of justice was convened to review the allegations against Pesic, it would have required Damocles and the others in her group to come out into the open and share their testimonies.

Bosnia–Herzegovina was a divided nation these days; the majority Serb, the minority Bosniak, and there was a growing desire in the country to wallpaper over the past. There was even a monument in Visegrád to commemorate the Serbian soldiers who'd died during the war. He wondered how painful it must be to the town's Bozniak population – those who remembered, those who'd survived, those who had lost loved ones – to have to walk past it every day.

If the only eyewitness accounts directly naming Pesic were those of Hadzic and Salmani, two Muslim men who some media sources were *still* labelling as jihadi terrorists, what chance would there have been of any meaningful justice being handed out? Pesic might have been found guilty of belonging to the Scorpion paramilitary unit, but not of any specific war crime.

Boyd still felt queasy at the thought that he'd spent a night drinking with Pesic, swapping stories and sharing salt-and-vinegar crisps. He would never understand how a man who'd been part of such a horrific piece of recent history had been was able to live with himself, to get up every morning and face himself in the mirror.

'Bill?'

'Hmm?'

She nudged his arm. 'You're miles away, there.'

'Yeah, sorry. I was just… mulling things over.'

'Are you sure you feel ready to go back to work?' Charlotte asked, concerned.

'I'm sure,' he replied. 'And, anyway, Dr Munroe seems to think it would be better for me to keep busy than arse about at home all day.'

'What are you going to do about Ozzie?' said Charlotte. 'Now that Emma's working full-time? Poor old chap's going to need to be let out for a midday pee.'

'I'll have to shoot back at lunchtimes, I suppose, or ask the mad parrot lady next door...'

'I could do it,' she offered. 'On Tuesdays to Thursdays.'

'Huh?'

'If you trust me with your door key, that is. Although,' she added, eyes twinkling, 'you might come home and find I've pawned all your household possessions for some crystal med.'

He looked at her. 'You mean crystal meth?'

'Ah right, yes, *that*.' She laughed. 'You may have gathered I'm not that hip when it comes to recreational drugs.'

'I wouldn't say that,' he said, smiling. 'You were the life and soul of the party if I recall correctly.'

'Oh, God. Please don't remind me! Although –' she squeezed his arm – 'it was rather fun, wasn't it?'

EPILOGUE

July 1992

The corporal stepped out of the farmhouse into the waning sunlight, tucking his tunic back into his trousers and swigging thirstily from the water bottle.

What a day. He smiled as he emptied the last of the water from the bottle down his throat. *What a crazy fucking day!*

He pulled the balaclava off his head and ran a hand through his sweaty brown hair.

They were *almost* human, weren't they? These animals... They squawked and screamed like people, even looked like people. But of course they weren't.

He'd lost count of how many of these dirty Bozniak cockroaches he'd got rid of today. This morning on the bridge and then this afternoon sweeping the outskirts of the town. It was thirsty work. But, fuck, it was so much fun. Like a game.

He spat out a thick wad of phlegm onto the dirt track, then spotted the dead family's postbox. *Hadzic* was painted decoratively on the side of it. He kicked its wooden post and the postbox wobbled off the top and clattered down into the dirt, unopened letters fluttering out.

'Won't need that now, will you?' he muttered.

'Ho! Mazzie!'

Corporal Markovic turned to see the rest of his squad emerging out of the dusk. They were coming up the track, pulling a cart laden with looted possessions. One of them was kicking a severed head along the dusty path in front of him like a misshapen football.

'All right, boys? You all done?'

Most of them looked as though they'd had fun. Only one of them of them didn't look happy.

Markovic tossed the empty water bottle across the road at him. 'Cheer up, Pesic, you miserable little pussy – you can have it back now!'

Pesic scooped up the bottle. 'It is empty.'

'Tough shit. Hey... you! Pass over here!'

The soldier kicking the head chipped it over towards him. Markovic bent down, picked it up and jammed it on the end of the wooden post.

'There! Like American's Halloween, eh? What do you boys think?'

Most of them laughed. As the men left the Hadzics' home behind them, their shadows – cast by the setting sun – trailed in their wake. They looked very much like ghouls emerging from abyssal cracks in the earth's crust and bringing a taste of hell to its surface.

'Quick!' Markovic waved his men on. 'Next village. Before it gets too dark.'

THE END

AFTERWORD

It never ceases to horrify me how brutal and evil a species we can be. As you can imagine, as Boyd did the research reading on the horrors that occurred in Bosnia, so did I. I remember reading accounts of what had happened in passing back in the 90's, but nothing so horrific as the details that have been collated by eye witnesses and survivors since.

If there's anything to be learned from reviewing this kind of material its perhaps this – the potential for evil persists and lingers in the background of every nation and we have to be mindful of the little steps that can occasionally take a nation and its people towards a very dark place.

You know, they say a picture is better than a thousand words. As I was reading the witness accounts, a picture came to mind over and over, and you'll have noticed I couldn't help referencing it in the novel: Pieter Brueghel 'Triumph of Death'. If you have a moment, google the work. I suspect that very same image was the one Steven Spielberg was nodding to in the movie Schindler's List when the Nazis come to clear the Jewish ghettoes. I can't help think that war crimes past, present and, sadly, of the future, will continue to resemble that timeless painting.

DCI BOYD RETURNS IN

THE SAFE PLACE available to pre-order here

ACKNOWLEDGMENTS

As always with this series of books, there are a number of people I need to thank for their contributions. Firstly, my wife Debbie, who puts as much into polishing and publishing these stories as I do. She also has the thankless task of telling my where, how and why, the first drafts don't work... which is never easy to do with a grumpy, opinionated author who thinks he knows how to write.

Then there's Wendy Tse-Shakespeare, my copyeditor, who is not only the last line of defence to catch errata, but also continuity-Queen. If it wasn't for Wendy, Boyd would be clean shaven one day and sporting a full-on David Bellamy the next.

For details on rail 'rolling stock' that I needed details on I'd like to thank Louise Hutchison, a regular member of a place I like to think of as 'home' online; the UK Crime Book Club on Facebook. Seriously... if you're ever planning a life of crime, these folks collectively know everything.

Finally I owe a debt of gratitude to a group of people known as 'Team Boyd'. These are the early 'beta readers' and ARC readers that we turn to, pre-publication, to check that I haven't gone too far on a particular theme.

So... deep breath... thank you Leslie Lloyd, Lynda Checkley, Donna Morfett, Pippa Cahill-Watson, Marcie Whitecotton-Carroll, Deb Day and Andy White.

A special extra thank you to Lesley Lloyd for a suggestion she made about the ending. (Good shout, Lesley) and to Alyson Read who came up with that killer strapline on the book's cover!

Finally, finally – a thank you to you. If you've read this far in the series, then I think it's fair to say we're both staying on this train until the end. I suppose that makes us travel-companions...

You remembered the tickets, right?

ALSO BY ALEX SCARROW

DCI Boyd Series
SILENT TIDE
OLD BONES NEW BONES
BURNING TRUTH

Thrillers by Alex Scarrow
LAST LIGHT
AFTERLIGHT
OCTOBER SKIES
THE CANDLEMAN
A THOUSAND SUNS

The TimeRiders series (in reading order)
TIMERIDERS
TIMERIDERS: DAY OF THE PREDATOR
TIMERIDERS: THE DOOMSDAY CODE
TIMERIDERS: THE ETERNAL WAR
TIMERIDERS: THE CITY OF SHADOWS
TIMERIDERS: THE PIRATE KINGS
TIMERIDERS: THE MAYAN PROPHECY
TIMERIDERS: THE INFINITY CAGE

The Plague Land series
PLAGUE LAND

PLAGUE NATION

PLAGUE WORLD

The Ellie Quin series

THE LEGEND OF ELLIE QUIN

THE WORLD ACCORDING TO ELLIE QUIN

ELLIE QUIN BENEATH A NEON SKY

ELLIE QUIN THROUGH THE GATEWAY

ELLIE QUIN: A GIRL REBORN

ABOUT THE AUTHOR

Over the last sixteen years, award-winning author Alex Scarrow has published seventeen novels with Penguin Random House, Orion and Pan Macmillan. A number of these have been optioned for film/TV development, including his bestselling *Last Light*.

When he is not busy writing and painting, Alex spends most of his time trying to keep Ozzie away from the food bin. He lives in the wilds of East Anglia with his wife Deborah and four, permanently muddy, dogs.

Ozzie came to live with him in January 2017. He was adopted from Spaniel Aid UK and was believed to be seven at the time. Ozzie loves food, his mum, food, his ball, food, walks and more food...

He dreams of unrestricted access to the food bin.

For up-to-date information on the DCI BOYD series, visit: www.alexscarrow.com

Printed in Great Britain
by Amazon